Mile Marker Ten

A Novel
by

Michael Maloney

Mile Marker Ten is a work of fiction. All characters, with the exception of those listed in the Preface, are products of the author's imagination. Where real-life historical figures appear, the situations and dialogues concerning these persons are fictional and are not intended to depict actual events.

Cover painting by Maryland artist, Bonita Glaser
Cover design by Susan Maloney

ISBN: 0-9906833-3-8
ISBN-13: 978-0-9906833-3-9

PREFACE

Between 1745 and 1760, a turnpike was established across Maryland to provide a land route between the port city of Baltimore and the mostly-German settlement of Fredericktown, some fifty miles to the west. Stone markers were erected every mile along the north side of the road. Many remain to this day. Mile Marker Ten sits just to the west of the Patapsco River—in the shadow of the B&O railroad bridge.

The Ellicott brothers founded their mill town in 1772 at the intersection of the turnpike and the Patapsco River. Mills of various types were built on both sides of the river. The town thrived through the 19th century. It was an ideal location: numerous streams flowed through the town from surrounding high ground, providing abundant waterpower.

In 1808, the Union Manufacturing Company established a textile mill on the river about a half-mile north of the town. An Irish immigrant and industrialist named William Dickey purchased the mill at auction in 1887 and renamed it "Oella Mill". After it was destroyed by fire in 1918, it was promptly rebuilt and operated continuously until 1972. Today the building houses elegant apartments overlooking the Patapsco River.

After living on the outskirts of Ellicott City for more than twenty years, my wife and I moved into an apartment in Oella Mill in the fall of 2015. My daily ritual was to work through the morning and then hike into town for coffee in the afternoon, either at the Little Market Cafe behind Tonge Row, or at Bean Hollow in the old Easton Sons' building. Then, if supplies at home were low, I might stop in The Wine Bin for a nice Tuscan red, or, time permitting, browse in one of the many fine antique or art stores along Main Street. Gramp's Attic Used & Vintage Book Store was also a favorite location.

I had been working on my second novel, which was to be about a modern-day forensic accountant, but I found myself growing less and less interested in the project—too similar to other novels that line the shelves of airport bookstores.

On my walks through Ellicott City, I began reading the bronze plaques mounted on many of the old stone buildings. I discovered the Howard County Historical Society and their archive of books and other materials describing the area's rich history. I began reading old newspaper articles from the late 1800s and early 1900s. I zeroed in on 1908 and found several interesting stories that suggested the outline of a plot. Abandoning my forensic accountant, I began work on the novel you now hold.

Thus, this book is a work of fiction, but it is based on real events that took place in and around Ellicott City, Maryland in 1908 and 1909. Many of the characters are real (see list below), although the dialogue and situations are fictionalized. All of the quoted newspaper articles are real. I have made only minor edits for typos and consistency in the spelling of names.

Most of the street names are the same now as they were in 1908, with a few exceptions:

- Ellicott Mills Drive is new. Fels Lane used to extend all the way to Main Street, providing a route to the northwest.
- Mercer Street (where the Chemist has his shop) was a short spur off of Fels Lane. It is now little more than a driveway.
- What is now Church Road used to be called Ellicott Street in the old maps, although folks would commonly refer to it as "the church road" because Methodist and Lutheran churches were situated along its short length. For clarity, I refer to it by the modern name.

The following characters are historical:

- Martin Burke (1869-1944) – State's Attorney in Howard County
- James Clark (1884–1955) – Young lawyer starting his career in Ellicott City
- Linwood Cross (1876-1936) – Boarder at Angelo Cottage
- Daniel Easton (1883-1935) – Co-owner with his brother of Easton Sons' Undertakers

- Edward Hammond (1877-1928) – A lawyer in Ellicott City
- Katie Hatwood – William's Mother
- William (Billy) Hatwood (1881-?) – A laborer in Ellicott City
- Archdeacon Edward T. Helfenstein (1865-1947) – Rector of St. John's Episcopal Church, west of Ellicott City.
- Benjamin Hill (1866-1945) – Farmer in Clarksville
- Charles E. Hill (1876-1964) – Farmer in Clarksville
- John Hill (?-1898) – Patriarch of the Hill family, farmer in Clarksville
- James Hobbs (1854-1941) – Deputy Sheriff of Howard County
- George W. Howard (1860-1930) – Sheriff of Howard County
- Marion Morgan (1875-1932) – Laborer, boarder at Angelo Cottage
- Edward Burr Powell (1882-1975) – Lawyer and editor at the Ellicott City Times, son of William Powell
- William Powell (1853-1931) – Founder of the Ellicott City Times
- Matthew Powers (1883-1964) – Blacksmith, boarder at Angelo Cottage
- John Reichenbecker (1866-?) – Worker at Howard House Hotel and Restaurant
- Johanna Ray (1868-?) – Owner, with her sisters, of Angelo Cottage Boarding House
- Martin Rodey (1838-1909) – Owner of Rodey's Emporium at the bottom of Main Street
- Roberta Ray Sanner (1874-?) – Widow, manages Angelo Cottage boarding house, sister of Johanna Ray
- Bernard H. Wallenhorst (1840-1909) – Immigrated to the U.S. in 1866 and settled in Ellicott City as a local merchant and magistrate
- Rev. Immanuel Wegner (1884-1971) – Pastor of the German Lutheran Church on Church Road
- Ethel Wosch (1881-1955) – Julius' wife
- Julius Wosch (1873-1945) – Newly appointed chief of the Ellicott City Police

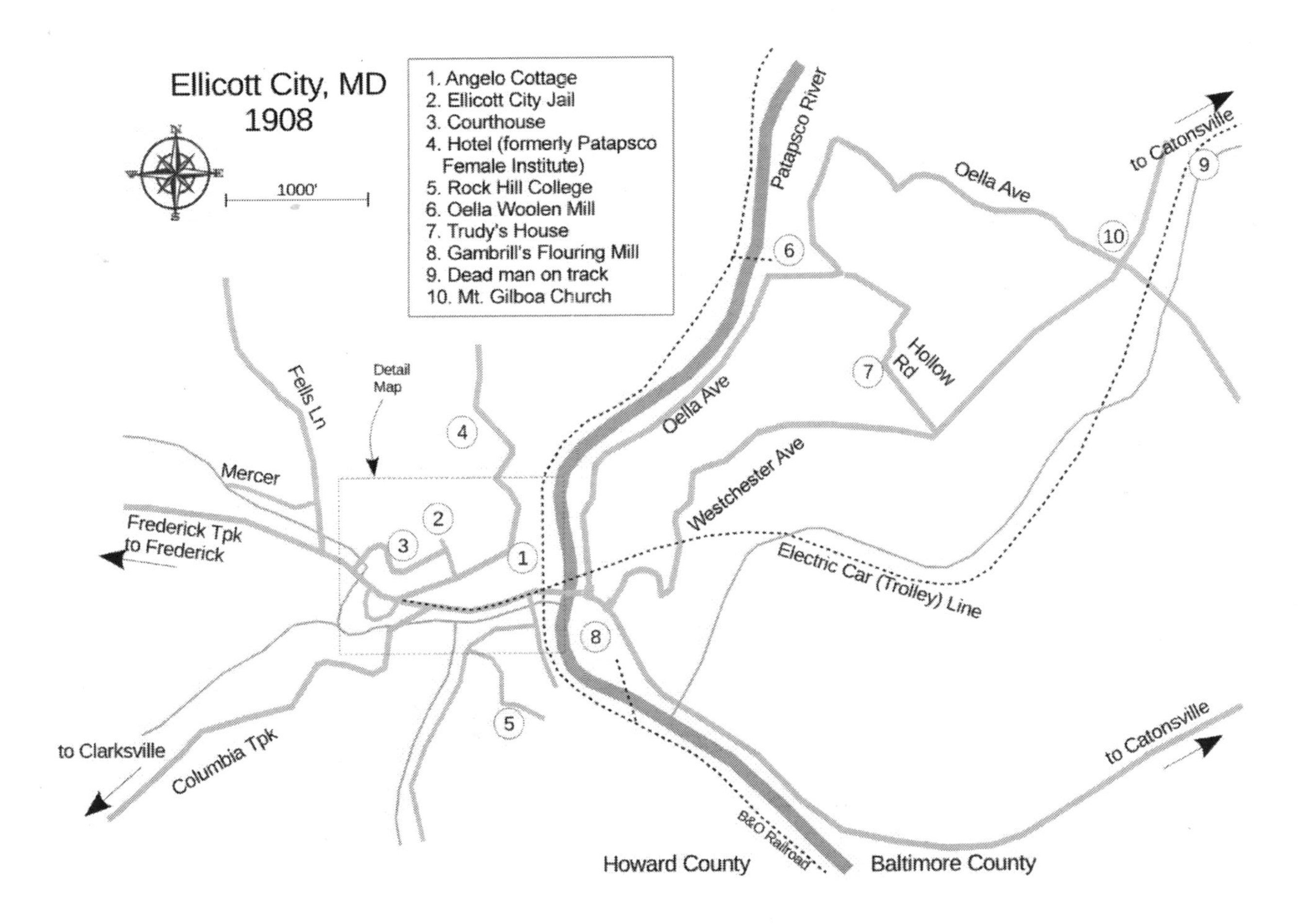
Ellicott City, MD
1908
1000'
1. Angelo Cottage
2. Ellicott City Jail
3. Courthouse
4. Hotel (formerly Patapsco Female Institute)
5. Rock Hill College
6. Oella Woolen Mill
7. Trudy's House
8. Gambrill's Flouring Mill
9. Dead man on track
10. Mt. Gilboa Church
Patapsco River
to Catonsville
Oella Ave
Hollow Rd
Fells Ln
Detail Map
Mercer
Oella Ave
Westchester Ave
Frederick Tpk
to Frederick
Electric Car (Trolley) Line
to Clarksville
Columbia Tpk
to Catonsville
B&O Railroad
Howard County
Baltimore County

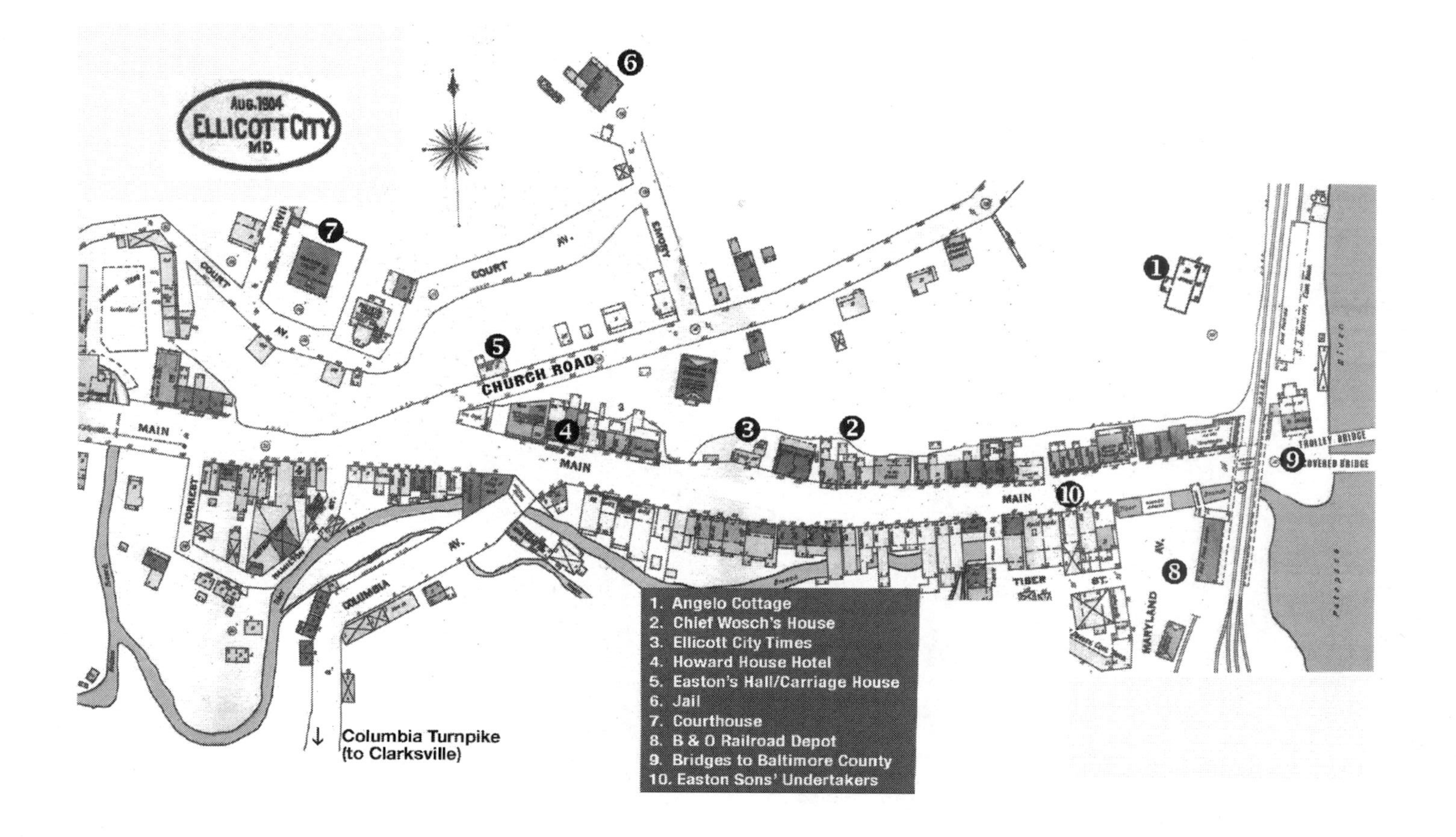
Aug. 1904
ELLICOTT CITY
MD.
CHURCH ROAD
MAIN
COURT AV.
EMORY
FORREST
COLUMBIA AV.
TIBER ST.
MARYLAND AV.
TROLLEY BRIDGE
COVERED BRIDGE
1. Angelo Cottage
2. Chief Wosch's House
3. Ellicott City Times
4. Howard House Hotel
5. Easton's Hall/Carriage House
6. Jail
7. Courthouse
8. B & O Railroad Depot
9. Bridges to Baltimore County
10. Easton Sons' Undertakers
Columbia Turnpike
(to Clarksville)

Dedicated to the good people of Ellicott City, Maryland, who endured a devastating flood on the afternoon of May 27, 2018. This was the second such flood in less than two years. Recovery efforts are again underway at the time of this writing. I have no doubt that the town will return soon to its former charm and beauty.

#ECStrong

MARCH
1908

MILE MARKER TEN

Wednesday Evening, March 11, 1908

The Chemist stood on the flat roof of Angelo Cottage in the crisp March air. He pulled the last match from a cardboard book and struck it against the front. Cupping the flame in his hands, he held it to the bowl of his boxwood pipe and puffed gently. He refolded the book and glanced at the ad on the front, proclaiming "Howard House, Ellicott City – Cuisine Unexcelled." He flicked the spent book over the side of the roof to the cliff below. He sucked gently on the ivory horn mouthpiece and inhaled deeply with satisfaction: Fine, aged, North Carolina tobacco from his supplier in Baltimore.

The prosaic name "cottage" did not do justice to this outlandish building—a stone castle replete with notched parapets. It was built in the 1820s atop a steep slope overlooking the Patapsco River and the north side of the then-nascent Main Street. The building had seen more grandiose days and now served as a boarding house.

Up here the Chemist felt calm and powerful. He indulged himself in the twilight tableau: Far along the river to the north he could barely make out the stark, brick buildings of Oella Woolen Mills. Across the river, to the east, colored men busily loaded wagons in the lumberyard. To the southwest, a shift was just ending at the cluster of buildings making up Gambrill's Flouring Mills. Below him, to the south, was Main Street, with its bustle of early evening foot and carriage traffic.

A squeal of brakes brought his attention back across the river. The six o'clock electric car was just now emerging from the gorge in the hills of Oella. It slowed as it approached the trestle bridge that carried it over the river into town.

His serenity was disturbed momentarily by the shrill but muffled voice of Mrs. Sanner, the boarding house matron, noisily arguing with her daughter on the floor below. The Chemist remained silent, not wanting to be admonished yet again by the unpleasant woman about the danger of climbing onto the roof.

He took another puff from his pipe and focused his mind. He had business this evening that would have a certain amount of risk to it. He had not been able to determine the identity of the man who had written to him, except that he was almost certainly a druggist, and that he was from Catonsville, or so read the postmark on the envelope. The letter had instructed him where and when to meet, and what to bring with him. It also hinted at grievous consequences should he not comply.

He once again considered his plan—the likely moves that his opponent would make and his own counter moves. Bold action might be required before the night was over. He extinguished his pipe and descended to his room to prepare.

The Chemist would not want to be recognized on this evening. To this end he had purchased patched, second-hand clothes from the bargain room at the back of Rosenstock's department store. He removed his normal fine attire, folding each article carefully and laying it on his bed. He donned the tattered replacements with no small revulsion. He had already washed the wax out of his thick handlebar mustache and had not shaved in over a week. A dark, wide-brimmed slouch hat, caked with dust, completed the disguise. For good measure, he would avoid the main roads and keep to himself, relying on the waning evening light for anonymity.

He could still hear Mrs. Sanner's endless tirade in her daughter's room. For a brief moment it reminded him of his own unhappy childhood.

His preparations complete, he descended the creaky staircase. His intent was to exit from the side door, through the kitchen, and onto the grassy hillside between the cottage and the German Lutheran Church next door. All was well until he entered the kitchen. To his annoyance, he found Mr. Marion Morgan, another boarder at the cottage, seated at the table. Morgan looked up from the watery soup that Mrs. Sanner had prepared for the house. He raised his bushy eyebrows in surprise at the Chemist's unusual appearance.

The notion that he now bore the same disheveled appearance as Morgan disgusted the Chemist. He never understood such men—

either shave, or don't, was his motto. But like many of the lower classes, Morgan shaved maybe once a month, leaving his face more often than not covered by untidy stubble.

Morgan said nothing. He set down his spoon, picked up his always-present snuffbox, and began to fiddle with the lid. The Chemist continued through the room. There was no point in offering an explanation. Morgan was beneath him—a common street laborer to whom, for reasons incomprehensible to the Chemist, Mrs. Sanner had taken a liking. Morgan didn't even pay for his lodging, but rather performed menial tasks, such as fetching wood and water in exchange for a small room connecting to the kitchen.

Finally free of the house, the Chemist walked past the privy and turned down the steep hill. He found the top of an old stone staircase that led to a short crooked path. Then he descended a set of wooden stairs between Rodey's Hall and the vacant stone building that used to be the Railroad Hotel. Finally, he emerged onto Main Street and turned left toward the river.

He ignored the bustling plaza in front of the B&O passenger station, keeping to the left to go under the railroad bridge. He was distracted by a commotion directly in front of him: A fistfight was just now breaking out on the trolley tracks between two young men who had likely spent the afternoon at O'Brian's, or Kramer's, or one of the many other saloons for which Ellicott City was famous.

One of the brawlers took an uppercut to the chin and, falling several steps backward, collided with the Chemist as he attempted to pass by unobserved. The Chemist was shoved back into the building. Attempting to retain his balance, his left foot violently struck the stone ten-mile marker protruding from the cobblestones. Cursing the other man, he hurried under the bridge and turned left along the west bank of the river through Ratcliff's coal yard. He passed the storage shed and continued northward through the narrow strip of land between the railroad tracks and the river. His left foot was tingling.

He continued northward through the brush along the river. He gradually became aware of a clattering sound, growing louder until it was quite clear over the rush of the water. He had been told that this was the sound of the looms. Oella Textile Mill operated around the clock. This must be one of the rare occasions when they opened the windows in the weaving room.

Remembering the contingencies of his plan, the Chemist stopped and selected a good-sized stone, about three or four pounds, from the rubble around the railroad ties. He tested its heft by taking a few practice swings with his left hand. Satisfied, he placed it in his coat pocket.

After walking about a mile, he came to a junction where a short spur of track separated from the B&O line and crossed over a trestle bridge to the mill. The clatter of the looms was quite loud here. He could see a boxcar on the other side of the river and several workers unloading heavy, tied bundles of raw wool. He climbed onto the narrow catwalk built along the side of the bridge and started across. It was precarious in places, with nothing to hold on to and the rushing river twenty feet below.

He made it across without incident and clambered down onto the cobblestones, noticing a feeling of pressure in his left shoe as he landed. He hoped he had not broken his toe. He had miles still to walk this night.

He ascended the winding hill of Oella Avenue, past Dickey's company store and numerous tenement houses, past the dilapidated school house on the dirt path they called Race Road, past more tenements and farm houses, and finally to the crest of the hill where the negro church stood. From here it was a short, mostly level walk to where the street intersected with the electric car tracks that ran between Baltimore and Ellicott City. According to the mysterious letter he had received, this was to be the meeting place. He pulled his watch from his pocket and squinted in the semidarkness. It was just after seven o'clock—about a quarter hour before the appointed time. He backed into the shadows of the woods, away from the gas streetlight, and waited.

This was the colored section of Oella. The old Banneker residence was just down the street. As he waited, several men passed by, likely returning from a day of labor at the lumberyard or one of the factories that hired negroes. It was odd that his opponent had chosen this place. After several minutes, he spied a white man walking toward him from the direction of Westchester Avenue. If the man was from Catonsville, as the postmark implied, perhaps he had taken the electric car to the stop next to MacDonald's store, and then hiked up the hill from there. As the man approached, the Chemist emerged from the darkness of the trees and removed his dusty hat.

The newcomer was startled at first and recoiled into the middle of the road. The Chemist stood still at the edge of the light from the street lamp and remained silent. He wanted the other man to make the first move.

The other man approached cautiously until he was quite close. They were about the same height, but whereas The Chemist was lean and muscular, this man had pudgy features—a man obviously unaccustomed to physical labor. He was breathing heavily and his face was moist from the exertion of his walk. He was clean-shaven, and over the stench of the man's sweat, The Chemist thought he could detect the scent of expensive cologne. He had an unwavering smirk—a sort of poker face, the Chemist supposed.

They sized each other up for a moment before the newcomer broke the silence. He laughed and took a step back, looking the Chemist up and down. "What a clever disguise. You look positively ... Oellan." Getting no response, he lifted his hands in surrender. "Very well, sir—I can see that you are all business. I am pleased that my letter sufficiently motivated you. It is good to finally meet you."

The Chemist finally spoke. "You have me at a disadvantage, sir. I do not know who you are."

The man waved the question away. "Who I am is of no import, except to say that I am, as you no doubt have deduced, well connected. I instructed you to meet me here this evening so that we might come to an arrangement concerning your business activities. Did you bring the money?"

"Shhh! Not here," the Chemist cut him off. "Too many colored folks passing by. We stick out like a sore thumb. Follow me." Without waiting for a reply, the Chemist plunged into the darkness, walking briskly along the trolley tracks to the north. His damned left foot was starting to ache now, but he forced himself not to limp. He sensed that it was important to show no weakness.

He heard the man lumbering behind him, breathing heavily again. They came to a small clearing after about a quarter mile, just before a right bend as the tracks ascended into Catonsville. There was a shallow ravine to the side and the sound of trickling water. It was quite dark now, everything in silhouette.

The Chemist began the short speech he had prepared: "Sir, I am a humble druggist trying to make a living with a small shop in Ellicott City. I wish you no ill will, but I do not know how my business could have anything to do with you, and I certainly do not see..."

The man cut him off. "Come, come, my good fellow. Let us not feign ignorance. Allow me to recite a few facts. Firstly, you are not, as you claim, a druggist. I have it on good authority that no one with your name has a license to practice pharmacy in the State of Maryland. So at the very least, sir, you are a humbug."

The man continued before the Chemist could retort. "Secondly, you have been selling cocaine in sizable quantities to the negroes who work in the shirt factory, the quarry, Thistle Mills, and perhaps other locations. I dare say, sir, your present appearance notwithstanding, that you are doing a good deal more than—how did you put it—making a living."

He paused, studying the Chemist's face, before continuing. "Fear not, sir. I am not one to deprive a man of his livelihood. My associates and I merely want some small consideration. I will tell you that we have, in fact, quite a bit of influence within the Maryland Board of Pharmacy. I'm sure we can clear up your lack of credentials without any trouble. As for the cocaine, well, please, I want you to continue. I have a close relationship with your supplier and can easily keep tabs on your sales volume. Do take care, though, to avoid using the powder yourself. It has been the ruination of many fine, otherwise upstanding men such as yourself."

The Chemist was dumbfounded. How did this stranger learn all of this? About one item, though, the man was wrong. The Chemist had indeed passed the Maryland certification examination. But that was before—it seemed a lifetime ago, long before he had changed his name and moved here from Baltimore.

Seeing that his opponent was waiting for some kind of reply, he asked, simply, "What is it, exactly, that you want from me?"

The man clapped his hands and rubbed them together. "Ah! Now *that* is the right question! Oh, nothing too burdensome. As I say, we would never deprive a man of his livelihood. Shall we say one hundred tonight, as I instructed in my letter, and twenty-five a week going forward? I do hope you have brought the money, or we may have a problem. I'd hate to have to walk back into town to find the sheriff. I believe his name is Wo..."

He never finished his sentence. The Chemist had silently removed the stone from his coat pocket and swung it in a wide arc. He heard, and felt, a satisfying crunch as the stone made impact with the man's right temple. He fell to the ground without another word, landing with his head face down in the gully.

The Chemist's heart was racing. He took several deep breaths to calm himself. He had planned for this contingency, and had followed through on his plan. He had hoped it would not come to this, but his opponent had forced his hand.

The Chemist sighed in resignation and slowly began his remaining tasks. He grabbed the man's feet and dragged him back into the clearing. He took out a fresh book of matches and struck one for light. The right side of the man's head was caved in, and he was bleeding profusely through his nose. He wouldn't be alive for long.

Where was the man's hat? He had been wearing a dark porkpie hat. It must have fallen into the ravine. The Chemist descended the short slope, favoring his left leg, and took several minutes striking matches and searching the area. It was to no avail. He was running out of time and would simply have to rely on the incompetence of any investigators.

He removed the man's fine coat and set it aside. He had some trouble placing his own tattered coat onto the man's bulkier frame. He searched the man's coat and trouser pockets, which yielded forty dollars in a silver clip but no identifying papers. He had hoped to at least learn the man's name.

His plan in this contingency had been to drag the body into the ravine. Not many people passed this way on foot. Let the rodents work on him for a few days and he'd be unrecognizable. But now a different idea came to him that had a certain dramatic appeal.

He dragged the body across the trolley tracks, leaving the man's head on one rail and his knees on the other. He took out a small bottle of whiskey that he had brought for this purpose, and spilled it on the man's chest. He slipped the empty bottle into the man's breast pocket. Finally, he set his dusty slouch hat over the man's ruined face. The eight o'clock electric car should be along soon. It would come around the bend from Catonsville at a good speed and would not have time to stop, even if they did see the man on the tracks.

Satisfied with his work, he started to don his opponent's fine black coat, only to discover the right shoulder and sleeve were soaked with a warm, sticky substance—blood, no doubt. He sighed heavily. He considered putting the soiled coat back onto the body and returning with his tattered one, but he had already soaked it with whiskey. And there was no time; he would have to take the bloody coat with him. He rolled it into a bundle and set off down the tracks back toward Oella Avenue.

This time, he allowed himself to limp. He was pretty sure by now that his toe was broken.

Instead of retracing the circuitous route he had used to get here, he walked straight down Westchester Avenue. He soon emerged at the flouring mill and hobbled through the cluster of buildings to the covered wooden bridge. His foot was throbbing now. He remembered the old times when he could take solace in a stiff drink at a time like this. But those days were gone for good.

Halfway across the bridge, he glanced both ways and, seeing no one, hopped up on his good leg and tossed the soiled coat through the latticework under the roof. The river was high with recent rain. With any luck the current would carry the coat all the way to Baltimore.

MANGLED BY CAR
Unidentified Man Killed on
Ellicott City Line Tracks

An unidentified man was instantly killed about 7:30 P. M. yesterday between Rock creek and Oella avenue by a westbound Ellicott City car. His skull was crushed in, his legs and arms were all broken and his right leg was severed at the ankle.

Motorman Charles Zimmerman and Conductor Charles Russell were arrested and taken to the Catonsville Police Station where they were later released pending an inquest to be held by Coroner Whitely at Catonsville tonight.

Zimmerman says the man was lying across the car track and that as soon as he saw him he tried to stop the car but it had too much momentum. The car passed entirely over its victim.

The man was smooth-faced, of medium build, with dark hair, and wore a dark coat, gray trousers and a black slouch hat. No papers were found in his pockets, and he had but 5 cents. He was roughly dressed.

[Baltimore Sun, March 12, 1908]

A STICKLER FOR FORMALITY

Thursday, March 12, 1908

The Honorable Justice Bernard H. Wallenhorst, Sr., sat at the busy lunch counter in Kraft's restaurant on lower Main Street. It was just after noon on a rainy, but unseasonably warm, Thursday. Another downpour had just started, and several pedestrians had ducked in and now waited by the door for it to pass.

The judge ignored the commotion and concentrated on his meal and his newspaper. He was an elderly but virile man in his late sixties. His dark hair was impeccably groomed in well-lacquered swirls, with just a touch of gray on an upraised wave in the front. His well-trimmed mustache wrapped around the corners of his mouth to join a luxurious goatee that flared out at the bottom, covering the top of his black silk bowtie.

He stabbed the last morsel of weisswurst with his knife, swirled it in mustard, and gingerly placed it into his mouth. He took a sip of coffee and then dabbed at his lips with his napkin. He adjusted his copy of the Baltimore Sun so as to read below the fold.

After a moment, he grunted and slapped at the paper with the back of his hand. He turned to the woman seated on his left. "Have you seen this in today's paper, Mrs. O'Flynn?" The slightest hint of a German accent betrayed his immigrant background.

The woman on his left was Mrs. Gertrude Leary O'Flynn. At thirty-five, she retained a youthful air. Her dark hair had been teased up, parted in the middle, and pinned in the back, thus showing her full cheeks and dark green eyes to good advantage. She was dressed in a typical woman's business suit—high-collared white blouse with a dark vest and ankle-length skirt, the hem of which was now soiled with mud due to the inclement weather.

She worked as a writer at the Ellicott City Times, a few doors up the street. As was her lunchtime custom, she had been engrossed in a novel when the judge spoke. It took her a moment to realize she was being addressed. She had told the man on numerous occasions that he should simply call her Trudy, as everyone else did. But the judge was a stickler for formality. She sometimes wondered if he called his wife "Mrs. Wallenhorst" during their intimate moments.

Trudy leaned forward and scanned the proffered newspaper column. It was about the unidentified man found on the electric car tracks. She was always amazed that the Baltimore Sun managed to get so much information so quickly.

"Yes, Edward and I were talking about that this morning. He wants me to write something for this Saturday, or perhaps next." Trudy was referring to her employer, Edward Powell, the editor and part owner, with his father, William, of the local weekly newspaper. "He was on the telephone with Julius this morning, trying to get more material."

As if on cue, the door to the street opened again, and in strode Officer Julius Wosch, the newly appointed chief of the city's Police Department.

Behind the counter, a waitress approached with a steaming pot of coffee. She motioned toward Judge Wallenhorst's empty cup. He nodded, sliding his cup and saucer across the countertop. She topped it off.

"Thank you, Viola," said the judge. He pointed to the article in the newspaper. "This electric car accident last night, where the man was killed—this happened up where your family lives, yes? Near that church where your people go, Mt. Gib, Gibbon..."

"Gilboa," the waitress corrected. "Mt. Gilboa Methodist Episcopal Church. Trudy lives up that way too."

"Ah, just so ... Gilboa," repeated the judge. "It is where you coloreds worship on that side of the river, is it not so?"

Viola smirked and shook her head. "Well, not alls of us goes there, sir. Why Lawdy, somes of us jes' lies around drinking da whiskey oh sniffing da white powdah."

Trudy tittered into her sandwich, but the sarcasm was lost on the judge. He responded ponderously, "Yes, yes. I have come to know that cocaine powder is indeed becoming a problem among the negro people. I have seen more than one case in my courtroom. Ah, Chief Wosch—do join us."

Julius Wosch had finished hanging up his coat and shaking the water off of his pant legs. He was a tall, dashing man in his mid thirties with full, dark hair. He had kind eyes and a well-waxed handlebar mustache as wide as his ears. He had the same German air of formality as the much older judge. He claimed the stool to Trudy's left and set his policeman's cap on the counter. "Good day, your Honor, Mrs. O'Flynn. What's good today, Viola?"

"E'rything's good, of course. Corn chowder ain't half bad. S'got bacon in it. Trudy's having egg salad. You want coffee, Hon?"

Wosch nodded. "Please. And a bowl of the chowder would be fine, with a slice of black bread."

When Viola had moved on, Wosch leaned close to Trudy. "So," he said. "I was just visiting the Times and spoke with the elder Mr. Powell. He said you would have questions for me about the unfortunate incident up in Oella last night. I understand that you are writing it up for Saturday's edition, yes?"

Trudy started to speak, but Wosch cut her off with an upraised right hand—a consummate cop gesture. "I am speaking both officially and as a friend. I have *no* information to share. The incident occurred across the river in Baltimore County—out of my jurisdiction—and so is being handled by the Catonsville police. They have not as yet requested our assistance. You will have to telephone Mr. Whitely. He's the coroner there."

Viola returned and set a bowl of thick yellow chowder in front of the policeman. She put out a fresh cup and saucer and proceeded to fill it from the tin coffee pot, which seemed to be always attached to her hand. As she poured, she asked Trudy, "You heading up the hill normal time today?"

Trudy nodded, "Yes, about five. Billy says he's getting off early. We can all walk together." Viola nodded and returned to her duties.

As a newspaper writer, Trudy felt obliged to at least try to get a few nuggets of information for her article. One technique Edward had taught her was to give air to her thoughts, hoping for some kind of reaction—either a confirmation or denial—from whatever official she was interviewing. "I understand, Julius. I've been thinking, though ... I assume the Catonsville police searched the area as well as they could in the dark last night. And I'm sure someone returned today to do a proper search for clues, although I suppose that would be difficult in this rain. Also, I hope they asked the local residents to see if anybody saw something strange around that time last night. It hadn't started raining then. You know, the folks up there—they keep a close eye on things, though I don't think they like to talk to the police much." Wosch said nothing, so Trudy continued, "Say, you know, I live very near there myself. I could walk up tomorrow morning and ask around, if you think it will do any good? You said yourself I was a big help with the Huntley case last year." Trudy paused, hoping for a response.

Chief Wosch listened impassively. He now smiled and changed the subject. "How many weddings has our good Reverend Ridgely done this week? I hear he's been slacking off. If he is not careful, Reverend Branch will eat his lunch this year. And then what will happen to our city's reputation as the marriage capital, or 'Gretna Green', of the state?"

Trudy slapped him playfully on the shoulder. "Okay, I get it. No comment. Ridgely has done only five so far this week, but I believe three are scheduled for Saturday. Myrtle Robinson has wed Richard Hudson and will be moving to Baltimore. I just wrote it up. You can read about it on page five this Saturday."

TO ELLICOTT CITY BY TROLLEY
Northeast Baltimore Improvement Association Has Excursion

Members of the Northeast Baltimore Improvement Association went on an excursion to Ellicott City by trolley last night. It was the annual trolley ride of the association, and 10 cars, which left North Avenue and Caroline Street at 6 o'clock, were filled.

Banners bearing the name of the association were displayed on the cars. President W. W. Parker gave out horns, sirens, and a variety of souvenirs.

Supper was served at the Howard House, followed by dancing, games, a frog race, peanut race, and other contests for prizes.

[Baltimore Sun, March 4, 1908]

BRIEFS

George M. Henault, of Prince George County, has petitioned the Legislature to change his name to Wm. Jennings Bryan Number 2. Mr. Henault explains his reason for his petition is his great admiration for the "peerless one."

The automobile business does not effect the horse business at all. Horses of all classes average $20 a head more now than they did in 1902. Breed more horses.

Mr. Taft is playing politics for all there is in it, while the understrappers of the War Department have to attend to the Government business, which Taft is paid to do.

The members of the Lutheran Church of Woodbine will hold an oyster supper for the benefit of the church, Thursday night, March the 12th. All are cordially invited to attend.

[Ellicott City Times, March 7, 1908]

POLICE RESPONSE UNGRACIOUS WHILE SAM FARES BETTER

Thursday Afternoon, March 12, 1908

After returning to the newspaper office, Trudy sat at her desk and collected her thoughts. She turned to a fresh sheet on her notepad and made sure her fountain pen was primed. She plucked up the earpiece of the candlestick phone on her desk, tapped the handle a few times, and waited for the operator to come onto the line. "Hi, Millie, it's Trudy down at The Times."

Millie was the daytime operator for the Citizens' Telephone Company. It was a locally based company trying to compete against the much larger Chesapeake & Potomac, or C&P. Both were part of the Bell System and could thus intercommunicate. Citizens' exchange office was two blocks up the hill on Main Street, just across from the firehouse. "Oh, hi Trudy! Hey, you'll never guess what I heard about Sam Mueller. It's probably too juicy for you to print, though. He's ... hang on, there's another call coming in."

Trudy knew that Millie often listened in on calls after making a connection, even though she wasn't supposed to. If a party said something startling, he or she might hear an audible gasp or a judgmental "tsk." Millie was a great source of tips for the local personals section.

At length, Millie came back on the line. "Hey Trudy, so where was I?"

"You were about to tell me about Sam Mueller. Sorry to scoop you, dear, but I already heard. He's having an affair in Baltimore. That's the reason for all the 'business travel'. I hear his wife is livid. But, hey, I don't have much time right now. Can you connect me to Catonsville—A Mr. Whitely at the coroner's office? Sorry, I don't have the number."

"Sure, honey, but they're on C&P. Hold a sec while I get Dot on the line."

"Oh, sorry. I could have just walked to her office." The C&P exchange was the next building up the hill from the Times' office.

"No problem, hon. Sit tight."

Trudy heard a series of clicks and then Dot's voice. "Operator—is that you, Millie?"

"Yeah, hi Dot. I've got Trudy on the line for a Mr. Wrightly at the colonel's office in Catonsville."

"Sure thing, hon," replied Dot. "Hey, Trudy."

"Hi Dot," said Trudy. "How's Sam doing?"

"A lot better since Dr. Sykes pulled the molar. Thanks for asking. I'll have to call the Catonsville exchange for the number. Please hold."

After another series of clicks a nasally voice answered, "C and P. Number please?"

Dot said, "Hi Polly, this is Dot over at Ellicott City. I have Trudy on the line for a person to person with Mr. Knightly at Mr. Cornwell's office."

Polly said, "Trudy! How have you been, gal? Say, you know, I was just thinking about you. There's a new land investor in town, just down the street, a Mr. Harold—quite a dish. Money, too. I hear he's from Philadelphia. He's supposed to be at the subscription dance at Egge Hall tomorrow, why don't you come on out? I'll introduce you."

Trudy had been a widow for six years. Her friends were always trying to set her up with bachelors who were advancing in age. "Sorry, Polly. Can't make it. Besides, you know I already have two boys in my life." She was referring to her sons, Colin, 12, and Liam, 8. "Who needs a man?"

That drew a laugh and general agreement from all the ladies.

Polly asked, "So what was that party? Mr. Litty, was it? Never heard of him, but I can connect you to Dr. Cromwell's office. Maybe he's new there."

Dot said, "No, it's Dr. Cornwell. You know, corn, like in fritters."

Millie corrected, "No hon, I think she said Colonel—like in the Navy."

Dot countered, "Sam was in the Navy. I don't think they have Colonels. They have Captains."

Polly was confused. "I don't think we have a captain's office in Catonsville. I can try the Annapolis exchange?"

Trudy interjected, "Coroner—the Coroner's office. And the man's name, unless I have it wrong from Officer Wosch, is Whitely."

"Oh, him," said Polly with undisguised scorn. "I saw *him* at lunch today and he was huffed to be tied. He batty-fanged Officer Norris right there in front of everybody. You sure you want to talk to that podsnapper, hon?"

"I'm afraid I have to, Polly. Please connect me."

After more clicks and an extensive pause, a woman's voice came on the line. "Coroner's office, this is Evelyn speaking."

"Hey, Ev, this is Polly. I got a person-to-person for your boss, from Mrs. Gertude O'Flynn at the Ellicott City Times. He still in?"

"Oh, hi Trudy. Hold on. I'll see if he's finished with his meeting."

After a lengthy pause, a gruff man's voice came onto the line. "Officer Norris. To whom am I speaking?"

"Oh ... good afternoon, Officer Norris. I was holding for Mr. Whitely. This is Mrs. O'Flynn from the Ellicott City ..."

"Yes, yes. Mr. Whitely asked me to take the call. He's tied up with important matters. You can put Mr. Powell on now."

"Uh, Mr. Powell isn't here. He asked me to follow up on the electric car incident in Oella last..."

"Am I to understand that Mr. Powell is too busy to call and wants me to talk to his secretary?"

Trudy said, "Officer Norris, I am a *writer* at the Times. I have a few questions about ..." Trudy heard a derisive laughter on the line.

"Writer, indeed! Do you handle the gossip column or the recipes?"

Trudy controlled her indignation and kept her voice even. "Actually, I do handle both the personals and the recipes. I also do news reporting and features from time to time. Can you tell me if the police found anything when they came back to search the area today?"

"Today? Do you pester your husband with such absurd questions? Perhaps you have been indoors all day polishing your nails. The rain has been relentless, and the area was trampled last night by God knows how many people. There is no point in going back."

Trudy considered, but decided against, responding to his crack about her husband. "So then, I will write that no proper search has yet been done. Have you established the identity of the victim?"

More derisive laughter, "Really, Mrs. O'Flynn, I assume you read the story in the Sun. There is no way to identify such a body. He was probably a drifter who passed out on the tracks after one too many drinks. There was an empty whiskey bottle in his coat pocket. We will have to wait to see if anyone is reported missing. Now I do have *important* work to do. Please stick to your clothing ads and wedding announcements, and leave this to the professionals. Good day." Trudy heard a click and then silence.

"Trudy, honey," said Polly's voice, "He's a typical bully. He get's chewed out so he takes it out on you. A real razzle-dazzle. I wouldn't worry about it. The word is, Norris is a real flapdoodle in the sack."

The bawdiness of this comment drew laughter from the operators, who had all remained on the line.

The Calamitous Life of A. Emmett Harriman

By R. L. McReedy-Knibbs

Author of "The Overly Zealous Metaphor" and "Confessions of Alois Swoboda"

Reprinted by Permission on These Pages in Serial Fashion

INSTALLMENT THREE – THE YOUNG DRUGGIST

Thursday July 10, 1890

Clarksville, Maryland

Now I ain't going to lie. Course I took my sweet time in delivering Mrs. Bainberger's headache pills. Then I had myself a smoke and a few snorts from the bottle I keep in the knot of the big oak tree round the corner. I figured Pa was probably snoozing away the day as was his custom. And I was right, too. Pa always hollers at me, telling me I'm slamming the door every time I ingress or egress. I read those fancy words in a ghost story last week and had to look them up in Mrs. Wilson's dictionary. I like to spring high-falutin' words on folks and see them either get a look of confusion or contrary-wise just go on with what they were saying, pretending they understood. Either way, it's good sport.

So, course when I come in, I open the door real slow so as to make the hinges squeak extra loud. Then I give it a quick push at the end so it bangs against the wall.

Pa stood up behind the counter, squinting at the light from the open door and scratching his belly. He was supposed to take his monthly bath today in the washtub out back, but from the looks and smell of him I figured he ain't got round to it yet.

"Dammit, Gus," huffed Pa, still scratching, "why ya gotta be such a foozler?" He hobbled to the washbasin and scowled at himself in the mirror as he slicked back his few remaining strands of greasy hair with spit-moistened hands. All this did was accentuate his bulbous, well-veined proboscis. (That's another one of my words.) Pa turned and eyed me vexatiously.

I looked down at my worn shoes—one's got a hole in the toe. "Sorry, Pa," I said with as much sincerity as I could muster. I hate it when Pa calls me by my first name, but at least Gus is preferable to my Christian name, August. Who in Sam Hill wants to be named after a month? I prefer the sound of "Emmett." I figure it kind of makes me sound like a gun-slinging cowboy from the penny serials.

I set myself down on the rickety stool at the end of the counter and picked up the old issue of the Baltimore Sun I was reading before my delivery. I found my place in a story about two ladies who dressed up like men. Then they tramped on freight trains from Wilkesbarre all the way to Kansas City. I imagined one of them being real pretty with dark hair and powdered face, and smelling nice, too, in spite of wearing a derby hat and dusty coat.

"Ain't you got no more work to do?" Pa grumbled, nodding at the stack of prescription papers in the basket on the counter. "They ain't gonna fill themselves." The old man set himself back down on his chair behind the counter and rubbed his rheumatic knee. He adjusted the pillow under his rump and felt around on the floor to the side of the chair. He found his bottle, raised it to his lips, and then wiped his mouth with the back of his sleeve. "When you're done with those, you can sweep the dang porch." He took another drink and set the bottle down. "Dang people draggin' in their dang mud." He lowered his slouch hat over his eyes and leaned back, all the while muttering, "bunch a no-account, lick-spittle ... put up with this twaddle no..." His head fell back and he lapsed into an uneven snore.

Now let me tell you—I was fourteen years old at that time, and I'd been doing darn near all the work at the pharmacy since I was eight. Pa used to be a pretty good chemist, or so Mrs. Wilson told me, but after Ma died, he took to the bottle like a fish to water, like a pig to, well, you know. Anyhow, Pa pulled me out of the school on account of I was already good at reading and figuring. So now I filled the prescriptions, ordered the supplies, kept the books, and kept the shop clean and orderly while Pa supervised, or so he liked to call it, with his bottle of whiskey.

I didn't mind filling the prescription bags. The hardest part was deciphering the chicken scratch that Doc Wilson called handwriting. Then I'd have to look for the jar on the shelf, count out the pills, and write the name on the front of the bag. Most of the medicines were patented then, but every now and then I got to mix up concoctions by myself with the various powders and liquids. That was my favorite part. We had a big book we kept on the shelf called *American Dispensatory*, by John King, M. D. Pa had bookmarks and plenty of scribbling in the margins in the back section where the recipes were.

I started filling the first bag, which was for Dr. Batty's Asthma Cigarettes. That was an easy one. After that, I could tell from Pa's snore that he was well into his forty winks, so I snuck over and took a pull from his whiskey bottle. I winced at the taste. Pa liked Old Taylor when he could get it, but today he was working his way through an unmarked bottle of local moonshine.

I knew darn near as much about the pharmacy trade as Pa—heck, probably more. So I'll tell you a secret. Last fall, when I was opening a box of pills, inside there was an advertisement for a correspondence course offered by the Practical Druggist Institute in New York. I figured I'd eventually start out on my own, so I might as well get a diploma sooner rather than later. So I filled out the application and sent the money. Since I took care of the accounts, Pa was none the wiser. But I did have to lie about my age on account of they said you were supposed to be at least sixteen.

I was on the fourth bag when I heard a buggy pull up outside and then heavy footsteps on the creaky porch boards. The door swung open and banged against the wall. Pa actually fell off of his chair this time and I had to stop myself from laughing.

Everyone around these parts knew Mr. John Hill on account of him owning so much farmland up in Dayton—it was up the old Linden road a ways to the north. Everyone treated him like his name was Rockefeller. He was a tall man, thin as a rail, with a pockmarked face. He shaved his mustache like one of the Amish and grew his gray beard long, which fanned out below his chin like the end of a broom. At the advanced age of nearly seventy, Mr. Hill was a chronically wrathful man. I ain't never seen him crack a smile—not even once.

His boy, Charley, followed the old man in. Charley and me were good friends, at least I thought so then, before things changed. We was the same age and used to go to school together—that was back when Pa let me go to school. I caught Charley's eye as he came in and made a face, trying to make him laugh, but he just lowered his eyes. He warn't no fun around his old man.

What you need to know about Charley back then is that he always looked up to me on account of I was smart and already making a living and practically a man. Charley himself was about as sharp as a bag of night crawlers, and he was a troublemaker to boot, but you'd never convince his old man of that fact. He was always playing hooky from school and finding me out on my delivery routes. Then we'd go looking for mischief, or maybe just go hang out by the creek. It was Charley that showed me how to drink whiskey without gagging and roll cigarettes from tobacco he pilfered from his old man. He also had a mean streak—as likely to wallop you as well as shake your hand.

Mr. John Hill took in the unruly scene before him. A wave of rage that could curdle milk washed over the man's face.

Pa arose straight away and brushed himself off. He made his voice real soft and gentleman-like. "Mr. Hill. You're lookin' hale. How might I be of service?"

Mr. John Hill looked down at Pa disapprovingly. He started to speak but then had a fit of protracted obstreperous coughing and expectoration. (I learnt that in my correspondence course.) When he could finally talk, he croaked, "Do you know what time it is, sir?"

After momentary befuddlement, Pa took out his pocket watch and glanced at it. It evidently warn't in good order seeing that he shook it and held it to his ear. "Ah, I reckon it's about half three. Is it..."

"Three-thirty, and you are already blotto. I don't know why I give you my business. In the future, I may commence sending into Ellicott City for my wife's pills. Are they ready?" He added a condescending sigh.

Pa was a little fuzzy, having just awoken and bruised his rump when he flopped onto the floor. He turned to me and raised his eyebrows questioningly.

I hopped off my stool and started going through the bags in the "Done" basket. About halfway through I found the one labeled "Mary Hill" and handed it to Pa. He glanced at the information I had written on it—name, date, and the name of the medicine. He handed it to Mr. Hill. "Uh...Be sure to tell her to drink lots of clean water," he added sheepishly.

Mr. Hill grabbed the bag from Pa and took a quick look inside. He turned to Charley and barked, "Get on out and wait by the buggy."

Now I knew that Mr. Hill didn't much like me, but the conniption fit that came next knocked me and Pa into a cocked hat.

As he turned to me, the old man's face turned red as summer beet soup. "Heed me now, you little hornswoggler. You got most folks in this town flimflammed, but I see right through you. You stay plumb clear of my Charles, you hear? I'm telling you on account of he don't listen to me a lick—got as much sense as a bent nickel. And don't think I don't know how you are ever tempting him away from school—frolicking down by the creek, carrying on with liquor and cigarettes. Charles ain't no great shakes with school-learning, but he's a good boy. You, on the other hand, are a no-account weasel."

Then he rounded on Pa. "And you, sir, should be ashamed of yourself, liquoring up this early in the day, and I don't give a hoot how hot it is outside." He glared from me to Pa and back to me. After he got no response, he stormed out into the street.

Now Pa don't like to get cussed. And when he is, the first thing he does is come after me. So course that's what happened. "Dad Blazes, Gus, didn't I warn you about your tomfoolery with that man's boy! How'm I supposed to make a fist of anything in this town? Gonna ride us out on a rail if you don't ..."

I set myself down again on my stool. Pa went on for some time but I can't tell you what he said—might as well been a mule braying. I was looking at the ledger book. Then I interrupted Pa's tirade and said, "Hey Pa, you know Mr. Hill ain't paid in a coon's age? He's running up quite a tab."

KATIE TO PREPARE MUSKRAT

Thursday Evening, March 12, 1908

The rain had cleared by five o'clock when Trudy exited the offices of the Ellicott City Times. She crossed the wet cobblestones in front of Odd Fellow's Hall and started down the hill. She stopped for a moment to admire a green-feathered hat in the window of Caplan's Dry Goods Store, but decided against the purchase. Her widow's pension from the Army was late again, and she wouldn't get her next paycheck from the newspaper until the following Friday.

She was startled by a loud pop. An automobile had backfired and was now lumbering loudly up the slope of Main Street. The engine was revving ineffectually, gears were grinding, and a cloud of black smoke belched from the tailpipe. She exchanged a disapproving look with another woman who had been looking in the store window. Trudy was not a Luddite, and she realized that if things continued the way they had been, the days of horse-drawn carriages were numbered. But still, the noise of it bothered her. It was such an uncouth way to travel.

She continued down the street and stopped just past Tiber Alley in Goldberg's Grocery Store to buy a pound of Arbuckle's coffee and a slab of butter. The prices and quality in town were much better than they were up at the Oella Company Store near her home.

She emerged from the store and continued on her way. Two doors down she came to the Easton Sons Undertakers building just as Daniel Easton was locking the door for the day. "Hello Daniel. How's business?"

The tall, well-dressed man finished locking the door. He turned to her slowly with squinting, bespectacled eyes. Daniel was only twenty-five years old, but he had adopted the cadence and mannerisms of someone much older. "Ah, Trudy O'Flynn. It is always a pleasure to see you," he said in his lugubrious baritone. "Business is grand. You can always trust an undertaker, you know. He will be the last one to let you down." He smiled expectantly.

Trudy rolled her eyes. Daniel was never without a bad joke. At least it wasn't the one about his clients dying to see him. Trudy changed the subject. "Daniel—did they ... ask for your services in that incident on the electric car line last night?"

"Ah, Officer Wosch did mention that you would probably be making inquiries. As you know, I am sometimes asked to care for the remains in these situations, but in this case, I was not. Mrs. Easton and I retired early last night and heard nary a knock on the door. I assume the body was taken to Henderson's in Catonsville. They are quite strict, you know, about crossing a county line when a death occurs under suspicious circumstances."

"Yes. Well, thank you, Daniel. And say hello to Ella from me. Remember, she needs plenty of rest in her condition." Ella Easton was seven months pregnant with their third child and having a difficult time of it.

After taking her leave, Trudy walked past the already busy saloons on lower Main Street and entered the plaza in front of the B&O train station. Her friend, Viola Snowden, was waiting on a wooden bench under an awning in front of the station. As usual, she had her nose in a book.

Viola was twenty-five and had been one of Trudy's students back when she taught at the Oella schoolhouse. Viola could not go to the whites-only school, but word had gotten round the neighborhood that a bright young colored woman was in need of a tutor. Trudy took the job and the two had been fast friends ever since.

Viola looked up from her book as Trudy sat next to her. "Billy said five. Should be out any minute. Glad this rain is finally done."

Billy Hatwood was Viola's next-door neighbor. A young man of twenty-seven years, he was good-natured and outgoing, but mentally not well endowed. He had come to this area from North Carolina with his mother, Katie, eight years ago after Katie had married a Maryland millworker. Alas, it did not work out. Her husband ran off to parts west with another woman, leaving Katie and Billy to fend for themselves. Katie found work cleaning and cooking in farmhouses in Oella, while Billy labored at Dorsey's coal yard and livery here in town.

There was one thing about Billy that baffled all who knew him. He couldn't read, and could barely write his name, let alone do anything with numbers. But if you put a banjo in his hands, he could play back any tune flawlessly, regardless of style, after a single hearing. He sometimes joined Trudy and her father-in-law at gatherings where they would provide Irish music for ceili dances or wakes.

Before long, Billy emerged from the gate of the coal yard in front of the freight depot. Smiling widely, he waved, adjusted his derby, buttoned his black coat, and started toward them.

When he drew close, Viola noticed his coat. "Billy, that's not the coat you were wearing yesterday. Where'd you get this one?"

"Hey Aunt Viola," said Billy. "You like it? Got it up on the bridge last night. It got caught up in the rafters after that white man throwed it." He modeled his new coat for them, turning this way and that with an unwavering smile.

Viola's tone was disapproving, "What do you mean, young man? What's this about a white man? I hope you didn't steal somebody's coat!"

Billy became defensive, "No. No. I promise, I ain't steal nothin'. I saw the man throwed it out halfway 'cross the bridge. I figured he ain't want it no more."

As the three started walking toward home, Trudy and Viola were able, with no small effort, to tease the story from Billy. He had gotten off late the previous night, well after dark. As he entered the covered bridge, in the feeble illumination provided by the electric lights at either end, he saw a man in the center of the span hop up on one leg and throw something through the open rafters between the side of the bridge and the roof. The man then came toward him, limping badly.

By now they were on the covered bridge themselves. Billy imitated the man's unsteady gait by hopping on his right leg and holding the wall with his left hand. "A'first I thought he was just corned. But I ain't smell no liquor on him when he passed. So when

I get to where I saw'd him jump, I look up, and there I see something." He pointed to the rafters. "I climb up and this here is what I found." He modeled the coat for them again, grinning as before.

"That ain't all," he continued. "The man shun't've throwed it away, 'cause he wasn't even wearin' one. He ain't had no hat neither. Just a limpin' along in his suspenders." Billy imitated the limp again. "I seen it myself. No hat."

They emerged from the bridge on the Oella side and started up Westchester Avenue. It was a steep, winding hill. They paused to rest when they got to the middle of the bridge over the trolley line.

Trudy said, "Well Billy, I think it's a fine, new coat, although it looks a little big around the chest for you." There was more than ample material for Billy's slim frame. "Do you think Viola and I could take a look at it? Just for a minute?"

"Sure," replied Billy, and he started to remove the coat. "But, hey, we got to hurry on home on time. Katie's makin' burgoo. Viola, you comin' over with your little girl ain't you? I caught the muskrat myself yesterday down by the river. Gonna be good!" He rubbed his stomach.

He handed the coat to Trudy. The sun had not yet set and there was ample light on the open bridge. Trudy and Viola examined the coat inside and out. It was a fine, woolen men's overcoat—practically new. They found nothing in the pockets. Sewn behind one lapel was a label saying, "Zehner's Fine Apparel – All that's new and fashionable – Catonsville, Maryland."

As Viola handed the coat back, she said, "Billy! Look at your shirt! What have you been into today?" A brownish stain was visible on Billy's right shoulder and shirtsleeve.

He looked down and noticed the discoloration for the first time. "I dunno. Been workin' outside all day." He tried to brush off the stain with his hand.

Viola sniffed at the sleeve of the black coat. She rubbed the material between her thumb and fingers and then examined her hand. "It's from the coat. It doesn't smell like much though." She handed the coat back to Billy. "Just tell Katie to give it a good washing."

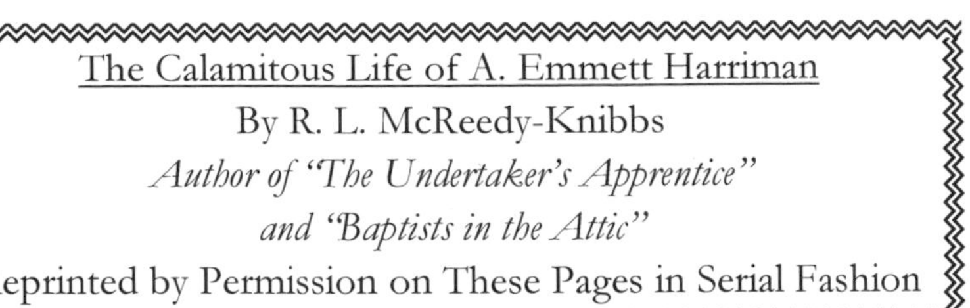
The Calamitous Life of A. Emmett Harriman

By R. L. McReedy-Knibbs

Author of "The Undertaker's Apprentice" and "Baptists in the Attic"

Reprinted by Permission on These Pages in Serial Fashion

INSTALLMENT FOUR – THE DAMNABLE DENTON

Wednesday July 23, 1890

Clarksville, Maryland

I remember that day real clear on account of it's the day when my life jumped the tracks and started careening into the swamp. (That's what's called a metaphor—I also took a correspondence course in fancy writing. They recommend using a lot of 'em.)

So I set out early in the morning on one of my deliveries, and before I left, Pa says to me not to get into any shenanigans and to hurry on back, but he always said that so I didn't give it no mind. Now I'm going to tell you what I reckon happened with Pa that day, but I don't know for sure on account of I warn't there. I'm going to tell it like I learnt the writers do in the penny serials with lots of fancy words and metaphors. Here goes...

Pa leaned back in his easy chair behind the counter at the dilapidated pharmacy, attempting to keep cool with a paper fan and a bottle of Old Taylor's. It had rained cats and dogs the previous night, making today's afternoon heat intolerable sticky.

Pa was feeling jittery. He wanted his wiseacre son to get home and then high-tail it to the post office to fetch the mail. The previous week, Pa had gotten a letter saying that his dear Uncle Beauregard down in Georgia had finally kicked the bucket. It was about dang time, Pa thought. The old coot had never taken much of a liking to Pa, and, as far as Pa was concerned, the feeling was mutual. Nevertheless and notwithstanding, Pa was hoping he might get hold of some money, or even land, from the probate court. He had been vexed lately on account of the money from Ma's estate was plumb near gone.

Pa took a pull from the bottle. He felt the soothing warmth coat his mouth and throat. He leaned back on his chair against the shelves, closing his eyes and muttering, as was his proclivity. "No account, pigeon-livered hubbub, gonna be hell to pay when..."

An hour or so later, Pa awoke from an unpleasant dream. "Ah! Vazey mutton-shunter! What in the..."

After a moment of confusion, he realized where he was—still in his own deserted pharmacy, and still hot as Hades in July, which was not far from the truth of it. He got up, smacking his lips. He looked disapprovingly toward the bottle on the floor aside his chair—empty as a church on a weekday. He sauntered to the door and squinted out into the street—still no sign of that malmsey-nosed offspring of his. Pa figured he was going to have to hoof to the post office on his own two feet.

He hadn't had sight of his boy since early in the morning when Emmett set off for Dayton on a delivery. He ought have been back hours ago—noon at the latest.

By mid afternoon, Pa figured he had waited long enough. He splashed lukewarm water onto his face from the bucket on the porch and used a stained ivory comb to straighten the sweat-soaked hairs on his head. He tucked in his shirt, tightened his suspenders, and straightened his vest. He donned his straw boater and headed unsteadily for the door.

Pa returned from his errands about an hour later. The exercise had left him spent. He had procured a new bottle of whiskey and wasted no time in unscrewing the top and taking a sustaining swallow.

There was still no sign of his laggard son.

He had collected two letters from the post office. He hastily tore open the thick one from Camden County, Georgia. It was from some lawyer in the probate court, written in fancy language in a florid cursive that was hard to decipher:

To all whom these present shall come, Greeting. Know ye that on the 17th day of July A. D. 1890, the last will and testament of Beauregard Sidney Harriman, deceased, was exhibited in open court (having been previously filed in my office) and in proper form of law...

Land sakes, get to the point, thought Pa.

...and ordered to be recorded a copy of which is hereto annexed and administration upon the estate of said deceased was granted to Mr. Denton A. Harriman, having taken the oath and performed all other requisites required by law...

Pa let out a heavy sigh. He had been afraid of this. His cousin, Denton, was a no-good, gold-digging jollocks if ever there was one. He'd be sure to cause trouble.

...in these precincts is hereby legally authorized to administer the estate of said deceased conveyed by said will according to the tenor and effect these of and according to...

"Come *on*," Pa grumbled aloud. He skipped to the next page where the actual will had been copied.

In the name of God, Amen, I Beauregard S. Harriman of the city of Marietta, county of Cobb in the state of Georgia, being of sound mind hereby make and publish this my last will and testament hereby revoking all wills by me heretofore made. I appoint...

"Balls! Get to it already!" Pa skipped down to the list of assets and assignments.

...my prize American Cream draft horse to my beloved nephew, August, if he come in person to claim it.

Pa quickly scanned through the remaining items. "That *can't* be all," he muttered.

But it was. He got to the end. There was no more mention of his name. (August was Pa's name too. That's also how come I hated it so much.) He read the whole list again to be sure. The house, the land, and the money were all going to the damnable Denton. Pa was getting ... a draft horse? And then, only if he traveled all the way to Georgia to take possession of it?

Pa felt a volcano of anger rising in his gut. He took a prodigious nip from the bottle and began pacing back and forth in the shop. Denton had perched himself there in Georgia, sweet-talking the old foozler in his final days. Pa stopped his pacing and checked the date on the will. Sure enough, it had been made only two months ago. Pa had seen the will from years ago with his own eyes—before he came to Maryland. Pa was counting on getting half of the damned land and half of the damned money. It was his damned right.

But what could he do? He took an ample pull from the bottle and continued his furious pacing. He was here and the humbug Denton was there. The court had spoken. Even if he had a mind to fight this thing, he'd have to wheedle for money to pay a lawyer in Georgia. Then he'd have to find a way to get himself down there full-chisel. And it probably wouldn't do a lick of good. He knew from experience how vexing it could be to try to reverse a court decision. The cutty-eyed Denton would have the land sold by then, and he'd have high-tailed it back to Tennessee.

Pa returned to the pharmacy counter, took another drink, and stared bitterly at the papers. He started collecting them together with a mind to burn them straight away. When he got to the bottom of the pile he noticed the second letter he had retrieved from the post office. "What's this, then?" He mumbled.

It was from some pharmacy school in New York. "I didn't order anything from..." He tore open the envelope and read the letter. It appeared to be addressed to his boy, Mr. A. Emmett Harriman. Pa's middle name was Lindsey, but he never used it.

It was a printed form letter with the blanks filled by hand:

Dear Mr. Harriman,

Congratulations! You have successfully completed our correspondence course in Pharmacy, Chemistry, Materia Medica, Toxicology, and Prescription Compounding. The Practical Druggist Institute of New York is well regarded and fully accredited in your state of __Maryland__. Enclosed please find your notarized, embossed, and fully ratified certificate signed by our president, the Honorable Dr. Alois Swoboda, M.D., Ph.D., D.D.S., J.D.

As directed by you when you tendered your final payment, we have forwarded a copy of your certificate and the application fee to the appropriate regulators in the state of __Maryland__. You will be receiving a license from the regulating body in that state in due course.

Enclosed was a separate sheet with a fancy script certifying that A. Emmett Harriman was qualified to practice pharmacy in any state in the union.

~ Meanwhile ~

So that's about how I figure Pa's day went. Now, while he was getting himself into a state of botheration, I was having myself an agreeable day. Here's what happened:

Pa sent me on my way early to make two deliveries out Dayton way, and I had good luck on the Linden Road. A farmer by the name of Oakley came passing by and said I could climb onto the back of his wagon atop some hay bales on account of he had his prize pig sitting with him in the bench. He took me almost the whole way before I had to jump off and make the rest of the way on foot.

So I made my deliveries in good time and, seeing how I was not far from the trail to the creek, I thought myself deserving of some recreation on the hot summer day. When I got to the clearing, sure enough, Charley Hill was already there along with his older brother, Little-John. They both set themselves on a rock, dangling their bare feet in the cool water, passing a whiskey bottle betwixt them. I took off my shoes straight away and joined them.

The brothers had poached the whiskey from their old man's supply. It warn't no secret in these parts that the venerated Mr. John Hill operated stills in the woods behind his farm. The negro farmhands ran the stills at night and every morning they come out of the woods hauling a wagon loaded with barrels and jugs. Charley once told me that their entire basement was full of whiskey.

After an hour of drinking, splashing, and catching frogs with the Hill boys, I made up my mind to take the entire day off. Pa could mind his own store for one afternoon. In the back of my mind I started fashioning a tall tale about what had delayed me—maybe something to do with helping out at Mrs. Wilson's place. But I probably wouldn't need it. Hell, the old man would likely snooze away the afternoon and wouldn't even notice I warn't there.

We splashed and swam in the creek through the morning and into the afternoon. Charley had pilfered a loaf of bread. Little-John had a sack with some jerky, pickles, and hard cheese. We had the whiskey and all the water we could drink from the stream. After our bellies were full, we had ourselves a series of contests—rock throwing, belching, and pissing.

At one point, Charley got riled and was fixing to whoop me when I started talking about Mahalie, the Hills' older sister. I was telling them about the time at the Hill's house, back when they'd let me inside—they don't anymore—when Mahalie lifted her skirt all the way up and showed me her quim, and she warn't even wearing any knickers! I swear it's the truth. So Charley started yelling at me to take it back and saying he was going to sock me in the mouth. Little-John, on the other hand, just wanted details about what it looked like.

The altercation didn't last long, and soon the talk lapsed into a comparison of what each of us knew about girls and their private parts. I was surprised at how little first-hand knowledge Little-John possessed, seeing as how he was almost eighteen. Before long, the heat and liquor got the better of us. The conversation wavered and we all set down in the grass and started in to snoozing.

Later, on the way home, I had no luck getting a ride. There warn't a single carriage on the road and I had to walk the entire way in the full heat. So I was plumb parched when I made the final turn and came in sight of the pharmacy. I recollect that before I went in, I stopped on the porch and dunked my head full in the bucket.

I figured I'd find Pa asleep in the chair behind the counter, so I was surprised to see him standing, beet-faced, by the window. He had some papers clutched in his hands.

THE MORNING DEW AND SAINT ANNE'S

Thursday Evening, March 12, 1908

Trudy, Viola, and Billy came at last to the level ridge at the top of Westchester Avenue. Trudy's companions continued northward toward the colored neighborhood. She turned left and walked a block down Hollow Road to the tenement house that she shared with her extended family.

She stopped in front of the small, frame house, closed her eyes, and stood still in the cool evening air. Her husband had been on her mind all afternoon since that rude policeman had mentioned him on the phone. She surrendered now to a moment of reverie.

Trudy had been only seventeen when, in the fall of 1889, she was forced to leave the Patapsco Female Institute after the headmistress found out she had become pregnant. She had been quite a troublemaker in those days. She and her bunkmate used to sneak into town regularly at night after everyone was asleep. On one such occasion, a local boy about their own age saved the two girls from being raped—and perhaps worse—by a gang of ruffians emerging from a local saloon. This boy was Thomas O'Flynn.

She remembered how they breathlessly evaded their attackers. Tom led them through alleys, behind buildings, into and out of basement windows, down a trap door, and at one point, along a foul-smelling stretch of Tiber Creek under an overhanging building. He seemed to know every shortcut and hiding place in the city. Tom became her companion and protector on her clandestine nocturnal outings after that.

One thing that had impressed her about Tom was how clean he always was. You could smell most boys his age from half a block away. Tom worked on the other side of the river, in Oella Woolen Mill. He told her that, after he got off his shift every day, he would hike two miles up the Patapsco and bathe at the head of the millrace. He did this religiously, regardless of the season.

She remembered the warm autumn night when she snuck out of the institute and met Tom just outside the gates. In the moonlight he guided her far up Church Road and then down a steep path that led to the Patapsco. They crossed the railroad tracks and forded the shallow river just below the dam. They arrived at the head of the millrace and paused expectantly, both knowing what was about to happen.

Each took turns undressing the other. Tom retrieved a cake of soap from a nook between two boulders. They bathed each other from head to toe and then made love on the grassy hillside to the sound of cooing frogs. It was the first time for both of them. Trudy shivered now, remembering the pain, thrill, and joy of that moment.

Some time later Trudy made the mistake of confiding to her roommate that she had missed her monthly blood. The headmistress found out that very day and sent word to her father in Richmond. Her father was a stern man whose reputation was more important to him than anything. He summarily disowned his own daughter. He sent a letter stating that he would pay no further tuition and recommended that she be immediately expelled.

She had been a good student, especially in music and writing, but she had no practical skills with which to support herself, let alone a child. Thomas did the honorable thing and proposed to marry her straight away. They had a quick wedding at St. Paul's Catholic Church, and Trudy came to live with Tom's family here in Oella.

She remembered when Tom first brought her to this house. Like all tenement houses, it was small, functional, and devoid of any frill. At the top of the stairs were two bedrooms. Tom's parents lived in one. Tom and Niall, his brother, shared the other. On the ground floor was a kitchen and living area with a potbelly stove in the corner. Tom and Trudy moved into a storage room that leaned off of the back of the house. Privacy was in short supply. Anyone needing to use the outhouse in the back would typically go through their room rather than out the front door and then having to walk around the house.

Trudy had been inspired by the unhesitating way she had been taken in and accepted by her new family. Tom's mother was especially fond of Trudy and fawned over her constantly, making sure she was well rested and had plenty to eat. This was to be her first grandchild and she wanted it "done proper."

But alas for Trudy, motherhood at such a young age was not to be. She miscarried two months after moving in with her new family. The midwife said it would have been a boy. Tom's mother was heartbroken and insisted on taking the little bundle to St. Paul's to be baptized. Trudy didn't think the priest would be willing to do such a thing, but she said nothing. She never even asked what had become of it.

One thing about that time had always given Trudy a sense of guilt: She felt almost no grief. It had been a time of rapid change. The fact that there would be one less complication in her life gave her a sense of relief more than anything else.

After years of trying, Trudy and Tom eventually had two boys: Colin was born in 1896, and then Sean in 1900. The little house grew steadily more crowded. Niall married, and now occupied one upstairs room with his wife and three children. Tom's father, Paddy, still lived in the same room upstairs, although alone now, Tom's mother having passed away in 1903. That was shortly after Tom was killed, fighting for the U.S. Army in the Philippines. Trudy recalled this, as always, with a pang of bitterness.

These days, she still lived in the back room with her two boys. She still had no privacy.

Trudy shook herself from her daydream. She ascended the steps to the porch and wiped her mud-caked boots on the mat. She pushed open the front door to a typical scene of early evening bedlam. Her eight-year-old son, Sean, and her seven-year-old niece were donning overcoats and boots, preparing for their job as "dinner toters." They would be bringing evening meals to Niall, his son, and a few neighbors who were working the late shift at the mill. Trudy put down her parcels and helped her niece with the troublesome top button of her coat. "Be careful on the steep part at the bottom of the hill," she said. "With all of this rain, it's sure to be a slippery mess."

Catherine, Trudy's sister-in-law, was stirring a pot on the stove while her four-year-old son sat below her, playing with wooden blocks and pulling on his mother's skirt.

"Where's The Old Man?" Trudy asked, referring to her father-in-law. Nobody called Paddy anything other than "The Old Man" these days.

Catherine had abandoned the pot on the stove and began packing a satchel of food for the dinner toters. "He's out back again—says his stomach's acting up. He's out of his something-bark elixir. He wants someone to go into town for it tomorrow."

Trudy nodded and rolled her eyes. The Old Man was a bit of a hypochondriac. He had a long list of elixirs, pills, ointments, and powders that he used on a daily basis. He was very particular about where each medication was procured, requiring the children of the house to make frequent visits to the various pharmacies in town. He used Dr. Martin's Elixir for his stomach, Ayer's Sarsaparilla for his cough, Doan's Kidney Pills for his urination problems, Johnson's Blood and Liver tonic for ... Trudy wasn't quite sure. And there were several others.

The Old Man did have real health issues, most notably his poor breathing. He had started working at the mill right after he arrived in this country, back when it was still owned by Union Manufacturing Company. It was a cotton mill back then, before William Dickey bought it at auction and converted it to wool. Paddy spent many years working in the carding room, one of the first steps in textile processing. The air there was always saturated with cotton fibers. Most of Paddy's boyhood friends who worked in the room were long gone. He was lucky to still be alive at seventy-two.

Trudy's older son, Colin, was scratching a pencil on a tablet under a kerosene lamp on the family table. Relieved of her overcoat and rubber boots, Trudy crossed the room and stood behind the boy. She placed a hand gently on his head and examined the paper he was working on. "Long division?"

"Yeah. It ain't hard, but it's boring. I don't see the point. How's this going to help me at the mill?"

Trudy leaned close to his ear. "Remember our deal, young man. You may start at the mill after your birthday, but you have to keep up your studies at night."

The boy sighed heavily and continued his labor. Colin would be turning twelve in August and already had a fierce independent streak. Thanks to a 1902 Maryland law, for which Trudy had canvassed tirelessly, children younger than twelve could no longer be employed in mills and factories. From twelve to sixteen, a child could work only with the permission of a parent.

Trudy had seen first hand the difficulty of escaping mill life. The work was physically and mentally exhausting, leaving little time for self-improvement. After her miscarriage, she had begun working in the weaving room alongside her new mother-in-law. The whole family would trudge down Hollow Road every morning before the six o'clock whistle. The ten-hour shifts seemed interminable. At night she would wake in a start from a recurring nightmare in which she was working the loom all by herself. She would let her attention waver for a moment and was struck by the shuttle as it shot through the warp.

From what she had read about labor problems at other mills around the country, she knew that Oella Mill was better than most in terms of the way they treated their employees. The Dickey sons who now owned the mill actually worked there daily and knew most of the employees by name. Still, she wanted a better life for her boys. But she had to agree with The Old Man and her brother-in-law that the extra income from Colin's half-wages would be a help to the household.

She credited her albeit-incomplete education for her own escape from mill life. After several years of working at the mill, and two more miscarriages, she started helping the neighboring children with their schoolwork in the evenings. She was good at it, and word got around. One year, one of the teachers at the Oella schoolhouse took ill, and they offered Trudy the job. She jumped at the chance.

Managing a large group of mixed-age children in a room that was often either freezing or sweltering was challenging, but she loved it. The children were eager and full of promise. There were occasional discipline problems, like when the older boys would fight over whose turn it was to fetch water from the pump up the hill, but for the most part she spent her time filling her students with the love of history, reading, music, and mathematics.

In those days Trudy had been a voracious reader. In addition to books and fiction serials, she read the Ellicott City Times every week and the Baltimore Sun whenever she could get her hands on a copy. She wrote frequent letters to the editor of both papers, commenting on opinion pieces she disagreed with, or factual errors that she found. To deliver the letters she would hike into town every few days.

It was on one of these trips that she met Edward Powell, the editor at the Ellicott City Times. She had decided early on that it made no sense to send a letter through the post to the Times when she had to pass by their building on Main Street to get to the post office. So instead, she would stroll into the office and drop her letters off with a secretary. Edward was standing there one day when she did this, and was delighted to make her acquaintance, having enjoyed reading her letters for months. He took her out to lunch and offered her a job on the spot.

After the family finished their meal, they dispersed to work on various chores. The Old Man reached atop a high shelf and retrieved a jug of local moonshine. He poured himself two fingers and set the mug on the floor by the chair next to the stove. He took out his fiddle, applied rosin to the bow, and plucked off a few loose horsehairs. He tuned the fiddle and started into a reel. Trudy recognized the tune as "The Morning Dew." He began playing slowly, gradually accelerating to the tune's normal frenetic tempo. It was one of those minor-key tunes that made Trudy imagine the workings of some fine and complicated machine, like one of the looms at the mill. It was impossible to keep one's foot from tapping during such a tune.

Trudy retrieved her tin whistle and joined The Old Man just as he was transitioning to St. Anne's Reel, a livelier tune in D major. She had read somewhere that there were three types of Irish music: tunes that made you cry, tunes that made you sleep, and tunes that made you hop with joy. This was the latter type. From St. Anne's they went into another reel, and after that a jig. The music went on for some time while the children engaged in impromptu dances.

Trudy recalled a warm summer evening years ago when they were playing tunes like this on the front porch with a few neighbors. A young negro man came walking down the hill from Westchester Avenue with a banjo slung over his shoulder. He introduced himself as Billy Hatwood and asked if he could join in the music making. The Old Man reluctantly agreed, grumbling something under his breath about not wanting to play Camptown Races. Billy took no offense. He was very amiable, with a wide smile that never left his face. He sat on the railing, tuned his banjo, and immediately launched into the tune they had been playing when he arrived. It was a complicated, five-part jig called Doctor O'Neill. They asked where he had learned it, and he replied, grinning, that he heard it for the first time as he walked down the lane just now. That was when they learned about Billy's uncanny ability. They liked the rhythmic drive that the banjo added to their ensemble. After that, Billy was always welcome in their gatherings.

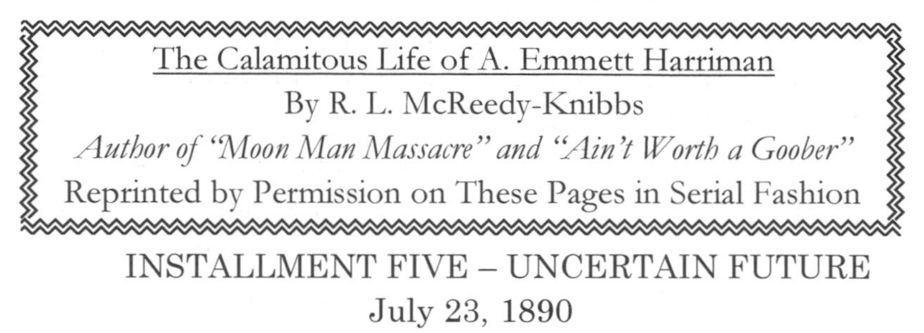

The Calamitous Life of A. Emmett Harriman

By R. L. McReedy-Knibbs

Author of "Moon Man Massacre" and "Ain't Worth a Goober"

Reprinted by Permission on These Pages in Serial Fashion

INSTALLMENT FIVE – UNCERTAIN FUTURE

July 23, 1890

Clarksville, Maryland

It was plain as the nose on your face that Pa had worked himself up into a lather about something. But I figured it couldn't have been on account of me being late, 'cause, to be honest, that happened most days. So I tried to make myself all casual, and I walked past him to the end of the counter and set myself on my stool. "Hey Pa, I made the deliveries," I said as cheerful as I could. I snatched up the newspaper and began leafing through it.

I started to read an article about a new machine in Buffalo that can make ten million match sticks a day out of pine logs, but out of the corner of my eye I could see Pa just staring at me with that crumpled paper in his hand. I could hear his weazy breathing from clear across the room. Then I noticed the near-empty bottle on the shelf behind the counter—a different bottle from the one he was working on that morning, so I figured he must be even more corned than usual for this time of the afternoon.

I pretended to read and waited. After a while he stirred. "Well ain't you all puffed up like a peacock," he grumbled. "You're just gonna set there. Of all the uppity, ungrateful, ... and after all I done for you."

Now before he said that, I figured that the thing that had got Pa into such a state was something to do with Uncle Beauregard's will. I knew he was waiting for news about it. Then it dawned on me—that paper in his hand. He must have gone and fetched the mail.

"Hey Pa—what's that you got in your hand? Did you hear about the will?"

Pa adopted the sarcastic manner and singsong voice he usually saved for when he was talking ill about some townsfolk after they left the store. "Well, I just don't know, dear son. It appears to be a letter from some highfalutin school all the way up in the State of Nee-ooooo York, addressed to somebody named 'Mr. A. Emmett Harriman.' But that don't sound like me, and I don't recollect any occasion to have business with them. Ain't you..."

"Hey—that's for me. Let me have it." I started toward the old man but Pa took a step backward and moved the paper behind his back.

"Let you have it? Oh, step on over here—I'll let you have it sure enough." Now he held the letter high above his head.

"C'mon Pa—It ain't like that. I was gonna tell you if I passed."

"Oh, was you, now? When did you reckon that was gonna be? After you skedaddle to New York and set up your own store? You was gonna set yourself down and write me a letter and say 'Dear Pa, I got my own shop now. Please send my inheritance.' Then you'd be all Billy Noodle up there, hobnobbing with your Wall Street buddies and cavorting with plug-ugly wagtail Yankee strumpets in some rum hole. You'll be hanging out like a hair in a biscuit. I know ..."

"Inheritance? Pa, you ain't got a two nickels to rub together. You're three months behind on the rent for this here store and that ratbag room upstairs where we sleep. You keep talking, but you ain't made a fist of nothing since Ma died. You take any extra money we make here and buy whiskey. We ain't never going to..."

I stopped short when the significance of what Pa had said dawned on me. "Wait... you thought I was gonna move to New York? So ... I passed the course? Let me see that letter." I moved toward Pa again.

Now reader, after I've had time to think on it, I knew I was right about Pa's lowly financial state, but I see now that speaking my mind out loud in that manner just blackened Pa's mood even further. Remember that he had just learnt that he was plumb cut out of Uncle Beauregard's will, and now with me being so ornery and all, I reckon it just put him over the edge.

Pa set into shouting like I never heard him done before. "I ain't gonna abide any more of your twaddle. Stealing my hard-earned money and sending it to a bunch of Yankee scammers, and then telling me I can't take a drink from time to time when I never done nothing but provide for you your whole miserable life. Why, that's it! I ain't had cause to do this lately, but that's the last straw!" He reached behind the counter and came out with a leather strap. "Here's your letter. Come and get it." He commenced swinging the strap in wide circles.

Reader, something snapped in me that day, too. I reckon knowing that I passed the pharmacy test filled me with manly gumption, and I warn't about to take no more whippings from nobody, specially my good-for-nothing Pa.

The two of us started in at each other, and the powerful ructions that ensued are still talked about in Clarksville to this day. It began with shouting and fisticuffs. Then we got to throwing things—glass jars of pills and powders, bottles of all manner of acids, oils, formaldehyde, and other solutions. Pretty soon an unholy concoction was brewing on the slippery floor. But we kept at it—tools, furniture, the balance scale, even the cash register became projectiles. A crowd gathered outside the pharmacy and peered in through the open door as the battle raged on. At one point Pa's easy chair came crashing through the front store window followed by Pa himself. He yelled something about 'gibfaced, pigeon-livered Sherman,' and ran back into the store full-chisel.

By the time the deputy sheriff arrived, we were still going at it like a couple of gamecocks although more slowly on account of we were both tuckering out. The lawman quickly separated us. He brung me outside by the scruff of the neck and told Tom Cady to take me down the street to Doc Wilson so he could make sure I didn't have any serious injuries. Then he took Pa away to spend the night in the drunk tank. I could hear the old man caterwauling the entire way.

Doc Wilson looked me over and, aside from copious contusions and abrasions, and a sprained wrist; he said there warn't nothing wrong with my internal workings. Mrs. Wilson gave me a blueberry tart she just baked and asked if I'd like to stay in their spare room upstairs. But I said no and that I'd just as soon head on home. So I came back to the destroyed pharmacy, lit a kerosene lamp, limped up the stairs, and fell into bed.

Pa didn't come home the next day or even the day after that. The deputy sheriff came by and told me that Pa was still in the drunk tank, and that the Lutheran pastor had visited him. He said the old man had found religion and he even took an oath of sobriety. Now this warn't the first time I heard that, so I didn't expect nothing to come of it.

I got out the broom and the mop and spent my time cleaning up the store as best as I could. More than half of the jars and bottles were broken. I placed anything that was salvageable in the front corner of the store by the boarded-up window. Among these was a glass-stoppered bottle of muriatic acid that Pa bought long ago when he used to mix his own remedies. It was a good thing that hadn't busted or it would have burnt a hole in the floor.

I started making a list of supplies that we would need to reorder. I had some money put away that Pa didn't know about, so I warn't worried about that. Mrs. Wilson was always kindly to me, and she brung me meals in the mornings and afternoons.

So you see, at that time I was figuring that we'd eventually reopen the pharmacy and things would go on more or less like they always had, except for one notion that kept popping into my head: Now that I had my own diploma, what did I need Pa for?

On the third day after the fight, early in the morning, Pa come walking through the front door like a dog with his tail between his legs. One eye was bandaged and his arm was in a sling. He nodded to me and then set himself in his easy chair by the front door. Pa started saying something about how he come to understand that this was the Lord working in his mysterious ways, and that God had forgiven him for his drinking and so Pa would forgive me for being so ungrateful, and that we both needed to pray real hard—or some such twaddle that the preachers are always peddling.

Now I ain't making excuses for what I did next, and I sure had me many hard lessons since that time about taking "responsibility for my actions," as the doctors I seen are always saying. But try to understand, reader: Pa warn't going to change, never. We'd been down that particular road a time or two. He'd be back to his drinking within the week, guaranteed. So, judge me if you want to, but I figured I was just doing what had to be done. Hell, why don't we call what *I* did the Lord's work? But ain't no preacher ever going to say that.

So I stood up and stomped toward the door. "Okay, Pa, there's fresh water on the porch if you get parched. I'll be back tonight." On my way out I stooped to pick up a bottle from the pile of salvaged supplies.

After I left, I spent the day by the creek. I might have liked some friendly company, but Charley and his brothers never showed. I figured their old man must have put the fear of God into them to keep clear of me on account of word of the fight at the pharmacy was all over the county. So I just sat there with my feet in the creek, making plans for how things were going to be different from now on and how I was going to make a success of the pharmacy and make lots of money and buy me some fancy clothes and maybe my own buggy and be a respectable man. Then maybe I'd marry Mahalie and settle down and have me some boys of my own. I had it all worked out.

So about an hour before sunset I figured I had waited long enough, and whatever was going to happen would have happened by then. I made a point of walking the long way around and entering town by the deputy sheriff's house. Sure enough, he and his wife were sitting on the porch enjoying the cool evening air.

The lawman saw me come out of the woods and up the road. He got up from his rocking chair and came out to meet me. "Son, I'm afraid I got some bad news for you. It's about your Pa."

I didn't say nothing.

"Well, there's no easy way to tell you, so I'll just out with it. Your Pa—well, he passed this morning.

The pastor stopped by to check on him, and found him on the floor. The doc said it looks like his heart or maybe his ulcers gave out. Lord knows he wasn't in the best of health. Sam's got him over at the undertaker's."

My mind was racing but I held my tongue. My plan worked.

The deputy sheriff put his hand on my shoulder and adopted a comforting tone. "Son, I know he wasn't an easy man to live with, but he's with the Lord now. Look—maybe you shouldn't go back home. You got any kin nearby you can stay with?"

I shook my head.

"Well, anyway, you should be with other folks. Don't worry about your Pa. We'll figure out the arrangements. You could stay here if you..."

I shook my head again. "I thank you kindly for the offer, but I reckon I'll be all right." I walked off in the direction of the pharmacy.

The sheriff called after me. "Emmett, I'll come by to check on you in the morning. If you change your mind, come on back here."

When I got back to the shop, the first thing I did was to take the bucket of discolored water from the porch and dump it in the ditch alongside the house. Then I went to the pump, rinsed the bucket, and then rinsed it again. Some of the galvanized coating on the inside had dissolved. It would probably rust before long.

EDITOR PREVAILS OVER OBJECTIONS

Friday, March 13, 1908

Trudy had not slept well. She had not actually seen the body of the man on the tracks, but that didn't stop her overactive brain from producing gruesome images all night. Each time she awakened, she thought about the case and realized that she had many questions but no answers.

It had already been an eventful morning. After leaving her house, she met Viola on the corner of Westchester Avenue, as was their custom. When they were almost at the bottom of the hill, Viola mentioned that a young neighborhood boy had found a fancy porkpie hat in the creek near Oella Avenue. Trudy insisted that Viola take her back up to the boy's house. This took some persuasion because it meant Viola would be late for the breakfast shift at Kraft's diner.

They were in luck. The eight-year-old was just about to leave for his job at the lumberyard. (Child labor laws were not enforced for negroes.) The boy proudly showed Trudy his new possession, and, since it was on his way to work, he took her to the spot in the stream where he had found it.

The hat was practically new and had survived a night in the stream with little damage. It was dark green, almost black, with a wide light gray ribbon around the base of the crown. Trudy looked on the inside and found a label that was very similar to the one she had seen in Billy's coat: J. Zehner's Men's Apparel.

Later, after arriving at work, Trudy took out a pad of paper. She always found making lists to be helpful in organizing her thoughts. She primed her pen and wrote across the top: "What We Know." She underlined it. Under this heading she wrote:

- *Man run over by electric car in Oella*
- *Driver claims man was impossible to avoid*
- *Man roughly dressed – no money save for a few coins*
- *No identification. Body unrecognizable*

She had failed to get any better description of the man from the Catonsville police or her contact at the Baltimore Sun. Earlier this morning she had tried to telephone the undertaker to whom they had taken the body, but the woman who answered insisted that he was "unavailable to reporters."

There was one bit of information she learned from Officer Norris that hadn't been in the Sun. She wrote:

- *Whiskey bottle in coat on body*

That might be a clue, a coincidence, or even a red herring. If it was a murder, perhaps the killer had planted the bottle.

Next she wrote down what she had learned from Viola and Billy:

- *Limping white man on bridge – no coat or hat*
- *Man discarded expensive coat – tried to throw it into river*
- *Stain on coat – Blood?*
- *Label on coat for Zehner's store in Catonsville*
- *Fancy hat in stream – same label*

This was compelling. The two labels tied the coat and the hat together. The limping man on the bridge must therefore be associated with both. The location of the hat meant that the limping man must have, at some point, been near where the body was found. The significance of the limp was unclear. Perhaps he had been in a fight?

She started a new heading and underlined it: "What We Don't Know." Under this she wrote:

- *Identity of man on the tracks*
- *Identity of limping man on the bridge*
- *Murder or accident?*
- *If murder, what motive?*

Determining the identity of the limping man would be problematic. Billy didn't get a close look at him in the darkened bridge, and he didn't see where the man went after he crossed into Ellicott City. She couldn't question every man with a limp in the city.

Without knowing the identity of the victim or murderer (she had, by now, convinced herself that this was no accident), it was impossible to discern the motive. That would have to wait.

The only obvious lead was the label for the clothing store. She would ask Edward if she could take the electric car to Catonsville next week to visit the shop.

As it happened, Edward Powell was just now walking toward her desk with a folded newspaper under his arm. "Good morning, Trudy. I suppose you've read the Sun already?"

"Good morning, Edward. Uh, no. I had an errand to run. I got in a bit late. I want to talk to you about..."

Edward unfolded the newspaper and dropped it onto her desk. He made a mock gesture of surprise toward the ceiling. "Wonder of wonders! I know something before the omniscient Gertrude O'Flynn." He searched the newspaper for a moment and pointed to a small piece halfway down the right side of the page:

CAR VICTIM IS IDENTIFIED

> The man who was killed by an Ellicott City car between Rock Creek and Oella avenue Wednesday night was identified late yesterday afternoon by J. W. Wilson, colored, of Oella, as that of Ignatius McCurley, who until recently lived at Clarksville, Howard county.
>
> [Baltimore Sun, Friday, March 13, 1908]

He gave Trudy a moment to read and then said with unveiled satisfaction, "It looks like the mystery of the man on the tracks is solved. So you can get back to your story on..."

"J. W. Wilson—Johnny? Johnny Wilson? You've got to be kidding. He's..."

"Nevertheless," continued Edward, "You need to get back..."

Trudy interrupted again, "Wait. You don't understand. Johnny Wilson—that can't be right. I don't believe it. If you met Johnny, you wouldn't either. Everybody in Oella knows Johnny. He's always either drunk or asking for money to buy liquor."

Edward tried to say something, but Trudy was just getting started. "McCurley? Come to think of it, I met a man named McCurley some time ago. It was ... it was at the Christmas dance last year at the mill's company store. He worked at the mill for a while—at least a year, I think. I didn't know he was from Clarksville. I'm pretty sure my brother-in-law knows him quite well. At the party a group of folks were all toasting him and bidding him farewell. I think he was supposed to be moving to Iowa or Indiana or someplace. I don't remember his first name, but McCurley isn't a common name in Oella."

Again Edward tried to speak, but Trudy was unstoppable, "And come on, Edward. How is poor, drunk Johnny Wilson going to identify such a body? How did the Sun describe it? Crushed. They said his skull was crushed. When I spoke with Officer Norris yesterday, he said it would be impossible. Here's what I think..."

"But..."

"I think the cops are anxious to be rid of this case because it is an embarrassment and just might involve a little police work. So they paid poor Johnny to pretend to identify the body, or more likely they just gave him a pint of booze."

Edward waited a moment to make sure the tirade was over. "Nevertheless, we are out of time for getting anything original into tomorrow's edition. We can't just reprint the Sun's story. You can spend a bit of time on this next week, a *small* bit. If you come up with anything interesting, we can always publish it on the twenty-first."

Trudy started to show Edward the list she had been writing, "But I have this..."

Edward waved her off. "No. Not for this week. Save it. Now you know I need the finished copy for your piece on Springfield Asylum. I needed it yesterday but I wanted to see what you turned up on this other thing. You may have until..." He took out his pocket-watch and flipped open the cover. "It's almost ten o'clock now. Have it on my desk by eleven-thirty."

<u>The Calamitous Life of A. Emmett Harriman</u>
By R. L. McReedy-Knibbs
Author of "The Murdering Spinsters"
and "Swoboda's Ten Steps To Great Wealth"
Reprinted by Permission on These Pages in Serial Fashion

INSTALLMENT SIX – THE LAW

Tuesday, July 29, 1890
Clarksville, Maryland

I figured I should turn up at the funeral for Pa, just to keep up appearances. There warn't many people in the church on account of, as you know by now, Pa warn't what you might call a popular man. The only folks who showed their faces were a few neighbors who lived on either side of us, although you could tell that even they didn't savor the notion of attending, and were probably just here for the refreshments that would be served after the service.

When I made my "ingress" at the door of the church, the preacher's wife come up at me and wrapped me in an embrace that I thought would squeeze the life out of me. She was a big woman—I could hardly reach my arms all the way round and I recollect my hands grabbed hold of what must have been her fleshy shoulder blades but that they felt like what I imagine bosoms must feel like. I also remember that she smelled like cheese. She spent the whole service blubbering and making an awful fuss. I reckon this must be her job at funerals where her husband preaches—kind of setting the tone.

The preacher blathered on and on about how Pa found God in his last days on this earth, and that it was a great miracle, and that Pa had vowed to quit his drinking, and how his tears flowed like the River Jordan on account of all his past sins, and oh my, how the Lord works in mysterious ways! He went on to say that he had it on good authority that Pa had been accepted through the Pearly Gates and was up in Heaven this very minute smiling down on the sorry lot of us.

They were going to bury Pa in the pauper's section of the cemetery off Linton Road. So that meant he warn't going to have any headstone, and that he might share his grave with three or four other poor folks. That didn't matter a lick to me—hell, I even hoped they'd put Pa on the bottom. I warn't about to waste any of my money on what you might call a proper burial. Not after I was the one slaving away in the shop for years while Pa sat on his haunches in a stupor. No sir.

And, let me tell you, I had me some money all right—almost five hundred dollars by then. Pa ain't looked at the books in years and I been sending money every month to an account at the Patapsco National Bank in Ellicott City. I remember when I opened the account, I didn't want to use my real name just in case they sent a letter, and it somehow got back to Pa. So I changed it a bit but kept my initials the same. It was amazing that you could do just about everything by post these days. I never had to show up at the bank in person—not even once.

So, to get back to my story, after the funeral I skipped the refreshments and all the polite hobnobbing and such, and I went back to the pharmacy and opened for business. I had the shop pretty much cleaned up by then and had replaced most of the supplies. I even had eleven prescription bags in the "Done" basket that Doc Wilson wrote before the fight between me and Pa.

I settled into Pa's chair behind the counter—it was my chair now. I passed the early afternoon happily sipping on whiskey and reading my serials. I figured folks would drop buy to pick up the bags and drop off new prescriptions like they always did.

Well reader, I've had years to think back on that day, and you can probably see already that at the age of fourteen, I might have been clever with book-reading and tricking adults into doing what I wanted, but I was plumb naive when it came to the ways of the world. I had it in my fool head that life would just go one like it always had, so consider my stupefaction when the deputy sheriff and Mr. John Hill came marching through the door late in the afternoon.

Mr. Hill looked even more sour then most days. He said "Look at him sitting there like his good for nothing old man. He reckons it's going to be business as usual. I got news for you, boy. You got no kin, and you ain't no adult. The juvenile court will decide what's to become of you. You best get on upstairs and pack your things. This town will be glad to be rid of you."

"Now, John, you don't have to go on that way about it," said the deputy sheriff in a more friendly tone. "Son, look, seeing how you're only fourteen ..."

"Almost fifteen," I countered.

"Okay, okay, almost fifteen, then. Well according to the law, that makes you still a minor. And the law says you got to have a guardian. Now John here says you ain't got no kin. You sure that's the case? No aunts or uncles ... nobody?"

No clever words came to my mind. Pa talked from time to time about relations down in Georgia and Tennessee—his Uncle Beauregard who just passed and some cousins, but I ain't never met them and didn't want to.

I knew it warn't going to do any good even as I said it, but I looked defiantly at the lawman and said,

"I pay the bills. I work the shop. I can take care of myself."

"Well son, now I'm sure that's true enough. Lord knows you been taking care of your Pa for years now, but again, according to the law, you ain't old enough to be here living on your own."

The deputy sheriff had always treated me kindly on account of he felt sorry for my situation. I figured he was telling me that the law said I had to get out of town. So my mind started to wander, thinking about where I might go and maybe it wouldn't be so bad to get a fresh start somewhere and ...

"Come on now boy, we ain't got all day," grumbled John Hill. "You must have some effects you want to take with you up in that filthy room upstairs. If you got any decent clothes, now would be the time to put them on."

"John, settle down," said the deputy sheriff. Then he turned to me and explained what was what: "Emmett, the law says we got to take you to orphan's court. There are a number of places where they might send you. It'll be okay."

John Hill couldn't help adding gleefully, "The judge is a friend of mine. You'll like him. Wallenhorst is the name—stern but fair."

So they made me get out Pa's old worn suitcase and pack everything I wanted to keep, which warn't much. They told me not to expect on coming back. I had never had any cause for fancy clothes, so I'd have to go to court as I was. I took my favorite books and the little bit of cash that I had. At the last minute I remembered: I went to the stack of papers on the counter and found the letter and fancy graduation certificate from the Practical Druggist Institute in New York. I rolled them up, tied a string around them, and put them in the suitcase.

The sheriff drove me in his own carriage to Ellicott City. It was a little over ten miles. I had made the trip on foot lots of times, running errands for Pa, so I was pretty familiar with the dusty roads.

The sun had just set when we arrived at the courthouse on the hill overlooking the town. But to my misfortune, it was closed. There warn't nobody to "process me," as the deputy sheriff called it. So he told me I'd have to spend the night in the jail behind the courthouse. He acted real sorry about this and said he hoped they'd be in time so that I could stay the night at the orphan's house in town, but it was too late. He made arrangements with the jailer for me to have a private cell so I wouldn't have to put up with the miscreants in the drunk tank.

Nobody brung me any supper that night. Later, I didn't want to sleep on their filthy mattress on account of I figured it must be crawling with lice and other nasty things. So I slept on the floor, which was concrete and cold even in July. When morning finally come, a guard let me out of the cell and took me to a room to wash from a long trough where all the other prisoners were washing and spitting and who knows what else. Then they set us at a long table to dine on mealy porridge and lukewarm tea. After breakfast, it was back to the cell. And, let me tell you, it got mighty hot in that cell as the day wore on.

I didn't know what to expect at the hearing. It was almost noon before the guard finally come and told me it was my time. Even though I put on clean clothes that morning, it didn't do a lick of good. I was soaked with sweat from sitting in the hot cell all morning.

The guard brung me into the courtroom and told me to take a seat near the back. I looked around and was surprised to see Charley Hill sitting in a bench in the middle of the room next to his old man. Charley stole a glance at me and made a quick smile before his father noticed and smacked him on the head. I recollect that it made me glad to have at least one friend there.

The judge was a prim looking, middle-aged man named Wallenhorst. He was all business-like, and after hearing each case he'd tell everyone what was what in a clipped German accent, and then give a quick bang of his gavel. I tried to imagine what it'd be like to be a judge. I didn't think I'd mind all the book learning you'd have to do, but I figured it would vex me something awful having to be all respectable all the time.

There was another bang of the gavel and I heard the clerk call out, "Is August E. Harriman present?" I raised my hand and the guard brung me to the front and pointed at a chair in the middle of the room facing the judge. I flopped myself down. I remember being kind of dizzy and I had a pounding headache from the heat and from not getting any sleep. Also, to be honest, I could have really used a sip of whiskey about then.

A pudgy bald man with sweat stains on his armpits did most of the talking. They called him the State's Representative. He said that I was now an orphan with no means of support, and so I'd have to be sent to the Maryland House of Refuge for Wayward Boys. But first, he said, there was another boy in the courtroom who would like to offer testimony on my behalf.

I watched as Charley Hill came up and was sworn in as a witness. He took a seat in a chair to the side of the judge. I tried to lock eyes with him but he was looking at his old man. The State's Representative started into asking him questions.

"Do you know August Harriman, who is sitting here?"

"Yeah, I heard that name afore, but Emmett hates it. He likes to be called Emmett 'cause he says it make's him sound like an outlaw."

"An outlaw? Does he want to be an outlaw?"

Charley again exchanged a look with his father. "I dunno."

"Very well—we shall call him by his middle name. Have you ever seen 'Emmett' engage in drinking alcohol or other such lewd behavior?"

"Alcohol? I dunno, but he drinks whiskey all the time."

Some folks in the room laughed. The judge banged his gavel and told the State's Representative to go on.

"And where does he get this whiskey?"

Again, Charley exchanged a look with his father. "I dunno, but he always brung it with him when we was at the stream near my house. He says to me to drink it, else he's gonna wallop me."

My mouth dropped near to the floor listening to this hogwash. "That's a damn lie!" I shouted as I stood up.

Judge Wallenhorst banged the gavel. "Ze defendant vill be silent!" A guard come up and pushed me down into the chair by my shoulders.

The State's Representative asked Charley another question, "and has he engaged in other lewd behavior?"

"What you mean, lewd?"

The State's Representative rolled his eyes. "Immoral, lascivious, ... dirty."

"Oh ... yeah, plenty dirty I reckon. Once he said he made my sister pull up her dress over her head. Said he felt her cunny."

And so it went on like that for a while. The State's Representative seemed to know every secret that Charley and me had between us, and each time he'd ask Charley something, Charley would lie and then I'd stand up and yell some unchristian words and the guard would push me back down into the chair. The judge must have been pretty vexed with me by the end of it.

Finally, John Hill himself took the witness chair and said that I was a bad influence on all the boys in Clarksville and that he had never seen me even once without smelling alcohol on my breath.

In the end, Judge Wallenhorst ruled that, in my current state of insobriety, I'd be a danger to the other boys at the Maryland House of Refuge, and that I should first be sent to the Bayview Sanitarium in Baltimore to cure my addiction to alcohol.

The gavel banged, and the next case was called. A policeman appeared and ushered me out the back door. I don't think I was in my right mind. It was like dynamite was going off in my head. Just before they pushed me out the door I hollered out, "You'll be sorry, Charley Hill—you and that German judge, too!"

I spent two more hours in my cell and then they took me to Bayview that very afternoon.

ALL THAT'S NEW AND FASHIONABLE

Monday Morning, March 16, 1908

Trudy departed her house at the accustomed time. She met Viola for the walk into town. The sky was gray. The air was cool and ever so slightly scented with cow manure. Viola made some remark about a patch of early daffodil sprouts on the side of the lane.

At the bottom of Westchester, Trudy bade goodbye to Viola and, instead of crossing the covered bridge into town, ascended the stairs to the trolley platform. A car was just now squeaking and squealing its way across the trestle bridge. When it stopped, she climbed aboard and found a seat. She was on her way to Catonsville.

The car ascended through the cut in Oella and soon came to the spot where the man had been run over on Wednesday night last. The location was discernable only by the trampled ground and brush. Dried mud was spattered everywhere. Trudy wasn't sure what she had expected to see.

She brought her thoughts back to her plan for the morning. She would go to J. Zehner's clothing store. She would not mention the black coat—it was too commonplace. Even now, as the car made its way along Edmonson Avenue, half the men she saw along the street wore something similar. But the hat—now that was distinctive, especially the unusual green color. She would focus her inquiry on that.

She got off of the car on Frederick Road in Catonsville and had no trouble finding Zehner's. It was on Ingleside Avenue just off the turnpike. The store had just opened when she pushed on the glass door, causing a set of chimes to jingle. She was apparently the first visitor of the day. The clerk was not at the counter, so she began browsing through the aisles.

Near the back, she found rows of pegs mounted on the wall displaying hats of all shapes and sizes. Being the fashion of the day, there were more derbies than any other type. Most were black, brown, or dark gray. But there were also fedoras, stetsons, newsboy caps, a couple of stovepipes, and ... there, on the bottom row: a dark green porkpie with a wide, light gray ribbon.

She took it off of the peg and examined it. She was pretty sure this was identical to the one that the boy had shown her in Oella. It had the same label sewn inside, just above the brim.

"A very attractive hat for your husband, madam," said a sonorous deep-pitched voice behind her.

Startled, Trudy dropped the hat on the floor. The shopkeeper retrieved it and brushed it off. "Forgive me, madam, I did not mean to sneak up on you. The floors in here are quite silent. I am sometimes told that I should harumph or cough occasionally, or that I should feign a head cold and sniff loudly, or perhaps I should drag my feet audibly on the floor, but alas, I am not prone to any such afflictions."

"Oh," stammered Trudy. The man standing before her was quite odd-looking. He was tall and extremely thin. His head was completely bald—shaved in fact, and he wore thick, round eyeglasses. This, combined with his large front teeth and open mouth, reminded Trudy of the unflattering caricatures of Chinamen that frequented political cartoons. Except that he wasn't Chinese. Baggy white sleeves protruded from his vest. A tape measure hung from his left shoulder.

Trudy recovered her composure. "Good day, Mr. ... Zehner?"

The man smiled and bowed his head. "The very same." He handed her back the hat and his hands joined in the manner of prayer. "As I was saying, this would be an attractive hat for your..."

"Oh, no. You don't understand." Trudy screwed up her courage and decided to forge ahead with the little ruse she had worked out. She didn't like being dishonest, but she didn't want word getting around that she was investigating a murder. A white lie would cause no harm.

"I was very much hoping you could help me, sir," she began. "You see, I attended the subscription dance this Saturday last at the hall on Egges Lane, and I met a certain gentleman."

This piqued the shopkeeper's interest. "Go on," he said.

"This gentleman and I had several dances together, and we discussed at some length a certain business arrangement that would be very advantageous to us both. I told him that I must think on it, and so he gave me his card. But you see..."

"What sort of business?" inquired the shopkeeper. He noticed another customer now entering the store and was starting to wonder if he was wasting his time with this woman.

Trudy hadn't been prepared for this question. She improvised, "Oh, ... it has to do with real estate. But that's not important. You see, I misplaced his card and have looked everywhere. So I was hoping ... I know this will sound silly, but he was wearing a very attractive hat that was a dead ringer for this one. He told me how wonderful your store was and how attentive you were to every detail. So I was hoping that you could..."

"Do you remember his name?"

Trudy let out a nervous laugh. "You must think me very scatterbrained. He introduced himself early in the evening, and we had a delightful time together, but, no. I seem to have completely forgotten his name. But this hat, sir—you can't have sold many like it. I was hoping you could tell me..."

The man was shaking his head. "Madam, I don't give out information about my clients. I'm sure you understand that..."

Trudy had taken out her handkerchief and began dabbing her eyes. "Yes, yes. I understand completely, but you see..." She sniffed loudly. "I'm sure the man would want me to contact him. I do ever so want to see him again. If you could just..."

The man let out a heavy sigh. "I shall help this other gentleman and then I will see what I can do." He walked off to attend to the other man in the store, who was now fingering his way through a rack of dress coats.

Trudy began idly looking at an assortment of bowties, remembering how she used to shop for her husband at Rosenstock's and Caplan's. Tom used to favor bowties on the rare occasions when he had to dress up. Soon she would be shopping for her eldest son, Colin. He'd be giving up his boyhood shorts and would want to wear long trousers.

Mr. Zehner once again startled her from behind. "Excuse me madam. I can think of two gentlemen who have recently purchased a headpiece similar to the one you were admiring. There was a Mr. Zehlendorf at the Catonsville Bank. You will find it on Frederick Road a few doors to the right. Then I believe there was a Mr. D'Ignoto. He has a pharmacy on Bloomsbury two or three blocks to the south. And if you could, please do not mention that it was I who gave you this information. I want my customers to know I respect their privacy. And now, if you will excuse me, I am somewhat pressed for time, as you can see." Without waiting for a reply, he hurried off to help another customer who was now entering the store.

Trudy visited the bank first. The interior had that ostentatious decor that banks everywhere seem to favor: mahogany desks, dark wood panels covering the walls and ceilings, expensive chandeliers, marble tiled floor. She asked the woman seated in the lobby for Mr. Zehlendorf and was directed to a glass-enclosed office near the back. She walked in the indicated direction and found the office. His name was stenciled on the glass door.

The office was empty, so she entered, and was about to take a seat on the chair in front of the desk, when she noticed a coat stand in the corner. A black overcoat hung on a hook, and a dark green hat was hanging on top. She took the hat down and examined it more closely. It was the right color and material, but it was a derby, not a porkpie, and with no gray ribbon. And it was well worn—not new.

She was hoping that her search this morning would turn up a missing person, not someone with a similar hat. This was not her man.

She turned around with the hat still in her hands when a short, portly man in the doorway cleared his throat and said, "May I be of service, madam? You are not a hat-thief, I trust?"

Trudy was embarrassed. "Oh, forgive me Mr. ... Zehlendorf?" The man nodded. She decided to be blunt to save time. "I am looking for the owner of a hat of similar make and color to this one. You have not misplaced such a hat in the past week, have you?"

"Indeed not madam. May I inquire...?"

"Forgive me sir, but I just remembered an appointment for which I am dreadfully late." She handed the man his hat, and walked quickly through the lobby to the front door of the bank. She felt embarrassed. She was not good at this kind of sleuthing.

It took Trudy a while to find the pharmacy on Bloomsbury Street. It was not well marked, and she inadvertently walked past it twice. The blinds were drawn on the glass storefront, with only a small hand-painted sign over the door saying, simply, "Druggist." It did not look inviting. She screwed up her courage and pushed the door open into the dim interior.

It was an old shop. A strange assortment of fragrances assaulted her nose: aging wood, fresh paint, antiseptic chemicals, and cigar smoke. Floor to ceiling shelves lined the walls containing a hodgepodge of jars and bottles, each with a neatly printed label. There were also stacks of cigarette packs, cigar boxes, snuffboxes, and books. A small soda fountain with three stools was near the back where the pharmacist was helping a customer.

Trudy looked around the shop while she waited for the pharmacist to be free. Three bare electric bulbs hanging in the center of the white-painted tin ceiling illuminated the space. When she turned around, she was startled to see a man sitting in a chair next to the door. She had not noticed him upon entering. He was a large, muscular man with a misshapen nose. His massive head was capped with a straw boater, unusual for this time of year. He ignored Trudy as he read a newspaper with a smoldering stub of a cigar gripped tightly in his teeth.

"Yeah? Can I help you?" said the reedy voice of the pharmacist behind her. The other customer was now leaving the shop.

Trudy turned to the druggist. "Good day, sir. I am looking for a Mr. D'Ignoto. Is this the right pharmacy?"

The man paused for a moment, and then said. "Uh, Vinny moved back to New Jersey. I'm running the place now. Is there something you need?"

"New Jersey? Oh." Trudy was unsure how to proceed. "That is surprising."

"Why is that surprising? It's where we're from. I'm his ... cousin."

Trudy let out a long sigh. She shook her head. "I guess I have been on a wild goose chase—and all over a silly hat. Well, thank you Mr. ...?"

"What's this about a hat?" The burly man by the door had gotten up and was brushing cigar ash from his sleeve. His voice was gruff, matching his overall appearance.

Trudy suddenly felt uneasy. She tried to make light of the situation. "Oh ... It is of no great consequence. You will think me silly. I live in Oella. Someone there found a hat similar to the one Mr. D'Ignoto wore, so I thought..."

"Wait," interjected the pharmacist. "Where's 'Wellah'? Is Vinny there now?"

Now Trudy was confused. "Didn't you just say he moved to New Jersey?"

The pharmacist paused, exchanging a glance with the burly man before continuing. "Here's the thing, Miss ... Mrs.?"

Trudy replied, "I don't believe I caught your name either."

"Our names ain't important," said the burly man.

Trudy did not well tolerate rudeness. "Well then, I suppose neither is mine. Good day." She started to move around the man toward the door.

The pharmacist came quickly round the counter. "Wait, wait, miss. We got off on the wrong foot. My name's Angelo Scuderi. I'm gonna level with you, miss. The truth is that Vinny—Mr. D'Ignoto—is a business associate of ours. We've been looking for him since Thursday. We came to collect ... I mean we showed up for ... you know, a business meeting, and he never showed. You know Vinny, so you know he ain't like that. A punctual, fussy man. So, if you've seen him, my partner and I would very much appreciate it if you'd..."

"I haven't seen him," Trudy said curtly. "In fact, I've never met him." The man's candor had diffused the tension somewhat, but she still wanted to leave. "A boy in the neighborhood found a hat that I think belongs to him. So I..."

"That hat!" The burly man chuckled and shook his head as he returned to his chair by the door. "Vinny always did dress like a dandy." He took out a book of matches and relit his cigar.

The door opened abruptly, and a uniformed policeman entered. "Hey Gino, I dunno about..." He stopped short when he saw Trudy in the room.

"Just a sec, Norris," said the pharmacist, holding up a finger. "Miss, I..."

The man named Scuderi had wanted to ask Trudy more questions, or at least find out what her name was. But Trudy had taken the opportunity afforded by the distraction to move toward the door. She mumbled something as she pushed past the cop and was gone.

She wasted no time in hurrying back to the station and was relieved to see the car to Ellicott City pulling up just as she arrived. She found a seat and caught her breath. After the car pulled away, Trudy let out a sigh of relief.

When she had calmed herself, she pondered the curious exchange. She would have a few more items to add to her list.

It was pretty clear now that the druggist named D'Ignoto was the dead man on the tracks. The accident had occurred on Wednesday night, and the two men in the pharmacy had been looking for him since the day after that. So why had they not reported him missing? And they were obviously very friendly with that cop. What was going on there?

Trudy had felt relieved when the cop had shown up, allowing her to make a hasty retreat. She now remembered that the pharmacist had called him "Norris." Was this the same Officer Norris who had been so rude to her on the telephone? There was a good chance of it.

When she added it all up, it wasn't good. Some nefarious activity must be going on in that pharmacy, and they don't want any attention drawn to the operation.

So then, who was the limping man whom Billy had seen on the bridge? She'd have no way of finding out without doing a lot more digging into what was going on in that pharmacy. And she was sure she did not want to do that.

Also, there was no point in going to the police with her new discoveries. Scuderi and that other man appeared to be in league with the Catonsville police, or at least with Officer Norris. She did trust Chief Wosch in Ellicott City, but he had no jurisdiction here, and had made it very clear that he wanted nothing to do with this case.

So, it was a dead end. She decided that when she got back to the Times office, she would finish writing up her notes and file them away. Life would go on.

IMMIGRATION EVILS

Messrs. Editors:

I was reading an editorial in THE SUN on "Immigration" while on a train going to New York on March 5, and now at my earliest opportunity after returning to Baltimore I write a letter to your most valuable paper to say a few things on that subject. Your sentiments are just those that should be entertained by all Americans. It is strange that this idea apparently has not entered the heads of those who control immigration. America is the dumping ground for all beings who are distasteful to the Eastern Continent. I have been informed (I hope it isn't true) that inspectors are paid so much a head to pass immigrants, and that there is a company which makes a business of inducing foreigners to come to "free America"–yes, free; too free for our own good. Any criminal anarchist, Black Hand or what not, can be dropped here, provided he hasn't trachoma and has a sufficient amount of cash. Not a word is said about his past. Then we wake up and look for causes only after some terrible calamity has befallen us. After the anarchist or Black Hand has killed some of our best people, thousands of dollars are spent to search him out, send him to trial and, if he is not hanged or electrocuted, keep him in prison, or in the popular place now for criminals–the lunatic asylum.

Why is it that Italians, from whom come most of the anarchists and Black Hands, are allowed here, and Chinamen, who never disturb anyone and are seldom in court except for gambling, and that among themselves, are debarred? Is there a single thing admirable to be said of the Italian that can't be said of the Chinaman, except personal appearance, and neither is responsible for that.

But why say anything? We vent our feelings and things go on just the same.

Signed, AN OBSERVER.

[Baltimore Sun, March 15, 1908]

MAY
1908

AGGRIEVED, MORGAN DEMANDS MORE

Tuesday, May 12, 1908

The Chemist smoked his pipe pensively on the roof of Angelo Cottage. It was late on a warm May evening, and the house below him was quiet for a change. The indomitable Mrs. Sanner must have already retired to her chamber on the ground floor. The Chemist took time to reflect on how events had unfolded since that fateful evening in March, and on the actions he might now be forced to take.

At the time, it seemed that his plan had worked flawlessly. The hapless police, as expected, were not interested in looking beyond the obvious circumstances of the mysterious "man on the tracks." They were all too happy to call it an accident. Then came a supreme stroke of luck when a colored man in Oella actually identified the victim as some vagrant from Clarksville. Even the Chemist could not have foreseen that.

There had been two hiccups: Injuring his left foot had prevented him from conducting many aspects of his business in the weeks following the incident. This was a minor and temporary inconvenience. The broken toe was almost healed now, and he barely noticed it, except when he put his weight on it in a particular way.

The more serious problem was his fellow boarder, Marion Morgan, who had seen him depart that evening dressed in uncharacteristic, ragged clothes. He realized after the fact that he should have been more careful. He could have changed outside after leaving the cottage, having left the old clothes in a sack hidden in the bushes. It was an unfortunate error for which he was still paying.

The day after the incident, Morgan had become suspicious and had asked many probing questions. This had been especially annoying as the Chemist was trying to bind his painful foot so that he could walk down the hill to his pharmacy. Morgan wanted to know where he had gone, why he had been dressed that way, and how he had hurt himself. Fortunately, Morgan was not a clever man, and it never occurred to him that The Chemist's actions could have been in any way connected to the dead man on the tracks.

After that, Morgan had begun loitering near The Chemist's pharmacy—observing who came and went. He even followed The Chemist on a nocturnal visit to a foreman at the Oppenheim Shirt Factory, up the hill on Fels Lane. It wasn't hard, even for Morgan, to figure out that the Chemist was selling drugs illicitly.

Business was indeed booming. When, in June of 1906, the Maryland legislature made cocaine and opiates illegal without a prescription, it created a black market overnight. The same thing was happening in states all over the country. The law placed no restrictions on wholesalers who sold to pharmacies and physicians. It only required a prescription for the person or animal actually taking the drug.

The Chemist didn't want to sell to drug users at all. In his experience, addicts were unreliable and indiscreet—always either high or anxious for their next fix. He had read stories in The Sun about pharmacies that engaged in that risky trade. The customer would come in with a password, saying that he wanted to buy "iodoform" or some other fictitious substance. The proprietors of such a pharmacies typically had to pay off policemen to look the other way. They also had to hire muscle in case things got nasty.

The Chemist didn't want any part in that. He liked being a lone wolf. He sold mainly to other distributors, and only those he trusted. A growing sales avenue lately had been selling to managers at factories, mills, and other labor-intensive, but low-skill, enterprises. They had found that clandestinely supplying cocaine to their workforce would increase the quantity and even the quality of the work.

After he found out what The Chemist was up to, Morgan had done what such wastrels always do: he tried to profit from his knowledge by blackmail. He threatened the Chemist, saying that he would turn him in to the police unless he was paid for his silence. He demanded five dollars a week. This was a sizable sum to a man like Morgan, but it was manageable for the Chemist, so he readily agreed.

That was a mistake. Morgan must have realized he had asked for too little, because he doubled the price two weeks later.

The Chemist was jarred from his reverie atop the cottage by a gruff voice calling his name from the yard below. He looked over the parapet to see Morgan beckoning for him to come down.

The Chemist sighed, tapped out his pipe, and went into the house. He emerged from the front door and found Morgan in the street in front of the German church. The man seemed agitated about something. His lower lip bulged in the front as usual, burdened by a plug of dipping tobacco. He spat on the ground as the Chemist approached.

"What do you want?" The Chemist asked tersely.

"Ya hear all the fussin' goin' on earlier?"

"No, I was out until quite late."

"Dang Mrs. Sanner give ma room away," said Morgan bitterly. "Says I gotta move out to the tool shed 'hind the kitchen for the summer."

"Oh ... I did hear that we would be having a new boarder. A Mr. Cross, if my memory serves."

"Oh your memory serves, all righty," grumbled Morgan. "Mister Linwood J. Cross," he said mockingly. "Mrs. Sanner says I gotta move 'cause he'll pay good money for the room. I think she might even be sweet on 'im, can y'imagine?"

"So ... what is your concern? Move into the shed then," said the Chemist. He was annoyed that Morgan was bothering him with such drivel.

"Hey, don't get all high 'n mighty. 'Member our deal, now. Maybe I'll just stroll on down to Main Street 'n find me a lawman. Bet they'll be mighty interested in what ya do at night."

The Chemist let a moment of silence go by, and then said. "I hate to repeat myself. I asked when I came out here—what do you want?"

"Well, I'm thinkin' to myself 'at maybe you might wanna move into the shed 'stead of me, or..."

"Out of the question," said the Chemist. "I'd sooner find a different boarding house."

"I was gonna say ... or we could double ma fee again," said Morgan, shrugging his shoulders innocently.

"Double? Again? I'm already paying you ten dollars a week. I think you have the wrong idea about the kind of money my business brings in."

Morgan spat out a sizable wad at the Chemist's feet. He then pulled a pouch of "Polar Bear" tobacco from his pocket. He took his time removing the paper wrapper from a fresh pack and cramming it behind his lower lip. He spent a long moment adjusting it with his tongue before he was ready to speak. "Twenny dowars ain't so much, and it's such a short little walk inna town. You think 'ere'll be police at Kramer's or O'Brien's this time a night?"

The Chemist was thoroughly disgusted by this man who, in many ways, reminded him of his father. He needed time to make a plan. "Give me until tomorrow. I'll have an answer for you at noon." He returned to the cottage without waiting for a reply.

He sat up late, ruminating over this increasingly undesirable situation. It was intolerable that a man like Morgan would have power over the Chemist. The disrespect showed by expectorating his filthy tobacco right at his feet was too much. The Chemist had always hated that habit. The Hill boys had tried to teach him to dip when he was young, but he had never liked it.

He had to find a way to be rid of Morgan, or at least to discredit him to such a degree that no one would listen to a word he said.

Dipping tobacco ... that gave the Chemist an idea. He sold the vile stuff in his pharmacy. Morgan's brand, Polar Bear, was among the cheapest. What if the Chemist offered to supply him with something better? The Old Weyman's sold for about three times as much. Morgan had probably never tried it. If it were to be laced with cocaine, the fool would assume that the tingling in his gums and the way it made him feel was due solely to the superior tobacco.

The next afternoon the Chemist met again with Morgan. He negotiated the price down to fifteen dollars and threw in a dozen tins of premium dipping tobacco. Morgan jumped at the offer.

BRYAN'S SON IN DANGER
Kidnappers Said To Have Planned To Get Him

Galveston, Texas, May 13 - William J. Bryan, Jr., 17-year-old son of the Great Commoner, had a narrow escape from kidnappers who, it is alleged, planned to hold him for ransom, near Seabrooke, in Harris county. The young man is a sportsman and well known in this section, which he has visited with his father.

Two Pinkerton detectives planned for young Bryan to accept the invitation for a hunting expedition arranged by the abductors, so that the officers could get hold of the kidnappers. However, a launch was sent after Bryan, with instructions to the man in charge to bring no one but Bryan to the spot where they were camped on the other side of the bay. Bryan was placed aboard, and the officers put off in another boat to reach the camp, but when they landed at the point five miles away they found the abductors had escaped.

Pat Crowe, the principal in the famous Cudahy case, was recognized and spoken to on the streets of Houston three days ago, it is declared, and officers have started in three directions after him and another man. A boatman who had been hired to help in the kidnapping got drunk and revealed the plot.

[Baltimore Sun, May 14, 1908]

ELLICOTT CITY DOWNS ALPHA TWICE

The Ellicott City High School defeated the Alpha Athletic Club, of Woodstock, twice Saturday at Ellicott City, winning the first game by 13 to 5 and the second by 12 to 2. The features of both games were the pitching of Gerwig, the catching of Mead and Stromberg's fine catches of difficult flies in left field for Ellicott City, while Maxwell carried off the honors for Alpha. The home team batted well. The High School will play Rock Hill College Victors May 30.

[Baltimore Sun, May 20, 1908]

SUFFRAGE A LONG TIME COMING

Wednesday Morning, May 20, 1908

Trudy stood sipping her coffee, looking out the front window of the Ellicott City Times building. Across Main Street and a few doors down was the white marble facade of Washington Trust Company. Above the high, arched front door, above the Diocletian windows built into the stone, was a narrow balcony right at the roof level, some thirty feet above the street. Atop that balcony, waving to the folks passing by on the street, stood a clown. He pranced back and forth on the narrow ledge. He would occasionally pause, reach into a sack, and toss a handful of paper-wrapped taffies to the crowd below. The clown's white powder face, red painted nose, and long green hair, were undoubtedly intended to be light-hearted and whimsical. However, judging from the reaction of those on the street, the clown was having the opposite effect. A crowd was gathering, looking up at the man's death defying act with horror. Several had been struck painfully by the thrown candies and now shouted their disapproval. Some teenage boys were making pantomime gestures urging the clown to jump. Trudy could see three different children crying as they clung to their mothers.

"What on earth were they thinking?" Edward Powell had approached and now stood behind her. "They are celebrating the second anniversary of the new building. This was intended as some kind of publicity gimmick."

"Indeed," said Trudy. "It is definitely working. It's a good thing you don't pay me enough to have savings. I'd rush over there right now to make a deposit."

"Be nice. Washington Trust is one of our best advertisers," Edward said as they began walking back toward Trudy's desk. "By the way, we're running a short piece on Bryan on page two, right after your piece on the boys' school. Have you had a chance to look at it?"

Trudy rolled her eyes as she sat and arranged the papers on her desk. "Honestly Edward, I don't know why you bother to ask my opinion on these matters. It is the official policy of the United States that women are incapable of political thought."

Edward chuckled. "We are a democratic paper, as my father is fond of saying. And I ask because I value your opinion. You are one of the few people around here to whom I can say that with any honesty."

"Oh, and if you were saying that to me without honesty, would I be able to tell the difference?" Trudy couldn't resist chiding Edward when he said things like this. Although Edward was her employer, they had a warm relationship and talked openly about many topics, some of which might be deemed inappropriate if overheard. When she first started working for the paper, she suspected that Edward might be interested in her romantically in spite of the fact that she was almost ten years his senior. Edward was twenty-six, a lawyer, a landowner, and the editor of The Ellicott City Times. He was clean-shaven, thin, and rather good-looking in a prim sort of way. Often, young ladies in town would imprudently approach him at social events rather than waiting to be approached. But Trudy had observed over time that Edward did not appear to be the least bit interested in women. This was perhaps the only way in which Edward bucked the will of his overbearing father, who was often urging him to marry and start a family.

"And not all believe that women are incapable of political thought," Edward continued. "You have many allies among men. We both know that some day in the not-too-distant future your suffrage movement will succeed. Though, it is a pity that the suffragettes have aligned themselves with the temperance movement. Men fear that the first thing women will do with the vote is outlaw liquor. But you'll see—the Democrats will make it happen. Bryan strongly favors suffrage, you know."

This elicited another eye-roll. "Thank God for the Democrats and Saint William Jennings Bryan. You do know he's going to lose, don't you?"

"Hardly, Trudy. Neither Gray nor Johnson stand a chance."

"Gray? Johnson? Oh, he'll get the nomination. That much is sure. The party bosses will see to it. They're already plotting to change the convention rules so that he'll be nominated on the first ballot—the will of the people be damned. Bryan practically owns the party. No, what I mean is that he'll lose to Taft. Yes, yes. Don't shake your head. Taft will be the Republican nominee if Teddy has anything to say about it. And then Bryan will lose to Taft just like he lost to McKinley—uh, twice as I recall, isn't that right?"

Edward ignored the dig. "I don't understand why you dislike Bryan so much. He's our best hope for ..."

"For what? How is his platform different from Roosevelt's—or Taft's? He's not going to do anything to break up the trusts, the banks, or the railroads. Nothing will change with the wars we keep getting entangled in—Samoa, Spain, Cuba, Puerto Rico, the Philippines, Guam, China. Good Lord, who's next—Germany? Really—it will be business as usual just like it was with your idol, Grover Cleveland. And by the way, I hear old Grover is not faring well. We should probably gather some biographical material."

"Yes, good point—I'll put Frances on it," said Edward. "But really, about Bryan, I..."

Trudy sighed heavily. "Why do I dislike him? I think it goes back to that awful speech you made me cover in Baltimore last year. What did he call it? His 'Prince of Peace' speech—that was it. Interminable, unenlightened nonsense is what it was. Does he want to be a preacher or a politician? And why spend so much time attacking Darwin? If the theory of evolution is true, it will be true with or without Mr. Bryan's assent. And by the way, you never did run my write-up of it."

"Hah! You know my father would never run such a piece. He said he didn't care for the tone. He places Bryan just under the good Reverend Frank Talmage. Oh, and this may be one of the rare weeks when we won't be running a Talmage sermon. But, seriously, ... I mean hypothetically, if you could vote, who would you ..."

"Eugene Debs. Hands down. He's on the right side of every issue I care about."

Edward grunted. "Debs! An avowed socialist? He has no chance. That would be a waste of a vote. Don't you see that a vote for Debs is a vote for Taft? We have to come together if we are to defeat the Repub..."

"When will the Democrats learn that they don't own those who are in favor of social justice, and that they won't win elections by declaring that they are less odious than the Republicans? They can either accept bribes from the trusts, or they can do the will of the people. They can't have it both ways."

Edward held his hands up in surrender. "Okay, okay. I give up. For what it's worth, I hope Bryan wins so that you will get the vote—and soon. Let's talk about your piece on the refuge."

"Here it is, ready to run. I already had Frances proof it." Trudy picked up a freshly typed sheet and handed it to Edward, who took a moment to read the draft:

> TREATED UNFAIRLY
>
> The investigation of the House-of-Refuge brings into the limelight the subject of fairness in the detention of unruly or criminal young people. Clearly the boys at this Institution are not treated fairly. In fact, by all the testimony produced, the reformatory measures are in the shape of harsh or brutal treatment. The employment given to the boys is of a class calculated to lower their natural compassionate qualities instead of encouraging them. Do such institutions actually reform? We fear not. Are they not self-acting machines for inculcating crime? We fear they are. The unfair treatment does not by any means exist only in the government of such institutions, but starts with the term of the commitment to them. The boy of 12 years of age who has stolen a banana, or who has run away from his home, is committed to a reformatory institution until he is 21 years old, which means nine years confinement, with only partial education, poor food, often harsh treatment and all the buoyancy of youth repressed. That our

> present treatment of the unruly young is wrong is proven by the large proportion of criminals in our penal institutions, who trace their criminal tendency to the associations formed and ideas gained while incarcerated during their younger years in what were supposed to be Reformatory Institutions.

Edward removed his spectacles and began rubbing the bridge of his nose. Trudy recognized this gesture as meaning that he was contemplating changes.

"I know of your fondness for rhetorical questions," she said. "Shall I add more?"

"Well, first of all, the state has officially changed the name of the institution to the Maryland School for Boys. So we should call it that. Then..." He paused for more nose rubbing. "It needs a better hook. How about 'natural *manly* qualities' rather than compassionate? And then ... maybe a few sentences at the end comparing the treatment of the boys to recent improvements at adult prisons. How about something like ... eliminating the lash, the knout, and the dark cell have made prisons better institutions?"

"The lash *and* the knout? Isn't that redundant?"

"Whatever," Edward said flatly. "This is fine. I'll take it from here. We're short a few column inches on page six. To be fair, we should have something explaining Johnson's platform ahead of the convention. You would be good for that, seeing that you think so little of Mr. Bryan."

1900 AND NOW

In the Presidential campaign of 1900, Mr. Bryan was the apparent choice of nearly every Democrat in the United States, east, west, north, and south. The Democratic Conventions of nearly all the states instructed their delegates to vote for his nomination. Maryland, Delaware and New Jersey are now against him as the undisputed leader of the Democrat party. New York and Pennsylvania, which are now against him, then instructed for him. The same is true of Minnesota and Michigan. In 1900 he was nominated by the convention on the first ballot. Such a thing is impossible this year, and his friends, evidently with his approbation, are seeking to bring about the abolition of the two-thirds rule to a bare majority. To do so would be folly, for it would only accentuate the prevailing opinion that with Mr. Bryan as the candidate, defeat would be inevitable.

[Ellicott City Times, May 23, 1908]

ACCUSED OF SELLING COCAINE

Evidence Against Negro Obtained By using "Pigeon"

Moses Gibson, colored, 520 South Caroline street, was fined $25 and costs by Justice Garland, at the Eastern Police Station, yesterday on the charge of selling cocaine. Susie A. Davis, colored, who was also charged with selling the drug, was dismissed.

According to the testimony of the negress, Ella Wallace, colored, 265 Chestnut street, gave her 35 cents to buy a package of "coke" last Wednesday. She said she bought the drug from Gibson. She was used as a "pigeon" by Sergeant Day and Patrolmen Porter and Davis, who arrested Gibson.

[Baltimore Sun, May 26, 1908]

MORGAN INCREASINGLY IRRATIONAL

Midday Tuesday, May 26, 1908

The Chemist had needed some time away from the volatile atmosphere at Angelo Cottage, and so he had strolled down to Main Street and now sat at a table in the front window of Stigler's Bakery. He was enjoying a steaming cup of coffee and a fresh blueberry pastry as he gazed idly at the bell cupola of the firehouse across the street.

It had been two full weeks since he began supplying Morgan with cocaine-laced tobacco. The Chemist was surprised that it was taking this long for his plan to come to fruition. The normal methods of taking cocaine were either by injection or inhaling the powder. If Morgan had snorted dry snuff in the English manner, it would have been easy to calculate the dosage. But most Americans either chewed moist tobacco or held a plug of it behind the lower lip—a practice called "dipping." Morgan was a dipper. The Chemist had been unsure of the rate that cocaine would be absorbed through the gums. He considered, but decided against, consulting one of the dentists in town who used it as a local anesthetic. In the end, he guessed at the dosage.

Shortly after starting to use the new snuff, Morgan became full of energy. He would quickly finish his chores at the cottage and then head into town looking for odd jobs—not that he needed the money with what the Chemist was paying him. He actually became more agreeable to Mrs. Sanner and the other boarders. This went on for more than a week, and the Chemist worried that his plan was failing. He had decided that in the next batch, if one were required, he would increase the potency.

Then finally, in the past three days, Morgan began acting increasingly irrational. To the disgust of everyone at the cottage, he dipped his tobacco constantly, sometimes even spitting the foul brown juice indoors on the floor. He had stopped washing and took on the haggard look of someone who is not sleeping well, or at all. His demeanor was wild, unpredictable, and irritable—thus the Chemist's desire to escape to town for a few moments of peace.

"More coffee, hon?" The girl behind the pastry counter was holding up a full pot.

"Uh, no, thank you, Shirley. I will just finish what I have."

Someone had thoughtfully left a copy of last Saturday's Ellicott City Times on the adjacent table. He picked it up and scanned the first few pages. The first was taken up by ads and the latest installment of the novel they had been printing in serial fashion—a romance called *The Princess Virginia.* The second page was mostly political prattle about the upcoming Democratic convention. But there was a short article on the Maryland House of Refuge that caught his attention since he had been a resident of that institution for many years. Except for a few nonsensical sentences at the end, including one rather glaring grammatical error, it was accurate and well intentioned.

He drained his cup, folded the newspaper under his arm, donned his straw hat, and left the cafe. He headed down Main Street, passing the Citizen's Telephone Exchange and Steward's Grocery. As he walked, he found himself thinking about his youth, and how he used to travel to Ellicott City from time to time on errands for his father. He would enter town right here after descending the winding hill of Columbia Pike. He recalled that he would frequently stop at the tollhouse some three miles from here. The toll man then was a friendly sort, and would always have a sustaining drink for him.

He crossed the street in front of Howard House Hotel. A large banner draped over the iron grillwork surrounding the porch announced that they had begun selling ice cream for the summer season. He continued a short way further and came to the Times' building. He took a moment to straighten his tie and suit jacket, and then pushed open the door.

The interior was much as he would have expected for a newspaper office—rows of oak desks, each with a typewriter, desk blotter, inkwell, and candlestick phone. Paper was everywhere: stacks of it on every desk, piles of newspaper on the floors. A cloud of tobacco smoke hovered at eye level, illuminated by the electric bulbs hanging on wires from the ceiling. An alphabetized mail cubby covered the wall to his right, overflowing in places with opened and unopened correspondence.

"Good afternoon, sir. Can I help you?" A mousy woman sat at the nearest desk with black hair piled atop her diminutive head in a complicated Gibson Girl pompadour. A simple string of pearls adorned her narrow neck just above a high lace collar. She appeared slightly cross-eyed. A nameplate on her desk said "Miss Frances Langenberger."

"Good day," said the Chemist. "I was just reading this article in your paper." He unfolded the copy of Saturday's Times and laid it out on the desk, pointing to an article halfway down the second column. "I wonder if you could tell me who wrote it."

Frances looked at the indicated column. "Oh, the Maryland House of Refuge piece—Trudy wrote that. I mean ... Mrs. O'Flynn. Did you want to leave a comment?"

"Really? A woman? Oh. Well ... I was hoping I could speak to the author in person."

"I'm afraid she's not here right now, sir. Her son is playing second base on the junior team up at the Rock Hill field. You could leave a comment, or would you like to speak to the editor?"

The Chemist was silent for a moment. "Uh, no. Thank you. So, it was a Mrs. O'Flynn you say? I will stop back some other time." Disappointed, the Chemist turned and left.

There was no more putting it off. He'd have to return to the cottage and see how things were faring with Morgan. He took the shortcut through the Howard House. Delicious aromas wafted from the dining room where several patrons were enjoying a late lunch. A chalkboard announced that today's special was end-of-season fried oysters. He climbed the steps, walked past the ice cream counter and out to the back patio onto the Church Road.

Looking for any excuse to delay his return, he crossed the street to the Carriage House under Easton's Hall. He had ordered a new Phaeton-model buggy with rubber tires from the Sears & Roebuck catalogue. Gaither's livery was supposed to send a man to assemble it today. It had cost him nearly seventy dollars, but it would be worth it to travel in the style he deserved.

He entered the dark interior through the wide sliding door and looked around. Alas, there was no one here yet. The wooden crates were still neatly stacked against the support-post in the center of the space. He would check back later.

He steeled himself for another unpleasant encounter with Morgan and walked the short distance up Church Road to Angelo Cottage. As he approached, he heard sounds of shouting, a door slamming, and then silence.

Mrs. Sanner greeted him at the front door. “Oh, Mr. Hardin, goodness, you’re home. Listen—I’m sure you’ve noticed that Mr. Morgan is increasingly unhinged of late. I am telling all the boarders that he is not to be admitted to the house. I have locked the door from the house to the shed where he’s staying. He will have to go in and out through the back door to the yard. And he will have to take his meals in town. He is not fit company. I sent Dot into town to warn Officer Wosch that there may be trouble—hopefully not. I just don’t understand it. He used to be such a nice man. He actually just threatened to...”

“Thank you for letting me know, Mrs. Sanner. I shall adhere to your rules, as always. Mr. Morgan will not be admitted by my hand.” The Chemist retreated to his room. His scheme was finally working.

DR. W. H. DULL IS PRESENTED

Druggist Accused of Trying to Bribe City Chemist

Dr. William H. Dull, druggist, 400 North Gay street, was presented by the grand jury yesterday on the charge of attempting to bribe City Chemist William E. Hoffman, Jr., in connection with an alleged sale of cocaine.

It is alleged that Dr. Dull called May 6 at the laboratory of the City Chemist and asked if he could make it interesting for Professor Hoffman to report that no cocaine was found in samples that had been left with him by the Detective Department. Dr. Dull was released on $200 bail for court.

[Baltimore Sun, May 26, 1908]

JAMES CLARK REQUESTS CONFERENCE

Thursday Morning, May 28, 1908

Being in a courtroom always filled the Chemist with a profound sense of unease. He sat by himself on a wooden bench at the very back of the room. Mrs. Sanner had insisted that all of her boarders attend the hearing in case they were needed to bear witness to Morgan's atrocious behavior. The Chemist worried that if Morgan saw him, he might become upset and say things that would be better left unsaid. He pulled his hat low over his eyes.

Mrs. Sanner decided yesterday that she could not take any more. She asked Morgan to leave and not come back. Morgan refused. Then, after a terrific argument, she banished him to the shed built off of the back of the cottage, locking the door that adjoined it to the house. At around eight o'clock in the evening, Morgan began shouting and pounding on the door with his fists. Mrs. Sanner wasted no time in sending her daughter, Dot, into town to fetch the police.

By the time Officer Wosch arrived, Morgan had broken the door in with a crowbar and was shouting incoherently at Mrs. Sanner and her older sister, Johanna Ray. Wosch arrested him on the spot and escorted him to the city jail. Magistrate Lilly was rousted, and a preliminary hearing was scheduled for this morning.

The hearing started on time at ten o'clock. The bailiff announced that the only charge against Morgan was disturbing the peace. This disappointed the Chemist. He had hoped for something more serious that would put Morgan away for an extended period of time. After the charges were read, Morgan's court-appointed attorney, a young up-and-coming lawyer named James Clark, immediately asked for a conference. He and the prosecutor were still in Justice Lilly's chambers, likely negotiating some kind of plea deal.

The Chemist pulled his watch from his pocket and glanced at it. The lawyers and the judge had been jawing in the back for almost thirty minutes. He lifted the brim of his hat and quickly scanned the courtroom. Mrs. Sanner and her sisters sat in the row behind the prosecutor's table. Morgan sat to the side in the front of the room.

He appeared to be muttering to himself, occasionally gesticulating with his hands. The Chemist thought he saw the usual bulge behind Morgan's lower lip. Evidently, the police had not taken his snuff away.

The hearing was sparsely attended—mostly by the residents of the cottage and a few neighbors. There was a woman separated from the rest, in the back row on the opposite side from where The Chemist sat. She was attractive in his estimation—about his age, in her early or mid thirties. She was slender, with simple, medium-length dark hair and a practical, small hat with a single feather. She had a pencil and a pad of paper and had been taking notes. He wondered if this might be Mrs. O'Flynn from the Times.

A door opened in the front. Everyone came to their feet as the judge reentered the courtroom followed by the attorneys. The lawyers took their seats as Judge Lilly silently read through a sheet of paper.

Lilly gazed down sternly upon the defendant. "Mr. Morgan, you have accepted the representation of Mr. Clark, is this correct?"

Morgan fidgeted in his chair. He said nothing.

"Mr. Morgan," the judge said more loudly.

"Eh? I ain't ... ten dowers a week. Ain't sleepin' in no shed no..." He lapsed into silence and looked around him for somewhere to spit. His attorney offered him a water glass.

"I need a yes or no, Mr. Morgan," said Judge Lilly.

"Okay then," Morgan said absently. He spat into the glass.

"Good, that is a wise decision," said the judge. "Your attorney tells me that you have pled guilty to the charge of disturbing the peace. We understand that you have been a model tenant until very recently, and Mrs. Sanner has attested that she does not want to see you in jail. Nor would it make any sense to impose a monetary fine on someone in your position."

This drew no response, so the judge continued, "Mr. Clark tells the court that you have agreed to leave town in exchange for a suspended sentence. The court accepts this arrangement. Your sentence shall remain suspended on the condition that you are no longer seen in Ellicott City or its environs. Be advised, however, that the court will revisit the matter and will look upon you harshly if you do return." He again waited for a response. Hearing none, he prompted, "Mr. Morgan do you understand?"

"Eh? I ain't ... all right now," said Morgan without looking up.

"Good. Officer Wosch, please see Mr. Morgan back to Angelo Cottage so he can collect his belongings, and then escort him to the city limit." He banged the gavel, stood, and departed the courtroom.

The woman on the opposite side of the back row was hastily writing notes on her pad. The Chemist rose and decided to approach her. He started toward the center, but quickly turned away and lowered his head. Officer Wosch was just now escorting Morgan down the aisle.

It appeared that Morgan was just now comprehending his punishment. "What? Leave town? Where'ma s'posed to go? Ain't goin' back to Rockville. Leave off ma now." He tried to free himself from Wosch's grip as they were passing the back row. Morgan violently jerked away from the policeman and tumbled into The Chemist. They both fell to the floor between the benches.

Wosch hauled Morgan to his feet. "This was all explained to you by the judge. You agreed. Now come along peaceably."

Morgan was anything but peaceable. "You got it wrong. It's 'at damned Linwood Cross took ma room." He again tried to free himself, but Officer Wosch held him fast. Morgan then saw the Chemist, who was just rising to his feet and brushing himself off. "It's HIM," bellowed Morgan. "It's all him! Take him. He's the one doin' the mischief 'round here. I seen him. Wait." Just before they disappeared through the door at the back of the courtroom, Morgan locked eyes with the Chemist and yelled out, "Later—Ain't done with you!"

TAFT TO RESIGN JULY 1
Expects to Leave Roosevelt Cabinet
Soon After Nomination

Though he refuses to announce his plans just now it is understood that if he is nominated for President by the Republican National Convention, which meets at Chicago June 10, William H. Taft will on July 1 resign as Secretary of War. He seems to be so confident of being nominated that he is getting his work in such shape that it may be easily turned over to his successor.

[Baltimore Sun, May 28, 1908]

COLIN SCEPTICAL ABOUT THE OH-TOPSIES

Thursday Afternoon, May 28, 1908

After school let out, Trudy's sons, Colin and Sean, were sent on a mission by their grandfather. The Old Man's bunions were acting up, he claimed, to the point where he could barely stand. And the only medicine worth a damn when dealing with bunions, he claimed, was a powder called Allen's Foot=Ease. He gave the boys the empty box so that they would be sure to accept no substitutes. At the bottom of the box, it announced that the trademark "FOOT=EASE," with the clever equals sign, was registered by the U. S. Patent Office. The scowling visage of Dr. Allen S. Olmsted on the cover advised that only boxes with his signature were to be considered genuine.

Colin was eleven years old, or "almost twelve" as he had recently begun telling people. He led his eight-year-old brother, Sean, down Hollow Road, past Oella Mill, and down the meandering stretch of Oella Avenue into town. They crossed the river through the covered bridge and entered the busy plaza in front of the railroad station.

They crossed the trolley tracks to the north side of Main Street and were greeted by Mr. Martin Rodey, who was standing in front of his five-story stone building. He often bragged that his was the tallest building in town, although it was difficult to tell since it was situated at the bottom of a hill. The ground floor was a general store. The top two floors contained a music hall where large meetings, concerts, banquets, and dances were frequently held.

"Good afternoon boys," Mr. Rodey said. "Where are you off to today without your mother?"

Sean was more outspoken than his older brother and was always forthcoming with information about his affairs whether it was solicited or not. "Hi Mr. Rodey. The Old Man sent us to fetch medicine for his sore bunions. He showed us his feet. They was red and kinda bumpy. He says they's so sore he can't hardly stand. Do you got bunion medicine in your store?"

"What good, helpful boys you are," exclaimed Mr. Rodey, patting Sean on the head. "But, no, I'm afraid we don't carry much in the way of medical remedies. You'll have to go up to Norton's for that. Say, how would you like a ginger cookie? My daughter just baked a fresh batch. They're in on the counter. Tell her I said it was okay."

The boys gladly accepted the treats. On their way out, Mr. Rodey said, "Good boys. Good boys. Say hello to Mrs. O'Flynn from me, and tell your grandfather I hope his feet are feeling better."

The two continued on their way up Main Street. They crossed back to the south side and entered Tiber Alley between Goldberg's Grocery and Kraft Meats. Five older boys were loitering on the wooden bridge over the Tiber creek. Colin and Sean joined the group as they leaned over the wooden railing. They looked down into the shallow creek as it emerged from a tunnel under the adjacent building.

The boys were taunting a beaver, which had evidently gotten confused and had swum up from the Patapsco. The boys were trying to hit the animal with rocks, sticks, bits of coal, or whatever projectiles were handy. The annoyed beaver finally swam to safety under the bridge on which they were standing.

"Hey Boog," said Colin.

"Hey Colin," said one of the boys as the group dispersed. Boog was fourteen and worked night shift at Oella Mill. "Watcha doin' in town?"

"We came to get some medicine for The Old Man," answered Colin quickly to prevent Sean from embarrassing him in front of the older boy with detailed talk of bunions. "You workin' tonight?"

"Course," answered Boog. "Hey, I'll go witcha. Ain't got nothin' to do 'til six."

"The creek sure smells today," remarked Sean, still leaning over the rail.

"Yup," said Boog. "I think it's 'cause of the hot weather bakin' all that shit from the outhouses, you know. But this ain't nothin'. I 'member I was down under the railroad bridge one day when a bunch a guts 'n livers 'n all kinds a nasty things came floatin' down. I had to get out right quick. It's 'cause of Easton's, you know. When they do the oh-topsies, you know, when they's cuttin' up dead people, they pull a lever and all the guts goes down a shoot into the creek. I ain't lyin'."

Colin was skeptical, but he was not about to challenge the older boy. So he said nothing. The three continued up Main Street and crossed over to John J. Norton's Pharmacy. Mr. Norton was standing in front of the shop, enjoying the afternoon sunshine.

"Good afternoon Colin, Sean, and uh ..."

"This is our friend, Boog," offered Sean.

"Ah, Boog, then. What brings you into town today?"

Sean said, "Hi Mr. Norton. We need to fetch some medicine for The Old Man. He's..."

"We need some of this," said Colin, cutting off his brother and giving him a nasty look. He showed J. J. Norton the empty box of FOOT=EASE.

"Oh, that," said Mr. Norton with undisguised disgust as he led the group into the pharmacy. "You know, that stuff doesn't work. I've told your grandfather as much on numerous occasions. I don't stock it, but I do have something every bit as good. I make it myself, right here. I call it Norton's Bunion Balm. It has spicy peppers mixed right in—warms the joints. I'll tell you what—I'll give you a jar for The Old Man to try. If he doesn't like it, he doesn't have to pay. How does that sound?"

"I don't know," said Colin doubtfully.

"Say, Mr. Norton," asked Boog, "Can we have a taffy?"

"Huh, what? Oh. Certainly boys, help yourselves."

The boys each took a taffy from the jar of paper-wrapped candies on the counter. There were several minutes of hard chewing before Colin could speak again. Mr. Norton helped another customer in the interim. When the other customer left, Mr. Norton retrieved a small jar from the shelf and offered it to Colin.

"Thank you, Mr. Norton, and I don't mean to look a grist horse in the mouth, like The Old Man says, but he said to only get the box with the picture of the angry man with the big ears. Do you think Johnson's might have it up the street?"

Mr. Norton shrugged and placed the jar back on the shelf. "Well, boys, I can't blame you for doing what you're told. Johnson's might have it."

"Thanks for the taffy, Mr. Norton," said Sean.

"Don't mention it," replied J. J. Norton. "Oh, and Colin, it's 'gift,' not 'grist'—you know, because it might have bad teeth. See you boys. Tell your mother hello for me." He turned to help a woman who had just entered the store.

The boys left the store and continued up Main Street.

"What did he mean about a gift of bad teeth?" Asked Sean. "Who would give away their bad teeth?"

"I dunno, a dentist maybe," replied Boog. "They must collect a lot of bad teeth. Maybe they give 'em out."

They crossed the street to find Harry Fissell standing in front of his grocery store with a tray of popcorn balls. "Hello boys. Would you like one?" he offered.

"Thank you, Mr. Fissell," said the always-polite Sean as they each took one of the sweets and started nibbling. "The Old Man needs medicine for his bunions. It's called Foot Tease. You got any of that here?"

"Foot EASE," corrected Colin, showing Mr. Fissell the empty box.

"Oh, no, we don't carry medicines. If you want fresh strawberries or asparagus, I'm your man. But for that you'll have to go across to Norton's or up to Johnson's. Now say hello to your mother for me."

The next building up from Fissell's was the Washington Trust Company. A scary-looking clown stood in the entranceway of the bank. The clown approached, apparently wanting to shake the boys' hands. They hurried past.

They entered Johnson's Pharmacy and found Mr. J. Hartley Johnson near the back of the store on a ladder placing some items on a high shelf. When he saw the boys, he descended and asked, disinterestedly, "May I help you with something?"

Sean said nothing this time. He had confided to Colin previously that he had always found Mr. Johnson to be rather frightening. He hadn't even wanted to come into the store.

Colin said, "Hi Mr. Johnson, we're Trudy O'Flynn's boys. Our grandfather sent us to buy some more of this. Do you have it?" He held up the box.

J. Hartley sneered. "No, I think not. What's it for?"

"Bunions."

The sneer deepened. "Oh, goodness no. I do have something better." He led them to the front of the store and retrieved a metal tube from the shelf. "I make this here in the shop."

"Johnson's Joint Gel?" Colin said, reading the label on the tube.

"Nope," said Boog. "The Old Man say don't 'cept nothin' else. Gotta be the Foot Tease."

Mr. Johnson grunted, "Well, I can't help you then. Try Seward's Grocery up the street. He carries that kind of snake oil. Now run along, I'm busy." He began ascending his ladder again.

They left the pharmacy and climbed onto the rock outcropping below Emory Church to rest for a bit. They laughed at some elderly men walking down the street wearing funny hats. They looked like a train conductor's hat, except for the bright purple ribbon over the visor. Boog explained that these were odd fellows heading down the street to the lodge.

Before continuing their quest, they took a detour through the Howard House to get free samples of ice cream. Then they crossed the street again and entered Seward's Grocery on the corner of Columbia Pike. Mr. Seward didn't carry the medicine they needed, but he did give each boy a handful of hard candies as a consolation.

"Have you tried Hardin's?" Asked Mr. Seward.

"No. Where's that?" asked Colin.

"It's a small druggist shop up on Mercer Street, behind the old courthouse. Do you know where that is?"

"I know," answered Boog. "I'll show 'em."

The boys left the grocery and continued up the street. They decided to stop and sit on a bench outside Joe Berger's Grocery on the south side of Main Street to eat their candies.

Boog sat in the middle with Colin and Sean on either side. He leaned close to Sean. "You see that dentist office over there? The sign with the big tooth on it?"

"Yeah. What about it? Is he giving away bad teeth?"

"No, not that. Did'ya know it's haunted with seven ghosts?"

"Naw aw."

"Yuh huh," countered Boog, and he told them the story of the dentist with seven ghosts:

"Once upon a time, they was a mysterious dentist by the name a Doctor Owings. He had his self a house down near the river—on the other side, near where McDonald's General Store is at. So he lived there with his wife and they's six young chilluns—three boys and three girls. The way I heard it, they was always cryin' 'cause they didn't get fed enough. They say old Doctor Owings was a stingy sort. They was cryin' like this: wuh, wuh, WUUHHOOOOOO!" The last noise became a creepy howl.

"Well then came the big flood back in 1868. You heard about that didn'tcha?" Sean nodded that he had.

"The house by the river was swept away 'cause it was made a wood. And the dentist's wife and all they's six chilluns, the three boys and the three girls—they was all drownded. Swept on down the river 'n they ain't never found a one of 'em. But not Doctor Owings. He weren't there when it all happened. He was pullin' somebody's sore tooth—some rich guy up on Church Road. Now some folks say the dentist knowed the flood was a comin' 'n stayed away from home on purpose. Others say it was just bad luck. And some even say that the old dentist made a deal with the devil and caused the whole flood his self. Ain't nobody knows for certain."

"Anyway, after the flood, he buys that building right there across the street and moves in. He starts up his dentist business again as if ain't nothin' happened. Got his self a new wife and they had another bunch a chilluns."

Boog paused for dramatic effect. "But the old wife and the six chilluns weren't about to just stay dead. They haunted the land down near the river. And when they built the old covered bridge they haunted that too. You could hear 'em a wailin' e'ry time you crossed, 'specially at night. That was 'till one night when a little girl that weren't afraid a no ghosts had a long talk with 'em. She told 'em that they's been hauntin' the wrong place and that they's father had his self a new family in that house right over there." Boog pointed across the street.

"So those seven ghosts, they packed up all they ghost-things—ya know, sheets and chains and such—and they come on up here. They's still there to this day. You can hear them a wailing if you walk by that house at night." Boog leaned toward the house with his hand cupped over his ear. So did Sean.

"wuh, wuh, WUUHHOOOOOO!" Sean jumped as Boog laughed.

"So you see, Doctor Gambrill has his dentist office there now. They say the seven ghosts want this building to always be a dentist office so that they can feel right at home. And I swear to God it's true. I ain't lyin'."

Colin and Sean looked at the building across the street with new respect. At length, Colin said, "It's gettin' kinda late. We ought to get goin'."

When they walked up to Mercer Street and passed by the old courthouse, they found a small store with a wooden sign nailed on the door that said "A. Everett Hardin, The Chemist." They entered.

The interior was dim. A single electric bulb hung on a wire over the counter. A man sat near the back at a small table. He was smoking a pipe and reading a book by a small lamp. He looked up when the three entered and called out, "Can I help you boys with something?"

"Yes sir," replied the youngest boy. "My name is Sean O'Flynn and this is my brother, Colin, and this is our friend Boog. We need to get some foot tease for The Old Man's bunions. Mr. Johnson said it was made out of some kinda snake oil, and Mr. Seward said you might have it."

Mr. Hardin placed his pipe in a metal tray. He rose and walked toward them slowly behind the counter. He was well dressed and smelled like fancy cologne. His dark hair was slicked back from his high forehead. His abundant mustache was impeccably waxed and curled at the ends.

Colin retrieved the empty box of FOOT=EASE from his pocket and showed it to the man.

"Oh, that," said Mr. Hardin. "Yes, I think I have it." He spent a few minutes rummaging around in a shelf under the counter. He pulled out a full box of FOOT=EASE and set it on the counter.

Colin picked it up and compared it to the empty box. "Yup, this is it. How much does it cost, Mr. Hardin?"

Everett Hardin cocked his head to the side and said, "O'Flynn, did you say? Are you on the junior baseball team, perhaps?"

"Yes sir," answered Colin with pride. "Do you have a boy on the team, too?"

"Oh, no. I'm wondering—is your mother the Mrs. O'Flynn who works at the newspaper?"

"Yes sir," answered Sean this time. "She works there every weekday. She walks down the hill with Miss Snowden who works down at Kraft's diner. We live up in Oella with our grandfather, The Old Man."

"I think I may have seen your mother this morning at the courthouse. Is she pretty—brown hair, small hat with a feather?"

"Yes sir, she's very pretty. She says that's her springtime hat."

"Well your father must be a very lucky man," said Mr. Hardin.

"He died in Philippians, back in oh-two," said Sean matter-of-factly. "I don't really remember him 'cause I was only two when he left. I was born in 1900. My mother calls me 'century boy' sometimes. Colin says he remembers my father a little."

"Oh, I am sorry to hear that," said Mr. Hardin. "But I think you mean Philippines. Philippians is a book in the Bible—you probably learned about it in Sunday school. The Philippines is a group of Islands in the Pacific that we liberated from Spain in the last war. We still have brave troops there, fighting the rebels."

"My mother says the whole country is rebels and they'd be plenty liberated if we'd just leave 'em alone," said Colin.

"Really? Your mother said that? Well, I suppose one can't expect a woman to understand such things." There was an awkward moment of silence and then Mr. Hardin said, "Say, how about a Coca-Cola?"

"Sure," said Boog.

He led them to the back of the store where the soda fountain was. Colin noticed that he was walking funny. "Did you hurt yourself Mr. Hardin?"

"The limp? No, it's nothing. A carriage wheel ran over my foot back in March and broke my toe. It's almost healed."

Mr. Hardin busied himself with the soda fountain and produced three glasses of fizzing brown liquid. "Here you go, boys. On the house." When the boys were seated at the counter stools with their drinks, he said. "So, tell me more about your mother. Does she have a paramour?"

"A pair of what?" asked Sean.

"No, no. I said 'paramour'—a sweetheart, an admirer? Does she go out socially?"

"Well, I don't know about that. She works a lot. She goes to Miss Snowden's house a lot. Sometimes she goes out and plays the whistle and sings."

"The whistle?"

Colin explained, "Irish music. She plays tunes with The Old Man, Billy Hatwood, Mr. Grady, and some other folks. The Old Man's teaching me to play, too. There's gonna be a wake this Sunday at Easton's hall for old John Murphy. She'll be there, but I don't think The Old Man can go unless his bunions get better."

"Easton's Hall on Church Road—I know where that is. I have a new buggy that I'll keep in the carriage house below the hall. I was thinking of buying an automobile, but the roads around here are just not good enough. Have you ever ridden in an automobile?"

"They ain't, but I have," answered Boog. "I gotta uncle in Baltimore who belongs to the automobile club. He took me for a ride once."

Mr. Hardin ignored Boog. "I'll tell you what. When they finish putting my buggy together, I'll rent a horse from the livery and we'll go for a ride. Your mother can come too."

"Well, thank you, Mr. Hardin," said Colin. "We gotta be gettin' back now. The Old Man is gonna be wonderin' what happened to us. So, how much does the medicine cost?"

The Chemist waved his arm in a dismissive gesture. "No charge, no charge. In fact, here." He took a moment to find a box on the shelf behind him. He handed it to Colin. "That's French writing on the box—fancy soap for ladies. Give that to your mother and tell her it's from me."

"Golly, Mr. Hardin, you sure are a nice man," said Sean.

"Don't mention it, my boy. I hope I get to know you boys better. So you say the wake is on Sunday? Tell your mother I may stop by. I live right up the street from there."

A NEW PLAN NEEDED

Thursday Afternoon, May 28, 1908

The visit from the boys had been a welcome diversion from the Chemist's deliberations. He was reminded of his own childhood in Clarksville—how he would roam about without a care in the world—until, of course, that awful day when Charley Hill betrayed him.

He drew his mind back to his present troubles. When Morgan had been dragged out of the courthouse this morning, he had shouted that he wasn't done. This could have been simply the rambling of a cocaine-addled brain, but perhaps he was serious. The Chemist prided himself on being thorough—on thinking through every contingency. He decided he would need a new plan in case Morgan threatened further mischief.

The memory of his childhood gave him an idea for how he might deal with Morgan once and for all. He opened the cabinet under the counter and began rummaging through his various supplies until he found the bottle he might need. It was a small bottle and only half full, but it would be enough.

As if on cue, the telephone rang. He picked up the candlestick and held the earpiece to his ear.

"Hello, Everett Hardin's Pharmacy. This is the chemist," he said into the mouthpiece.

There was a fit of coughing on the line followed by Morgan's hoarse drawl. "Told, Told ya I ... that you ... Ya got ma money for the week?"

Hardin played dumb. He didn't want to incriminate himself in case an operator was still listening on the line. He spoke in a friendly voice. "Sir, I'm afraid I don't know who you are, or where you are calling from." He paused for a moment and added, "So I don't see why you expect any money from me."

After more coughing, Morgan barked, "wait!" Hardin could hear scuffing sounds on the line. He envisioned Morgan going through the motions of unwrapping a fresh plug of snuff and situating it in his mouth. He also heard a click, which he hoped indicated that the operator had disconnected. At length Morgan spoke again. "Gaaa! I'm in, in Oella. Got, gotta friend works inna butcher shop up 'ere. And, and, and don't think that this mornin' changes nothin'. I still get ma fifteen dowers a week or ya, ya know what. Fifteen dowers. You can sennit to me, or, or walk on up 'ere yourself."

This is what Hardin had been afraid of. "Hold on a moment," he said. "There's a customer. I'll be right back."

He set the phone down and paced behind the counter, thinking quickly. He would have to put his new plan in motion right away. He went back to the telephone. "Operator ... if you're still listening, I have a question." He waited a moment but no reply came. Good.

He adopted his friendliest tone of voice. "Oh, Marion, I was hoping you would call. I spoke to Mrs. Sanner after you left. We all feel terrible about how this has played out—so much unpleasantness—the court, the police. We do hope that you found adequate lodgings for the night?"

There was a pause before Morgan spoke. "Wha ... Sanner said th-that?" He sounded confused.

"Of course, Marion. We are all very concerned about you. Mrs. Sanner asked me to tell you that all is forgiven, and you can have your own room back inside the house. As it turns out, Mr. Cross is a very disreputable man. Mrs. Sanner has insisted that he leave tomorrow. After that, there will be no more sleeping in the shed for you. Everything will be just like it was before."

"It weren't right—Mr. high-falootin' Linwood Cross. Who's he think ... Mr. high-fal ... Wait, You're sure Mrs. Sanner said I, I, can have ma room back? Tonight?"

"No, Marion, not tonight. I said Mr. Cross is leaving tomorrow—in the afternoon. Mrs. Sanner said it would be best if you two did not see each other. She doesn't want any fighting. She would like you to come back to the cottage tomorrow night. Say around nine?"

Morgan seemed unsure. "But ... but that judge said I ain't to be seen in town again, else he, he, he's gonna lock me up, and what about..."

"Marion, don't *worry*. Mrs. Sanner said all is forgiven. She talked to that nasty judge and Officer Wosch too. You are welcome back with open arms. In fact, they'll be having a little celebration at the cottage tomorrow night for your homecoming. And of course, I will have all of your money for you."

Hardin knew that a normal person would see right through such a ridiculous ruse, but he hoped that it would be persuasive to Morgan in his current state.

"Might need some more a that fancy snuff too. I'm, I'm almost out."

"Of course, Marion. I shall bring a whole case. So remember. Show up at nine, not before. Do you understand?"

"Nine," came the weak response. Then the phone went dead.

NEGRO TO WED WHITE GIRL
Student Says He Is A Son Of Maceo, Cuban General

Syracuse, N. Y., May 28—Joseph Antonio Maceo, a Cuban student at Syracuse University, and Alice Isabel Mackley procured a marriage license here today.

The groom gave his birthplace as Jamaica, West Indies. He says he is the son of the Cuban insurgent general Antonio Maceo, and that the Cuban Government is defraying his college expenses. The family of Miss Mackley strongly opposes the marriage.

Both bride and groom are Catholics and expect to be married in the Cathedral here.

[Baltimore Sun, May 29, 1908]

SURPRISE GUEST ATTENDS PARTY

Friday Evening, May 29, 1908

The three Ray sisters were holding a dinner party at Angelo Cottage for their boarders and a few invited guests. The esteemed Reverend Frank DeWitt Talmage was in town. He was a Presbyterian minister from Philadelphia, whose sermons were printed in newspapers all over the country and were a regular feature in the local Ellicott City Times. Johanna Ray was an ardent admirer and prevailed upon him to attend their little gathering.

Mrs. Sanner had invited August and Louisa Schotta, a young, newly-married couple in town. The Ray sisters knew their parents well, and endeavored to include them in social gatherings. Two boarders were also present, Matthew Powers, a blacksmith, and the newcomer, Lynwood Cross.

As the boarders were well aware, none of the Ray sisters could cook to save their lives. Thankfully, they had hired one of the chefs from the Howard House restaurant to prepare the meal. Thus they were to dine on turtle soup, stuffed smelts with Béarnaise sauce, roast saddle of venison, and rice pudding with compote of orange for dessert.

All were having a good time in spite of the lack of alcohol. The Rays were outspoken members of the temperance movement, encouraged in this pursuit by the good Reverend Talmage. They maintained a strict rule against drinking on the premises.

Everett Hardin had no interest in attending the party. He had given his regrets to Mrs. Sanner by telling her he had a social commitment that he could not break, but he hoped to be home shortly after nine o'clock.

Hardin spent the evening in his pharmacy on Mercer Street and returned well before nine. Rather than joining the party, he walked past the cottage and concealed himself behind a large boxwood in the front yard of the house just up the street. He was close enough to see the gathering through the open windows and even hear snippets of conversation.

At nine o'clock sharp, he saw the ragged figure of Marion Morgan lumbering up the hill with a sack thrown over his shoulder. Hardin was surprised at the man's punctuality, given his stuporous state. He watched Morgan walk the short path from Church Road to the cottage's front door. He crept closer, so as to better witness what transpired.

Morgan dropped his sack on the porch next to the bucket of drinking water. He flung open the front door and announced, "I'm home! And don't ya be worryin' 'bout none of it. Bygones, I say. I forgive ya ... Cross! What are ... ya ain't welcome here no more. Ya better be..."

Hardin heard Mrs. Sanner scream followed by the sound of breaking glass. Everyone started yelling at once. Hardin inched closer to the house but remained out of sight. There was a scuffle. The front door was flung open and Morgan was ejected onto the porch backward. He tripped over the full bucket of drinking water, spilling half of it, and fell hard on his rear end. The two boarders, Matthew Powers and Mr. Cross, followed, fists raised.

Mr. Cross said, "You'd best be gone. We're sending for the sheriff straight away."

Morgan was horribly confused. He sat up on the porch, shaking his head. "Wait! I was ... you ain't ... I'm s'posed ... Hardin said ... where's he, anyway? My ten dowers!"

"Get you gone now," warned Mr. Cross again. "You heard what the judge said would happen if you came back. The law will be here shortly."

Morgan had gotten unsteadily to his feet by this time. "Don't ya bother none. I ain't. Hey, where's that damned Hardin?" Mr. Powers started toward him, but Morgan had retrieved his sack and was walking toward the street. "You all are gonna be mighty sorry 'bout this. You can't treat. Wait, where's ma snuff? Hardin? Oh, he ain't even here." He continued to grumble as he reached Church Road and started unsteadily down the hill.

Cross and Powers followed Morgan to the street and watched as he receded down the hill until he was out of sight. Eventually they were satisfied that he wasn't coming back. They rejoined the party.

Hardin waited a few minutes more and then approached the cottage. Thankfully for his plan, the bucket of drinking water was still half full. He retrieved three items that he had secreted on the side of the porch: a drinking glass, a ceramic pitcher, and the sealed bottle of clear liquid that he had brought from his pharmacy. First he filled the glass with fresh, untainted water from the bucket. Then he carefully opened the bottle and poured the contents into the bucket. He threw the empty bottle into the bushes. Finally, he swirled the bucket until it was well mixed. He filled the ceramic pitcher from the bucket.

Hardin backed through the front door carrying the glass and the jar. At the sound of the door opening, all turned toward him, fearing that Morgan had returned. He placed the full jar on the bureau in the dining room. "I brought in fresh water for the guests." He then made a point of sipping from the untainted glass.

"Oh, Mr. Hardin," exclaimed the apoplectic Mrs. Sanner. She was sitting in the living room breathing heavily. Dot was fanning her mother's red face with a newspaper. "Mr. Morgan was just here. It was awful!"

"Marion?" said Mr. Hardin. "I thought he was gone for good. Did you send for the police?"

Linwood Cross answered, "We will let Officer Wosch know in the morning to be on the lookout. Morgan is gone now. Curious, though, he mentioned your name. He seemed to think you owe him some money."

"Oh, for ... that again? I borrowed a few dollars from him back in April and repaid it long ago. His memory is shot. Marion does not seem to be himself lately."

"About that, you are right," said Mrs. Sanner, gradually calming herself. "I just don't know what's gotten into him in the past two weeks. He was always a bit uncouth, but now he is absolutely loathsome."

Hardin nodded. "Well, I'll be in my room, catching up on my reading. Good night." He mounted the stairs and was gone before anyone could detain him further. He entered the room and switched on the electric light. He picked up his volume of Edgar Allen Poe and began reading The Masque of the Red Death.

He didn't have long to wait. A high-pitched squeal came from the floor below. It sounded like Mrs. Sanner's daughter, Dot, was in some distress. Hardin came to the top of the stairs and slowly descended to the living room.

Dot was running in circles, screaming and holding her mouth. Mrs. Sanner was following her, "What in the world is wrong, dear, would you sit still!"

Most of the guests seemed confused. Mr. Powers also appeared to be afflicted. He was doubled over, holding his stomach, in the dining room near the bureau.

Hardin ran to the man. "Good lord, what happened?"

Powers nodded his head toward the pitcher on the bureau. He grunted in his pain. "Water ... burns!"

Hardin lifted the pitcher and made a show of smelling the contents. He stuck his finger into the liquid and then quickly wiped it off on his vest. "Poison. Some kind of acid, I'll wager." He quickly took charge of the situation. "Mr. Cross—run to the neighbor and get some fresh water. I have some ipecac upstairs. Mary—run into town and fetch the police. The rest of you keep calm."

Mr. Powers and Dot were directed out onto the porch where Hardin administered a dose of ipecac syrup to each. Soon they began purging themselves in the grass.

By the time Officer Wosch arrived, things had settled down. No one besides Powers and Dot had partaken of the water. Wosch quickly determined that the water in the bucket on the porch was also tainted. Dr. Frank Miller arrived from town and examined the two victims, who were both now resting quietly.

AERONAUT WRIGHT IN PARIS
Goes To Demonstrate Capabilities Of Flying Machine

Paris, May 29.—Wilbur Wright, the aeronaut, arrived here today from America. The European representative of the Wrights, Hart O. Berg, of Philadelphia, says the purpose of Mr. Wright's visit here is to demonstrate the capabilities of the airship inventors' machine. The preliminary arrangements for the demonstrations are complete, and a suitable enclosed field two miles square has been secured in Western France. Parts of the aeroplane shipped here from America last year will be put together at the location selected and the motor to be used has been constructed in Paris after the same model as that used by the Wright brothers in their experiments in the United States.

The important features of the invention have now been protected by European patents. If certain tests are fulfilled at the coming experiments it is understood a company will be formed to exploit the machine.

The French Government, it is stated, has offered to buy the exclusive European rights for three years provided the machine, carrying the weight of two men, flies 30 miles, returning to the point of departure.

[Baltimore Sun, May 30, 1908]

WALL STREET MANIPULATION

The Wall Street speculators have advanced the price of stocks beyond the pre-panic level, and it is hardly necessary to say, that those with reduced incomes and smaller dividends, should not be in demand at higher prices on their intrinsic merits. As Harriman and Rockefeller are said to be engineering the advance, there is no doubt they can force prices even higher, but that is all the more reason for small fish to seek shallow water, or those big fish may swallow them up like the pike does the minnows. The Wall Street stock market is no longer run on business principles. It is now entirely at the mercy of the big speculators, who force prices up and down to suit themselves, and generally make money which ever way it goes. How can the ordinary business man compete in such a nest of manipulation?

[Ellicott City Times, June 6, 1908]

SEND ME BACK TO IRELAND

Sunday Evening, May 31, 1908

It was just after nine o'clock in the evening when Billy Hatwood and Trudy trudged up Main Street and rounded the corner onto Church Road, arriving at Easton's Hall. It was early yet—the wake for John Murphy was set to begin at ten. The street was dim and fairly quiet. It being Sunday, the dinner crowd at Howard House had long since dispersed.

Two carriages were stopped in front of the hall. The nearest was a small, one-horse affair, hired to bring Kitty Murphy, the deceased's widow, into town. John's much younger brother, Frank Murphy, stood on the curb and was now helping Paddy (The Old Man) O'Flynn with the step.

The other carriage was a hearse drawn by two-horses. Daniel Easton was descending from the driver's platform as Trudy and Billy approached. "Ah, Mrs. O'Flynn." He took Trudy's hand. "It is always a pleasure to see you, even on such a solemn occasion as this most certainly is. You have my heartfelt condolences."

"Thank you, Daniel. John Murphy was well beloved in Oella. It was good of you to offer the use of your hall. I expect there will be quite a number of people. They wouldn't have all fit at John's home, and also, you know, it's not in such a presentable state with Kitty's affliction being what it is."

"Indeed. Don't mention it at all." Daniel released Trudy's hand. "So ... Billy—I'm glad you are here. We now have four to carry the coffin into the hall."

"Yes sir, Mr. Easton. Trudy, can you hold my banjo? Where do ya want me, Mr. Easton?"

Billy joined three other negroes that Daniel had recruited from the dishwashing staff at Howard House. It was no easy feat to carry an occupied coffin up the staircase on the side of the building. Attempting to keep it level at the landing was especially difficult. Daniel led the way, supervising each step.

Trudy and The Old Man followed the procession into the hall followed by Frank Murphy, who assisted Kitty with the stairs.

Trudy thought it odd that, in all the years they had known John Murphy, they had never once met Frank, nor had they ever heard him mentioned. He evidently lived alone in Baltimore and was fifteen years younger than John. He had only shown up after a newspaper article appeared in the Baltimore Sun saying that John's body was at Easton's funeral home in Ellicott City, and that there was an unclaimed life insurance policy for several hundred dollars. Frank seemed to have taken Kitty in, but The Old Man was pretty sure he was a fraud.

They entered Easton's Hall through the side entrance. It was a wood-frame structure, built in 1889 by Mr. Benjamin Mellor. Situated near the bottom of Church Road, just across from the firehouse and the back of the Howard House Hotel, it was roughly fifty feet wide along the street. It extended thirty feet back where it abutted the granite cliff just below the courthouse. The lower floor was a carriage house with a large sliding door in the front. The upper floor was originally used by Mellor for his painting business. But when the Easton brothers bought the building six years ago, they cleared it out and now used it mainly for storage—even now four coffins were stacked against the far wall. They also loaned it out as a meeting space for large groups. It was a popular venue for concerts and dances owing to its excellent acoustics and buoyant floor.

Strings of electric lights suspended below the ceiling provided adequate light for the somber proceedings. The four pallbearers set the coffin against the back wall of the hall. Trudy affixed a candle to each corner and lit them as Daniel opened a panel to reveal the deceased's well-restored head and upper torso. Kitty, the bereaved widow, had not said a word. Frank directed her to the widow's customary place—a chair at the foot of the coffin. The Old Man pulled over his own chair, with difficulty because of his bunions, and sat next to her.

Trudy's brother-in-law, Niall, arrived carrying a large mirror on a wooden stand and a mantle clock. He set the mirror next to the coffin and covered it with a black cloth. The clock he placed on the foot of the coffin. It was stopped at five p.m., their best guess as to the time when the accident occurred that had taken John's life.

Kitty stood suddenly, took in her surroundings, and exclaimed, "My hat and parsley! What's become of my Mabel?"

The Old Man rose to her side. "Mabel? You mean that old mare you used to ride? Why Kitty, she passed many years ago. Calm yourself dear." He helped her back into her seat.

Kitty's grasp on sanity had been tenuous for the past few years, and her husband's death had pushed her over the edge. The day after John's accident, a policeman had found her wandering the streets of West Baltimore. When the officer asked her where she wanted to go, she adamantly replied, "Send me back to Ireland."

It took another day before they were able to learn her identity. She was returned to her home on Nine Mile Hill where they found John Murphy dead in the backyard. He had apparently fallen from a ladder that was leaning precariously against a tree. They brought his body to Easton Sons' in Ellicott City.

After much prodding, they finally were able to tease from Kitty the story of her husband's death. "Please Jesus, I told the old bosthoon, no more of your poteen until you get your arse into town and fetch the spondoolicks you are owed by that sleeveen, O'Brian."

They later asked Mick O'Brian, the saloon owner, about this, who did remember a small debt that he had once owed to John Murphy, but he claimed it had been repaid years ago. Kitty went on, "So I say to the old thoolamawn, by the jappers, your jug is locked in the cabinet and the key is on a string about the cat's neck. And where is the cat now, he asks me. When last I saw the scruffkin, it was aside the butter-box by the shed. God look down on us all!"

That was the last bit of sense they were able to pry from her. They surmised that John must have propped the ladder against the tree in pursuit of the cat.

By ten o'clock, the hall was nearly full. The Old Man, Trudy, and Billy Hatwood joined an ad-hoc band playing a variety of Irish and popular songs. The Old Man and a neighbor played fiddle, Billy picked out the tunes on his banjo, occasionally strumming syncopated harmonies more often heard in ragtime than in jigs and reels. Others in the band played the bodhran, or Irish drum, bones, an accordion, and a set of pipes. Mr. Rosenstock normally played his clarinet in a Klezmer band, but tonight he played Irish out of respect for John Murphy.

Liquor was flowing freely. Mick O'Brian had donated several bottles of decent Irish whiskey and then, of course, there were numerous jugs of poteen and other types of home brew in circulation. It was rumored that half the homes in Oella had stills.

After singing "The Wild Irish Rose" by popular demand, Trudy left the band and joined the line of people waiting to pay their respects to the deceased. As she waited, she heard bits of conversation. Many were curious about the mysterious brother, Frank, from Baltimore. Several were concerned about what would now become of Kitty in her befuddled state. It was widely assumed that she would be sent to the asylum in Catonsville.

When it was her turn, Trudy approached the coffin and crossed herself as she, from ingrained habit, prayed sotto voce, "Requiem aeternam dona eis, Domine."

Daniel Easton had remarked to her earlier that he had needed all of his considerable skill in making the face presentable after the corpse had lain in the yard for a day and a half. It didn't look much like the John Murphy she remembered, but rather a poor waxen imitation with an overpowering floral smell. His hands were crossed over his chest and enlaced by a rosary.

Someone from the crowd had now joined the band and was attempting, abominably, to sing "Danny Boy." The man had a passable tenor voice and could hit the high notes, but he had evidently forgotten most of the words, and was repeating "tis you, tis you" to cover the defect. Before long he was booed off of the platform.

Trudy crossed herself again and turned to the grieving widow. "Kitty, I'm so sorry for your trouble. Is there anything I can get for you?"

Kitty looked up with innocent eyes. "Oh, Deirdre, check on the cat if ye have a care. Tis an evil cold night and we're sure to be banjaxed."

At midnight, the music and revelry was stopped. The Old Man made his way to the side of the coffin. Frank helped him onto an upended soapbox. Trudy handed him a glass of whiskey.

The Old Man cleared his throat and began his eulogy. "Friends and relations—if you haven't done so already, pour yourself a wee smahan. Let us all raise our glasses and remember my dear friend, John Murphy. Tis a grand celebration we're having tonight, and I'm sure John is sore to be missing it. He always did enjoy a good ragairne." There was a flurry of movement while everyone procured a libation.

Glasses were raised and the Old Man continued, "What can I tell you about John Murphy? He was the best friend a man could ever hope to have in this life or any other. I've known John for near forty years, if you can believe that by my youthful appearance.

"I met John and Kitty on the boat—a steamship it was—on the way to Americay as the songs say. They had a berth next to me and my dear Abby, may the good Lord look after her soul. There was no privacy on the voyage so we all got to know each other rather more intimately than one might want. John and Kitty were from Dunshaughlin. We were from Killinkeyvin. There were a hundred Irish on that boat. The captain was a capable sailor for an Englishman, and we made the crossing without incident, although I must say, the smell of a hundred Irishmen after eighteen days with no washing is not something I would wish on anyone. Thank the Lord if you've never had to take such a voyage. We landed in Baltimore. There was no work there, at least not for Irish, so we asked around, and a priest—a German, as I recall, by the name of Father Furzen—told us to head west ... that there was millwork to be had here in Ellicott City. And that, there was."

Glasses were still raised. The Old Man plowed on, "That was the year eighteen seventy two. We felt lucky that we weren't rushed off to war like so many Irish who came in the decade before us. And after ... like my own dear son, Tom. God, how I miss him."

Trudy felt a lump in her throat at the mention of her beloved.

"Jaysus, how my mind wanders," continued the Old Man. "We're here tonight to honor John. Where was I? So John and I, with Kitty and Abby, came to Oella and found work in the carding room at Dickey's mill up the river, although then it was called Union Manufacturing, which is an odd name when you ponder it, because the last thing they would ever allow would be a union.

"So, we saw each other every day from dawn until after dusk. In the evenings we would gather at O'Brian's saloon and play the grand music from dear old Eireann."

"Now many of you younger folk may not know this, but John Murphy was just about as fine a fiddler as ever walked the earth. Many of the tunes I know, some we played here tonight, I learned from John. He was such a fine fiddler that the devil got jealous and made John stricken with the arthur-itus. It got so poor John couldn't move his joints even with the lubrication of John Jameson, and so he had to put his fiddle away."

"Oh," the Old Man noticed that everyone still had glasses raised. "Slainte." He raised his own and took a sip. Everyone in the room did likewise.

"So, in conclusion," he continued as he set his glass down and picked up his fiddle. "This ... this is John's fiddle, which he gave to me after he could play no longer." He paused for a moment, overcome with emotion. "John taught me this very tune. It's called Caoineadh cu Chulainn. I'm sure you all know the story of Cuhullin and his cattle-raiding, so we won't go into that here. This was the lament written for his passing."

The Old Man reverently raised the fiddle to his shoulder and played a short piece. All were silent as the sound of the fiddle filled the room with its mournful, soulful, arrhythmic keening. He finished the lament to a completely silent hall, paused for a moment, and then raised his glass again. "We Irish know that the word whiskey comes from the Gaelic word 'Uisce,' as in 'Uisce Beatha,' which literally means the water of life, or 'living water', as our Lord would say, please Jaysus." He extended his arm over the coffin and spilled a few drops over the lips of John Murphy. "To my friend, John, who's like will never be seen again. May God keep you, and may your glass never run dry!" He upended his glass into his mouth, set it down, raised his fiddle once again, and launched into a lively jig.

When he was finished, he turned to the grieving widow. "Kitty dear, do you have anything you would like to say?"

Kitty was still drinking from her glass. When she finished, she looked around and realized that everyone was expecting something from her. She said. "Me ma is after saying to stop at Callopy's on the way home for eggs, but please Jesus, not the brown ones. And to mind the puddles afore the coop." She noticed the half-full glass in her hand. "The Lord save us, I believe I'll have a smahan." She drained her glass.

The dancing and revelry continued. The crowd started to thin. It was almost one o'clock in the morning when Everett Hardin showed up at the door of the hall. He entered while Trudy was singing the final stanza of "The Parting Glass." The entire hall was hushed, listening to her dulcet, lilting voice.

A man may drink and not be drunk.
A man may fight and not be slain.
A man may court a pretty girl,
and perhaps be welcomed back again.
But since it has, so ought to be,
by a time to rise and a time to fall,
Come fill to me the partying glass.
Good night and joy be with you all.
Good night and joy be with you all.

Everett Hardin stood transfixed. After the song ended, a dance was called for. The band began playing. Trudy left the stage and made her way to the refreshment table. Hardin arrived at the table ahead of her. She noticed his stare as she approached. "You look familiar, sir. Have we met?"

Hardin's gaze was unwavering. "Madam—I am quite overcome by the song you just sang. I do fancy myself an appreciator of good music, but I have never heard anything quite like it."

Trudy blushed. "You are too kind sir. That song is a staple of Irish gatherings everywhere—especially at wakes. You are just arriving now? The wake is nearly done, except for the vigil of course. But as I say, you look familiar. Have we ..."

"No, madam, I do not believe we have formally met. You have probably seen me around town. I opened my pharmacy just over a year ago. You are Mrs. O'Flynn, are you not?"

"Why yes, sir, I'm afraid you have me at a disadvantage, Mr. ...?"

"Hardin. Everett Hardin." He took her hand and kissed it—a strangely formal gesture given their current surroundings. "Madam, I am a chemist. My shop is on Mercer Street—not as well known yet as Johnson's or Norton's, but I carry items that they do not, and I cater to various maladies that they ignore, particularly among the negro folk. Your two boys visited me last Thursday. They mentioned that you would be here this evening."

Trudy paused for a moment. "Oh, yes. Colin told me about their eventful afternoon. I think they visited every pharmacy in town." She paused, remembering, "Oh, and you also gave them some soap as a gift. Thank you, but that really was unnecessary."

It was Hardin's turn to blush. "Oh, do not mention it. I heard quite a lot about the grandfather's bunions. I trust they are improved?"

Trudy laughed, "much better, thanks to you. He's there now, playing in the band."

Hardin looked in the indicated direction. "Ah. Good." He grasped for some new topic. He was not good at the art of conversation. His gaze fell toward the coffin at the back of the room. "Forgive me, madam. I am not familiar with Irish customs. What is that next to the coffin, wrapped in the black cloth?"

Trudy followed his gaze. She took his arm as they walked toward the back. "That, Mr. Hardin, is a mirror. A wake is usually held in the home of the deceased. We are holding it here ... well, for many reasons. The custom is to cover all mirrors in the house until the body is buried. The Irish belief is that a soul could be trapped within a mirror. We cover them to prevent that from happening. Do you see the clock at the foot of the coffin?" He nodded. "Clocks are to be stopped in the house when someone has passed. I've never understood this one myself, but it has been explained to me that the stopping of time confuses the devil and gives the soul a chance to ascend to heaven, assuming it has not been entrapped in some mirror along the way."

Hardin was unaware that Trudy was making a joke and nodded solemnly. He found it difficult to concentrate with her holding on to him. He could feel her bosom pressing against his upper arm. At length he nodded his head toward the dancers in the center of the hall. "And what is that dance they are engaged in?"

They watched the dancers—lines of four people in rows from one end of the hall to the other. They were weaving in and out, occasionally clasping hands and spinning, but mostly performing complex footwork with their arms stiffly at their sides.

"That, Mr. Hardin, is called The Siege of Ennis."

"The Sea Govenn..?"

"The Siege ... of a town called Ennis. It's a dance that commemorates, or so I've been told, a battle in the west of Ireland some time in the late sixteen hundreds. Of course it was between Catholics and Protestants. It's ... well, if you're really interested, I'm sure the Old Man could bend your ear for an hour talking about it. But it is a diverting dance, and easier than it looks."

After the dancers had completed the pattern a few times, Hardin said, "You can feel the floor bouncing in synchrony to the dance."

Trudy laughed. "Isn't it grand?"

Hardin eyed the undulating floor doubtfully.

Trudy said, "I was on my way to the refreshment table. Would you join me for a drink?"

Hardin nodded, "If you mean lemonade, then yes. I never touch alcohol. I assume you are in the temperance movement, Mrs. O'Flynn? I have noted that most women are."

Trudy laughed as they arrived at the table. She poured herself a measure of whiskey. "Good Lord no, Mr. Hardin. I admit to having a fondness for Mother Jones and her causes, but keep Carrie Nation and her hatchets away from my liquor."

Mr. Hardin poured himself a small glass from a bowl of lemonade. He stood stiffly sipping from his glass as he frowned at Trudy drinking the amber liquid. The Siege of Ennis finished and a waltz began. Dancers broke into pairs. Hardin asked, "Would you do me the honor of a dance?"

"Well, I'm supposed to be playing in the band, but I suppose they can play one without me." She set her unfinished glass on the table and allowed Mr. Hardin to take her hand.

Hardin was an abysmal dancer. For an appreciator of fine music, as he had described himself, he had absolutely no sense of rhythm. He evidently did not realize that he was supposed to be leading, and he seemed to be favoring his left foot rather badly—something Trudy had not noticed before. As she tried to direct him around the floor, he stepped on her feet repeatedly. She also became uncomfortable at the inappropriately close manner in which he was holding her. She tried repeatedly, but without success, to maintain a respectable distance. She became increasingly annoyed and was starting to wonder if she had made a mistake in engaging him in conversation. He had seemed like a nice, albeit shy, man until now.

The dance ended and Trudy was able to extricate herself, Hardin asked if she would be his partner in the next dance.

"I'm sorry, Mr. Hardin, but at my age, one dance is enough."

Hardin was grasping for something witty and complimentary to say. He knew that women took great care in their appearance. He said, "I do believe you are very attractive for your age, Mrs. O'Flynn."

Trudy frowned. "Well, it was delightful meeting you, but now I really must rejoin the band."

"Very well, Mrs. O'Flynn, I hope to see you later..."

Trudy had already retreated toward the other musicians, where she remained for the rest of the gathering. Something about the encounter with Mr. Hardin unnerved her. He was a very strange man.

It was near two o'clock in the morning when the band finally finished playing. The crowd had dwindled considerably. Trudy discreetly glanced around the hall and was relieved that she did not see Mr. Hardin.

The widow Murphy had already left to spend the night with some Oella women. There was an argument about who would remain with the coffin for the vigil through the night. John Murphy's dubious brother, Frank, insisted that he would remain, as did Mick O'Brian. Frank and Mick had oddly become fast friends through the evening. The Old Man also wanted to remain, but Trudy prevailed upon him to take a ride home that had been offered by some neighbors.

Daniel Easton had reappeared and was directing a small group of negroes in cleaning the hall. Again, he asked Billy Hatwood to assist in the effort. Trudy felt that this was inappropriate, but Billy cheerfully agreed. He joined two other men carrying borrowed chairs back to Howard House. Trudy said she would bring his banjo and meet him out on the street.

Trudy donned her jacket. She wrapped Billy's banjo in its burlap sack and carried it down the steps at the side of the hall to the street. The sliding doors of the carriage house under the hall were open, and the electric lights within were illuminated. Trudy had not been in the carriage house for many years. She felt herself drawn in.

She leaned Billy's banjo against the wall and made her way to the very center of the space. Here a thick wooden post supported the center beam that ran the length of the building. She reached out and placed her hand on the rough wood, feeling, once again, a physical connection to this place.

She closed her eyes in reverie. Her husband, Tom, had worked here as a livery boy when she was still a student at Patapsco Female Institute, just up the hill. Tom had brought her to this place many times. She peered high along the wooden post—about as high as she could reach. There it was, barely visible above a shadow in the dim electric light—a heart with cupid's arrow carved with the initials T.O. & G.L., for Tom O'Flynn and Gertrude Leary. She flushed as she remembered the night when Tom had carved it. It had been very late. She was supposed to have been sleeping soundly in her dormitory. That was when they shared their first kiss.

"Mrs. O'Flynn, I am happy to see you. I had hoped to speak to you again." Mr. Hardin appeared in the doorway. "I do hope my lack of prowess as a dancing partner has not totally put you off. I used to be quite good, before I broke my toe this spring."

Trudy sighed and resignedly walked toward the door. "I wouldn't worry, Mr. Hardin. It was just a dance. I am waiting for..."

"It is serendipitous that I should meet you here. I keep a carriage right over here." He gestured toward the side of the building. "If you like I can send to Gaither's livery for a horse straight away and give you a ride home. It is a long walk back to Oella."

"Thank you for the kind offer, but I think..."

"It is new. It arrived just last week. Let me show you. It is a Phaeton buggy from the Sears catalog—leather seats, a cover in case of rain, although we will not need it tonight. It is right over here near the back." He began clearing a way through the clutter of carriages and spare parts.

"Really sir, I plan to..."

"It would be no trouble at all. It would be my delight. Please allow me to make up for my horrible dancing."

Trudy had been trying to politely demur, but she realized this was not going to work. "Mr. Hardin! Thank you, but no. I walked here with Billy Hatwood, the banjo player. I plan to walk back with him."

This seemed to confuse Hardin. "The banjo player? But ... he's colored."

"Indeed," said Trudy. She began walking toward the door.

Hardin intercepted her again. "Very well Mrs. O'Flynn, but ... may I call on you some time?"

"I believe you know where the Times' office is. If you ever have anything worth printing, please, stop by."

"I meant ... I meant socially," he said sheepishly. Hardin took a step forward and took her hand in his. "I mean if you are not already courting someone?"

"Miss Trudy?" Billy Hatwood stood in the street peering into the carriage house. "I'm ready now if you want to go."

Trudy recovered her hand and strode without delay to the street. "Thank you, Billy. I am quite ready." She took his arm, and they walked together down the hill.

The Chemist came to the door of the carriage house. He watched as Trudy and the negro walked arm-in-arm. He watched as they receded down the lane and rounded the corner past the engine house onto Main Street. Trudy seemed to be leaning into Billy. He heard her laugh at some shared joke. Were they talking about him? He silently seethed as he walked the short distance back to his boarding house.

FEATHERS AND EGGSHELLS

When your feeding is bringing a reasonable number of eggs, don't change your methods because "Sam Tryitall" has been around. If he was a leopard, he could change his spots. Don't trade a gold dollar for a lead nickel with a hole in it.

When your hen cackles, "go thou and do likewise," but keep your head level. Don't let an egg record or a blue ribbon make you an egotist.

If you make a good sale, cackle, but don't think you are the only cockerel on the perch. When you begin to be stuck on yourself, feel the top of your head, and you will surely find a soft spot.

The average length of an egg is 2.27 inches. The average diameter at the broad end is 1.72 inches, and the average weight is two ounces. When a rotten egg hits a politician's cheek, neither can be measured.

[Ellicott City Times, June 6, 1908]

NOT THE WILD WEST

Friday Morning, June 5, 1908

Chief of Police Julius Wosch sat on his usual stool at the counter in Kraft's Diner sliding the top half of his biscuit across his plate to soak up the last residue of egg yolk. As he chewed, he drained his cup of coffee and was about to ask for the bill when a newspaper slapped down onto the counter to his left.

"I was hoping I'd find you here," said Trudy. She took the stool next to Wosch. "Have you seen this?" She pointed to an article in the Sun.

The waitress approached from behind the counter. "You eating, hon? Or just coffee?"

"Just coffee, Viola, thanks." She waited while Wosch perused the article.

THREAT TO KILL FAMILY

Tinner Charged With Putting Acid In Water At Angelo Cottage Had Been Told To Leave

> Ellicott City, Md., June 4.–Marion J. Morgan, accused of putting poison in a bucket of drinking water at the Angelo Cottage, Ellicott City, was held yesterday under $5,000 bail by Justice William F. Lilly for a hearing at the fall term of the Circuit Court of Howard County ...

"I read that this morning." Wosch pushed the paper away and dabbed at his lips with a cloth napkin.

"Julius, I thought we had an understanding. I was at the hearing yesterday, as were you. Where did all of this extra information come from? Are *you* their source?"

Wosch chuckled. "Trudy, Trudy. I promised to share and share alike. I didn't give them anything that I hadn't already given to you. Lots of folks are involved in this. Maybe Morgan's attorney—that young one, James Clark—spilled the beans. Or perhaps ... I know that this is hard to believe for someone with your unimpeachable integrity, but sometimes newspaper reporters make things up. I spotted a few things that I know for a fact are not correct."

"Really? Which parts?"

Wosch sighed, "Mrs. O'Flynn, I can't spend all morning in this diner. I do have police work to do."

"Come on, Julius. It will only take a minute."

Justice Wallenhorst arrived and pulled the stool out from the counter on Trudy's left. He nodded to the two as he sat and removed his hat. "Good morning, Chief ... Mrs. O'Flynn. Ah—Mrs. Wallenhorst said to give you her thanks for the rhubarb bread. It was most appreciated."

"Oh, don't mention it. I hope she's feeling better."

"Thank you. Well, I seem to have interrupted an animated conversation. Please continue."

Wosch said, "Trudy was expressing surprise that the information in a Baltimore Sun article may not be completely accurate."

Trudy hit him playfully on the shoulder and then turned to the judge. "It's about that poisoning at Angelo Cottage. Are you familiar with it?"

"Yes, of course. I spoke to Justice Lilly at length about the ... Oh, thank you." Viola set a steaming mug of coffee in front of him. "I'll just have some bread and soft cheese, and maybe a boiled egg?" Viola wrote on a small pad and disappeared. "As I was saying, Justice Lilly and I spoke about the case." He sipped his coffee.

When the judge failed to comment further, Chief Wosch said, "Trudy, you heard my testimony in the hearing yesterday. I was there the morning after the incident. I interviewed everyone who was there. I took samples of the water to have it tested." He pointed to the sub-headline of the article. "Nobody ever called Morgan a tinner, or tinner's assistant. And that other bit, where is it?" He scanned the article. "There."

> ... Morgan, who had been working as a tinner's helper, had a bottle of acid in the house, and had several times told the women it was dangerous to

> handle it. Mrs. Sanner said that when she told Morgan to leave the house he threatened to burn down the place and kill them all.

"No one that I talked to ever heard Morgan say anything like this. Morgan of course denies the poisoning and says he knows nothing about any acid. No one heard any threats of arson."

Trudy said, "Muriatic acid—that's what the chemist's report said. So where did it come from?"

"It's one of the mysteries of the case. Morgan denied even knowing what it is."

Trudy had taken out her notebook and was writing. "What else in the story is wrong?"

Wosch sighed and looked again at the article. "Here—it says Reverend Talmage is a boarder at the cottage. He is not. He is a clergyman and temperance leader that Johanna Ray invited to the dinner. And look—They got Johanna's name wrong. They called her Josephine."

"Anything else?"

Judge Wallenhorst interjected, "I too, read that article this morning. Preposterous. It says that after the first incident, Mr. Morgan was given ten hours to leave the state. What law would be used to banish someone from the state? This is not the Wild West. Justice Lilly told me that there was an informal agreement that he would suspend the sentence on the guilty plea if Mr. Morgan agreed to depart from the city."

Wosch pointed to another section of the article. "Also, this is wrong. It says Powers went to Norton's Pharmacy in town for the emetic. He couldn't have. He told me he was doubled over in pain after drinking the water. It was that other gentleman who boards there—the quiet one—the druggist. Hardin, I believe is his name. Knowing John Norton, he may have told the Sun he provided the drug as a means to get some free advertising. Mrs. Sanner told me that Hardin just happened to have some in his room."

Trudy was writing and almost missed the mention of the name. "Hardin? Would that be a Mr. Everett Hardin?"

Wosch nodded. "Yes. That's the name. Elusive fellow. He was never around when I was there."

"I didn't know he boarded there," said Trudy.

Wosch went on, "I finally found him in his pharmacy up the road. He is an awkward fellow, for sure. He seemed very nervous—some folks don't like talking to cops, I guess. Anyway, it was a good thing he was at the cottage that night."

"Did you ask him why he just happened to have a quantity of emetic in his room?"

"I did," said Wosch, smiling. "He confided to me that he has limited confidence in Mrs. Sanner's cooking, especially the freshness of the meat she serves. He asked me not to mention that to her."

Trudy finished writing. "So, what will happen to Mr. Morgan?"

Wallenhorst answered, "He's being held for the grand jury. Justice Lilly set bail at one thousand dollars—not three thousand like the article says. But it might as well be a million. Mr. Morgan has no means to post that much money. He will remain in the city jail until the grand jury convenes for the fall session."

Wosch added, "I spoke with him last night after the hearing. He has the appearance of a very sick man. And I don't just mean mentally incapacitated as he was in court. He was sweating, feverish ... said he was in pain. He kept asking for his snuff. They called for Dr. Miller. I had to leave before he arrived."

Between Tears and Laughter

"Do you ever think, George, dear," said she, and her voice was soft and low, as befitted the perfect beauty of the night, "do you ever think how closely true happiness is allied with tears?"

"I don't believe I ever do," admitted George dear, "but I will, if you like."

"Yes," she went on, gazing up into his face, and her lips were very close to his, "when one is truly and wholly happy, George, dear, there is but little to divide a smile and a tear."

"Well, that's a fact," assented George dear. "But I never thought of it before. After all, there's nothing but the nose."

[Ellicott City Times]

AN INDUSTRIOUS MAN

Friday Morning, June 5, 1908

Trudy spent the next hour working on the final draft for the Morgan story. Edward demanded that she have it finished by noon. The conversation this morning with Wosch and Wallenhorst was helpful, but she felt there were still a few loose ends that needed to be tied up. She grabbed her hat and headed out.

She cut through Howard House, as everyone did, and started up Church Road. As she passed Easton's Hall, she shivered, recalling the uncomfortable situation with Hardin at the wake this past Sunday. Something about the encounter had disturbed her, and she had found herself brooding on it more than once this week. Something about the man's comportment was off.

She walked the short way up to Angelo Cottage. Mrs. Sanner answered the door after a single knock. "Trudy! Come in, dear. We're always happy to see you. It is such a relief that this dreadful business is over."

She directed Trudy to a small parlor at the front of the house. Johanna Ray sat at one end of a long sofa sipping tea from a china cup. She held the saucer in front of her chin and took dainty sips with quick, barely perceptible movements of the cup. Her thick, circular spectacles made her eyes appear twice their actual size. Trudy sat at the other end of the sofa.

Mrs. Sanner asked, "Can I offer you some refreshment, dear? Some tea, or fresh water?"

Trudy hesitated as she noticed the crystal pitcher on the sideboard.

Mrs. Sanner followed her gaze. She gave an exaggerated laughed and said loudly to Johanna, "Sister, do you see? Trudy thinks we are trying to poison her?"

Johanna rolled her eyes but remained silent. She continued sipping her tea.

"You needn't worry dear," said Mrs. Sanner. It's fresh, and it's not from *that* bucket."

Trudy said, "Thank you, but I'm fine. I just have a few questions about the incident. I'm writing it up for tomorrow's paper. Ah ... Is Mr. Hardin here?"

"I don't think so, dear. I haven't seen him all morning. He usually arises early and goes to his shop on Mercer Street. He's such a hard worker, and so polite. He is younger than he looks, you know. Don't let the graying temples fool you. I tell you, Trudy, if I were ten years younger... Ah, but you are not here to listen to me prattle about. What can we do for you?"

"Yes, thank you," said Trudy. "I was hoping to get some more information about Mr. Morgan's background. Where is he from? When did he come here? What line of work was he in? That sort of thing."

"Oh. Well. I believe I told all this to that reporter from the Sun. And what a rude man he was! Insulting, I would say. Anyway, Mr. Morgan came here five years ago, in the springtime."

"Clarksville!" The unexpected outburst came from Johanna.

"What was that, dear?" asked Mrs. Sanner.

Johanna rolled her eyes again but said nothing more.

Mrs. Sanner continued, "So, he had steady work as a baggage handler at the train station. He wore one of those blue hats with the shiny visor. Oh, and he was always helpful around the house—emptying pans, fetching water from the pump on Main Street, that sort of thing. And oh my, was he ever a help with the gardening! He had a real flare for it. We had the best tomatoes last year—as big as a melon, and you've never tasted anything so good. He would..."

"So, when did he start acting strangely?"

"Oh, yes. Well he hurt his back at the station last summer. Those steamer trunks are so heavy, you know. I believe it was in August. He was flat on his back for weeks. And did the mighty Baltimore and Ohio Railroad offer him any assistance? No, I should say not. The only word we heard from them was that they wanted the uniform back."

"He has been ill since then?"

"No, no. He was back on his feet in the autumn. But he had a hard time of it after that. He found odd jobs here and there in the city. He paid his board when he could, which frankly wasn't that often. But he was a gentleman until I had to ask him to move out to the shed. We have a tool shed that adjoins the house in the back, you see. It's clean and dry, and it was only for the summer months. We have our own expenses to worry about, you know, and Mr. Cross was willing to pay a premium over full board."

Trudy asked, "and when did Mr. Cross arrive?"

"Hmmm, about a month ago, I would say, I think..."

"May tenth," declared Johanna.

"Yes, that sounds about right—as I said, about a month ago. So I asked Mr. Morgan to move into the shed for the summer and I must say, he took great offense. It was shortly after that, I believe, that he became rather irritable and short tempered."

Trudy was writing this in her notebook. Before Mrs. Sanner could continue, she asked, "So, it was Morgan who brought in the pitcher of poison water?"

"Mr. Hardin," said Johanna.

Mrs. Sanner furrowed her brow trying to remember. "Was it? Are you sure, dear? Well, now that I think of it, I believe you're right. I recall Mr. Hardin standing right there with a pitcher in one hand and a glass of water in the other. He must have filled it from the poisoned bucket. I'm sure he feels awful about that. And you know, he drank a glass himself. The poor man must have been stricken too, but he thought only of the others in the house. Such a gracious man."

"Mr. Hardin was at the dinner party?"

Mrs. Sanner thought about this for a moment. "Yes. Well, no. I believe he arrived late—just after Mr. Morgan had been chased away. As I told you, Mr. Hardin seems to work all hours. He is such an industrious man."

It was a half hour later before Trudy was able to politely extract herself from the house.

Hardin stood in the shadows on the roof of the cottage. He smoked his pipe as he watched Mrs. O'Flynn withdraw down Church Road. He pondered whether something would have to be done.

Under a Serious Charge

M. J. Morgan, a young white man, who at one time was the baggage agent at the B. and O. R. R. Depot, in Ellicott City, but for some time past has been making his living in doing odd jobs around the town, is in jail under the serious alleged charge of putting a poisonous substance in a bucket of drinking water at Angelo Cottage, the home of the Misses Ray, where Morgan has made his home as a boarder for the past five years. It seems that Morgan recently created quite a disturbance in the Ray house, and made himself so objectionable that his arrest was requested. The arrest was made by Officer Wosch, who carried his prisoner before Justice Lilly, who upon promises of leaving the town, by Morgan, suspended sentence on the disturbing the peace charge. Morgan, being assisted by the officer, got his clothes together and apparently made off towards Baltimore county and promised never to return. About this he evidently changed his mind as he was seen to come into Ellicott City Friday night last. About the time of Morgan's return, the Ray family with some visitors partook of the water, kept in a bucket on the porch of their residence and noticed nothing in its taste to show it had been doctored, but soon afterwards, members of the family and guests began to feel burning pains and sickness, which could only be relieved by emetics. The water bucket was then examined and its contents clearly showed it contained foreign substances, which had not been noticed when the water was freshly drawn. Suspicion immediately pointed toward Morgan, and he was re-arrested and committed to jail, and a sample of the water sent to Baltimore chemists for examination. As a result of the water examination, by State Chemist Penniman, and additional testimony, Morgan had another hearing before Justice Lilly on Thursday, and was held for the Grand Jury at the September Term of the Circuit Court. Martin F. Burke appeared for the State, and James Clark for the prisoner.

[Ellicott City Times, June 6, 1908]

ELLICOTT CITY A GRETNA GREEN

Ellicott City, Md., Jan 7.—An examination of the marriage license records of Howard county shows that Ellicott City outstrips her rival Rockville as a Gretna Green, having issued just 217 more marriage licenses in 1908 than were issued in the county seat of Montgomery. In the course of the year, 664 marriage licenses were issued by Dr. W.W.L. Cissell, clerk of the Circuit Court, which is a decided gain over any previous year. ...

Most prominent of all these licenses, and one that created excitement among the residents of Baltimore and vicinity, was that issued on August 19, 1908 to Rev. George S. Fitzhugh, the retired minister, aged 64, and L. V. Shiflet, aged 10, both of Brooklyn, Anne Arundel county.

[Baltimore Sun, January 8, 1909]

DECEMBER
1908

GOOD REPUTATION OF ELLICOTT CITY TIMES AT STAKE

Monday Morning, December 14, 1908

Col. William S. Powell, owner and editor-in-chief of the Ellicott City Times, called the meeting to order by banging a ceramic ashtray, gavel-like, on the worn oak desk. The meeting room at the back of the Ellicott City Times building was crowded with reporters, feature writers, news gatherers, and clerical workers—every employee except the newsboys.

These types of meetings were called from time to time when important news was unfolding. Trudy was accustomed to being the sole woman present. She stood in the back near the door and was ignored, as usual, by the others present.

Trudy had a cordial, but formal, relationship with the elder Powell. She had great respect for his ability as a newspaperman. It amazed her that, even when extemporizing, he spoke in well-constructed, grammatical sentences fit for print.

"Gentlemen, I shall make this as brief as possible," announced the portly Powell, waving his hands in the air in an attempt to get everyone's attention. When the room had quieted, he began speaking, his mouth barely visible behind a colossal, bobbing brush of mustache. "This is a matter which gravely concerns us all. Indeed, the good reputation of this newspaper may well be at stake.

"I am sure that you have all heard by now of the unfortunate affair concerning Mr. A. H. Crawford. Or is his real name Cullen? I am not sure if we have established even that much. For those of you who have not been assiduously following the events, I shall briefly summarize the facts as they are known at present.

"To begin at the end, this Saturday last in the early afternoon, Mr. Crawford, or Cullen, committed suicide by shooting himself with a pistol in a privy behind a boardinghouse on Frederick Road in Catonsville. His arrest was in progress by a phalanx of police officers including Catonsville officers Cavey and Stevens, with whom we are familiar, and our own Chief Wosch. The lawmen ill advisedly let the man out of their sight for a moment, allowing him to confer privately with the matron of the boardinghouse. He thus escaped through a back door and hid in the privy, during which time a search was conducted of the grounds. Before they could find him, he put a gun in his own mouth and pulled the trigger."

He nodded condescendingly toward Trudy. "To the ladies present, I ask your forgiveness for the explicit nature of my description, but these are the facts.

"The events leading to this Saturday's shooting are ... complex, and not, at present, well understood. There are rumors that Crawford was, in some manner not yet determined, in the employ of the United States government. We have heard speculation that this was in some clandestine intelligence capacity. There are also allegations that he was affiliated in some way with Russian business interests, and even that he was a revolutionist or anarchist of some sort. As I said, the circumstances are complex and, on the face of it, contradictory. Now indeed, many of you know Mr. Crawford, as he was a frequent visitor at these offices. In the past several months, he has placed many advertisements in our pages offering loans for real estate and other assets. He has always paid for these ads with cash. It is now alleged that this loan business may have been a swindle.

"Much has been made in certain law enforcement circles, particularly in Baltimore County, of these connections to our newspaper. Therein lies our problem, gentlemen. These allegations could do great harm to this institution. We need to show that the Ellicott City Times was indeed a victim, and not an accomplice, in whatever machinations were perpetrated by Mr. Crawford.

"There is also the wrinkle involving Mr. Daniel Easton, an undertaker here in our city. Because of Mr. Crawford's connections to this town, Mr. Easton was mistakenly called upon to manage the remains, which he willingly did. Later, it was alleged by the Catonsville coroner that this action might have been a crime—to move the body to a different county. For a short while, it looked as if Mr. Easton was going to be brought up on charges. I believe this matter has now been resolved.

"I expect this story to be the focus of the paper this entire week. I expect to see a major feature in this Saturday's edition, perhaps as much as half of page four. My son, Edward, will make individual assignments. Let him know if you have any questions or suggestions."

William Powell left the room without another word. The meeting was adjourned.

G. K. CHESTERTON WILL HAVE TO WAIT

Monday, December 14, 1908

In the early afternoon, Everett Hardin sat atop a stool at Stigler's lunch counter across from the engine house. He blew on a hot spoonful of oyster stew as he opened a book he had just purchased at Caplan's. It was G. K. Chesterton's latest novel, *The Man Who Was Thursday.* He had been looking forward to starting it after reading a review in The Sun.

He set his spoon down and took a sip of aromatic tea as he turned the page. He remained focused on his book as another man took the stool next to him and ordered a ham sandwich with extra pickles. The man smelled of tobacco, whiskey, and pig manure. Hardin took another spoonful of stew and attempted to ignore the intrusion.

"Weather's turnin'. 'Bout time, too," the newcomer said to no one in particular.

Hardin kept his eyes glued to his book. He nodded and grunted in a manner that he hoped would portray a not-unfriendly acknowledgement of the remark, but without the invitation for further conversation. There was something oddly familiar about the man's voice.

Hardin's attempt to indicate that he did not wish to be bothered was too subtle for the stranger.

"Yep. Headin' dayown a Balmer. Got a room at da Belvedere. Bran new place." The man repeated the name of the hotel, lingering on each syllable, "Bell-Vee-Deer. Y'ever been 'ere?"

The waitress approached from behind the counter. "Coffee, Hon?"

"Yes'm," said the stranger, sliding his empty cup and saucer toward the waitress. "But leave a lil' room at da top."

She filled it and turned toward Hardin. "More tea?"

"Oh, no thank you, Shirley. I'll be leaving soon. Can you just put this on my tab?"

"Sure thing, Hon." The waitress wandered off.

"So, y'ever been to da Belvedere?" repeated the stranger, undeterred. As he said this, he retrieved a metal flask from within his coat, unscrewed the top, and poured a generous amount of clear liquid into the coffee in front of him. He nudged Hardin on the shoulder, saying, "Y'want some?"

Hardin could see that a brief conversation with this oaf would be unavoidable. He put a bookmark onto the page and closed his book. He turned toward the stranger for the first time. "No, I have never been to..."

Hardin's jaw dropped as recognition washed over him. Here, sitting next to him was a man his own age. He hadn't seen this man since they were fourteen years old. Time had not been kind to this man. Years of overuse of tobacco and whiskey had left his skin sallow and scabrous. His beard and bushy eyebrows were unkempt and dirty. Yet his identity was unmistakable. Here seated on the stool next to him was Charley Hill, his boyhood friend from Clarksville.

Hardin felt the flush of rage color his face as he remembered the last time he had seen this person—at that hearing so many years ago in the courthouse just up the hill. He remembered that pompous judge banging his gavel. He remembered the arrogant Mr. John Hill saying that he was a no-good troublemaker. And most of all he remembered Charley Hill's exact words as he cheerfully betrayed every confidence of their friendship, sending Hardin away for years of torture.

All of this took place in an instant. Charley Hill sat next to him with his whiskey flask extended. Hardin recovered his composure. "Ah, no, thank you," he said, waving off the proffered flask. "So ... why did you say you are going to Baltimore?"

Hill put the flask back into his pocket. "Name's Hill," the man said, extending a dirty hand.

The Chemist suppressed his revulsion. "Hardin," he said, briefly shaking the man's hand and then wiping his discreetly on a napkin. "I'm pleased to meet you, Mr. Hill. You are not from around here?"

"Nope. Got a farm out Clarksville way. Hey, you look a lil' familiar. Y'ever been dayown 'at way?" He took a sip of his whiskey-laden coffee and raised his bushy eyebrows.

To Hardin's relief, it appeared that Charley Hill did not recognize him. "No, I don't believe so." He decided to draw Charley out—to gather whatever information might be useful. "What kind of farm is it?"

"Well, it ain't all mine. My brothers help out. Wheat, mostly, some corn, and we raise us some hogs."

"Ah," said Hardin. "Wheat and corn ... the whiskey in your flask—a home brew?"

Hill looked around guardedly. "Well, I ..."

"Oh don't worry, Mr. Hill." Hardin laughed dismissively. "There are no revenuers here. Half the men in town have stills in their backyards, right next to their outhouses."

"All right," said Hill, nervously laughing in concord. As Hardin suspected, Charley's demeanor hadn't changed since he was a boy. He could never keep his mouth shut, and he never missed an opportunity to brag. "We make da finest whiskey in Merlin, or so folks say. An 'at ain't no lie."

"Didn't say it was," said Hardin, falling into Hill's clipped way of speaking. "So, what's your business in Baltimore?"

Hill leaned in close and spoke in a whisper. "Gotta wagonload a dis whiskey. I'm a sell it wholesale to da saloons dayown 'ere in Balmer. Ma brother says we're gonna make out like bannits. Dey're puttin' me up at da Belvedere. Maybe even fand me a strumpet layder. Gonna be a busy night." He winked.

Hardin rolled his eyes. "Good for you. And well deserved, I'm sure. So, will you be coming back through town tomorrow?"

Hill nodded, "Prolly 'bout noon. Got some supplahs comin' in dayown at da freight depot. Maybe I'll see ya agin'."

Hardin was getting up and wiping his mustache with his napkin. "Indeed. If you will excuse me, I do have an appointment. It was my pleasure talking with you, Mr. Hill."

The two men shook hands again, and Hardin stepped out into the street. His mind was racing with memories as he walked toward his pharmacy.

BRISK RIDE LEADS TO WELL FORMED PLAN

Monday Afternoon, December 14, 1908

Hardin returned to his pharmacy in the early afternoon. He found it difficult to concentrate on his work. His unexpected encounter with Charley Hill had released a flood of emotions and memories long suppressed.

He had been living for years with an all-embracing sense of numbness—something he had once tried to explain to that prison psychologist who found him so damned interesting—Knibbs was the name. He remembered describing the feeling in their meetings as emotional anesthesia—like ether on his soul. Eventually he had embraced this emotional nothingness—even thinking that it was normal.

But this year things had changed. He reflected on his brief attempt at a dalliance with that Ellicott City Times reporter, Mrs. O'Flynn. He didn't really know what had come over him, or what to call those feelings—desire, lust, love perhaps? Whatever word one applied to it, two things were undeniable—it had been sincere, and it had been rejected. The damnable woman had summarily jilted him—for a negro no less. He had decided then that he had been foolish to indulge his feelings and that he had clearly overestimated the woman's worthiness.

And now this—Charley Hill had reappeared. The numbness in his soul was replaced now with a white-hot rage. He recalled the promises of vengeance that he had made to himself so long ago. When he left the courtroom, his anger had been focused on three people: Charley Hill, Charley's odious father, John Hill, and the pompous judge at his hearing.

He recalled some ten years ago reading with satisfaction that John Hill had died. Later, after moving here to Ellicott City, he had seen the judge—Wallenhorst was his name—many times. It had caused him only a trifling sense of revulsion. Wallenhorst was no worse than others of his ilk. Not worth Hardin's scorn.

But seeing Hill was different. It was as if he were fourteen again, sitting in that courtroom, listening to his trusted friend betraying him—a betrayal that led to losing a decade of his life.

He still very much wanted retribution on Charley Hill. Hardin had the beginnings of a plan. He spent a few minutes consulting a map and then telephoned Gaither's livery to arrange for a horse for the afternoon. The ride would be enjoyable. The brisk air would calm him and allow him to think things through—to weigh moves and counter moves. He walked to Easton's carriage house and arrived just as the man was hitching a horse to his buggy. He would head up Columbia Turnpike toward Clarksville. This is the route Charley Hill would be taking on his trip home tomorrow.

He was surprised at the clarity of his mind. The fog of rage had lifted, leaving behind a cold determination. Fate had just handed him an opportunity for revenge, and of course he would seize it. He only needed a plan, the beginnings of which were now taking shape.

The horse lumbered up the hill for the first mile-and-a-half after leaving Ellicott City. When he neared Montgomery Road, the ground leveled out. It was a chilly day—just above freezing. The afternoon sky was steel-gray.

For his plan to work, he needed to find a spot that was secluded. The road thus far was fairly heavily traveled, this being one of the major routes into Ellicott City. He knew that in another mile he would come to the intersection of three major roads: The Columbia Turnpike, The Clarksville Turnpike, and The Old Annapolis Road. In recent years, a small collection of houses had sprouted up there. Some had begun calling it the town of Columbia.

He continued on. The road was fairly level now and the traffic became more sparse. After another mile he came to a tollgate consisting of a rope tied between two posts on either side of the road. A small brick house stood some fifty yards off of the western side of the road. Thick gray smoke streamed from the chimney. Hardin waited, but no one came. He got down from the buggy and walked to the house. He knocked, waited a minute, and then knocked louder.

The door opened slowly. A tall, incredibly fat man stood in the doorway in a soiled undershirt, his suspenders hanging loosely about his abundant hips. Hardin could feel heat radiating from within the house. He also detected the unmistakable stench of whiskey. The man was squinting out from the dark interior. He had obviously been napping.

"Yeah?" was all the fat man said, while scratching the back of his head.

Hardin pointed to the gate. "The toll—don't I have to pay it?"

The big man chuckled, "Well ain't you honest Joe? Most folks just ride on through. Well, since you're here, that'll be ten cents."

This sounded high, and Hardin wondered if he wasn't being taken for a sucker. But he paid the toll. Everything about this man boded well for his plan.

He climbed back into his buggy and drove on. After a hundred yards, the road veered to the right and a narrow wooden bridge crossed over a small stream. He stopped in a clearing just beyond. This would be perfect: It couldn't be seen from the tollhouse, and it was still about a quarter of a mile from the crossroads.

The only potential hitch in the plan was the possibility of witnesses. He hoped that there would be little foot and buggy traffic this time tomorrow. The weather forecast in The Baltimore Sun was calling for colder temperatures. He hoped they would be right for a change.

Finally, he needed to find an alternate way back into town. He didn't want to be seen returning after the incident. He had found a route on his map, but he needed to make sure all the roads were passable. He continued to the little town of Columbia and turned west onto Clarksville Turnpike. After a short distance, he turned right and continued northwest on an unfamiliar extension of Old Annapolis Road. A mile later he came to the Old Hammond road, which continued northward and met up with Frederick Road between the thirteen and fourteen mile markers. Relieved, he turned east and returned to Ellicott City.

He spent the evening thinking through various contingencies. He went to bed early. The next day would be busy.

CURED CHRONIC DYSPEPSIA

Mrs. W. Warner, New Orleans, La., after Suffering for Years from Dyspepsia, found Immediate Relief from the use of Duffy's Pure Malt Whiskey

Recently she wrote—"I have been suffering from dyspepsia for the last 12 years, and have tried almost everything, but failed to get relief. I was told to try Duffy's Pure Malt Whiskey. I went to the drug store and bought a bottle, and before I finished using it I was relieved. I have been taking Duffy's Pure Malt Whiskey for some time and am glad to say it was the medicine that cured me. I highly recommend it to anyone suffering from dyspepsia."

Caution—When you ask your druggist, grocer or dealer for Duffy's Pure Malt Whiskey be sure you get the genuine. It's the only absolutely pure medicinal malt whiskey and is sold in sealed bottles only—never in bulk. Look for the trade-mark the "Old Chemist" on the label, and make sure the seal over the cork is unbroken. Price, $1. Illustrated medical booklet and doctor's advice free. Duffy Malt Whiskey Co., Rochester, N. Y.

[Baltimore Sun, Reprinted several times in 1908]

A PLEASING SYMMETRY

Tuesday, Early Afternoon, December 15, 1908

Hardin stood in the back corner of O'Brian's Saloon, gazing through the grimy window while sipping a cup of tepid tea. He loathed the noise, decor, and the combined odor of bleach and vomit that such establishments offered. But in this case, he made an exception as it afforded him an unobstructed view of the plaza in front of the B&O Train Depot and the covered bridge over the river. Charley Hill said he would be coming through town on his way back to Clarksville from Baltimore. That meant he would be coming through that bridge.

He pulled his watch from his vest and noted that it was now almost one o'clock—more than an hour since his arrival. Was it possible that Hill had already come through town in the morning? Hardin didn't think so. That would have required leaving Baltimore early—unlikely given the night of debauchery that Hill had bragged he was looking forward to.

Hardin was also having second thoughts. His rage had subsided somewhat since yesterday. He reflected that, despite a few challenges, the year had been a good one, and his financial future looked bright. Perhaps he should just return to his pharmacy and put these foolish thoughts of vengeance out of his head. He could...

A nearly empty farmer's wagon emerged from the covered bridge. On the bench holding the reins sat Charley Hill. His face was red. He looked even filthier and more unkempt than he had yesterday. Hill pulled the reins and turned the wagon to the left, passing directly in front of the window where Hardin stood. Fresh hatred and excitement bubbled up from somewhere deep within him. He *would* soon take his revenge.

The Chemist watched as Hill pulled his wagon in front of a row of freight storage buildings just past the B&O depot on Maryland Avenue. Hill dismounted, fixed the brake on the wagon, and entered the depot. He returned after a moment with a porter who took him to a storage building, unlocked it, and swung open the wide door. The porter cupped his hands and called across the street, beckoning broadly with his arms. A negro emerged from the coal yard, listened to the porter's instructions, and then began loading sacks of grain into the back of Hill's wagon.

Hardin watched the negro work for some time. He couldn't be sure, but the more he looked, the more convinced he became that this was the same man with whom the O'Flynn woman had walked off after the wake back in June. He had the same stupid grin on his face. He couldn't remember the name—was it Hatfield?

He took the last sip of tea and set the cup on the nearest table. He perused the plaza through the window one last time and saw a young colored girl selling bags of roasted walnuts from a barrel in front of Rodey's News Stand. A hand-painted sign on the barrel announced "5 cents a bag." The girl was bundled from head to toe in rags against the cold.

A flash of inspiration came into Hardin's mind. He had been mulling over his plan all morning, and it had occurred to him that the biggest flaw was that he needed a scapegoat. The Ellicott City police were more tenacious than their Catonsville brethren—at least Chief Wosch was. He would look far and wide for the perpetrator ... unless one was handed to him on a platter.

He quickly thought through how he could modify his plan without incurring too great a risk. The walnut girl was the key. But he wouldn't want the girl being able to recognize him later.

The cold weather would be his ally. He wrapped his scarf loosely about his neck. He walked to the front door of the saloon and paused as he put his hand on the cold metal knob. He had an odd feeling—a premonition that this was somehow his Rubicon—a sense that he was about to set a series of momentous events in motion, and that there would be no turning back.

He almost fell forward as the door was pulled open from the outside. He recovered and moved to the side as Charley Hill swaggered into the saloon. Hill showed no sign of recognition as he pushed past. The cretin recognized neither the boy he grew up with nor the man with whom he had conversed less than a day ago.

Hardin pulled his scarf up over the lower half of his face and went out to the street, bracing himself against a gust of cold air. He crossed Main Street and stopped before the girl with the walnut barrel. She looked to be about twelve.

"Hello. What's your name?" asked Hardin.

The girl lowered her head, unaccustomed to being addressed in such a friendly manner by a white man. "Um, Ninah-Lou."

"Ninah-Lou—why that's a very pretty name. My name is Mr. Fate."

"Uh, okay. Ya wanna buy some nuts, Mr. ... Fate?"

"Oh, no thank you. I was hoping you could do a quick errand for me. Do you want to earn a dollar?"

"Um, my Pa gonna be back soon. He say I gotta stay here and sell these nuts. But ... you say a whole dollar?" The girl seemed confused.

Hardin retrieved two one-dollar coins from his pocket and handed them to her. "Yes, indeed—a whole dollar for you. Now do you see that negro up there?" He pointed to the freight depot. "The one loading that wagon?"

"Billy Hatwood? E'rybody know Billy."

"Hatwood," repeated Hardin. "That's right—Billy Hatwood. Now I need you to run up there and give him one of these dollars. Then you can keep the other. But you also have to give him an important message." He told the girl the message and made her repeat it back to him twice.

Satisfied that his plan was now in motion, he walked up Main Street and climbed into his buggy, which he had left in front of Goldberg's Grocery. He drove off up the hill, turning onto The Columbia Turnpike, following the route he had traversed the day before. As he rode, he pulled a round stone from his left coat pocket and felt its heft. He had found it just outside his boarding house. It was very much like the one he had used back in March on the man on the tracks. There was a certain pleasing symmetry that this task would be done in the same manner.

A HOE DOWAR

Tuesday Afternoon, December 15, 1908

Like every day, except for Sundays and the occasional holiday, Billy was hard at work at Dorsey's coal yard and livery. He cheerfully did whatever Mr. Dorsey told him to do, which now involved loading grain sacks from a storage shed onto the back of a farmer's wagon. It was a cold, blustery, dry day. Collars were turned up, scarves encircled heads, hats were pulled down low. Billy wanted to finish this job quickly so that he could get back to the bonfire in the livery yard.

The farmer and the porter from the depot stood to the side, engaged in conversation as they watched Billy work. Billy didn't expect them to offer help. That sort of thing almost never happened.

The farmer was talking about whiskey he made in Clarksville and how much better it was than the local swill. He would frequently pause from his bragging and offer instruction when he thought Billy wasn't doing something right. He wanted the grain sacks stacked crosswise like bricks, instead of one on top of the other. He wanted the corn seed stacked separately from the hog feed. There were also bags of nails and other hardware, which he wanted put in a special bin near the front of the wagon. Billy did the best he could to follow the man's conflicting instructions.

When Billy finished loading, the farmer said he was going to go to O'Brian's for a quick snort, and he'd be back in ten minutes. The porter told Billy to go and get fresh feed and water for the horses from the livery yard, and that Billy better have the horses ready to go when Mr. Hill got back, or else he'd have words with Mr. Dorsey.

Billy started his new task. He had just set the pail of water on the ground in front of the horses when the walnut girl came running up to him.

"Hey, Billy. I got sumpin for ya," she intoned flirtatiously.

"Hey, Ninah-Lou, ain't you supposed to be down there sellin' your nuts? You know your Pa get mad when he see you talkin' to me." He lifted a sack of feed and began emptying it into the horse trough.

"Don't ya wanna know what I got for ya?" She replied coyly. "Okay, well I guess I jus' keep 'em both. Spite a what that white man say."

Billy set the sack down stood upright, grinning at the girl. "Okay, Ninah-Lou, what you got for me?"

"Lookey here." She handed him a dollar coin. "Man named Mr. Fate say I gotta give it to you."

Billy looked with astonishment at the shiny coin in his hand. "Where you get this, Ninah-Lou? How come you givin' me a whole dollar?"

"The man give it to me. But he say I gotta tell you a message. He say to tell you Miss O'Flynn need you right away. He say she need your help with sumpin. He say she way up at the tollhouse out Columbia way, and I gotta give you that dollar so you can find someone give you a ride. He say it's important so you gotta go. You gotta, Billy."

Ninah-Lou heard her pa angrily calling to her from in front of Rodey's. "See ya later, Billy." She quickly leaned in and gave Billy a kiss on the cheek. She smiled and then skittered off back to her walnut barrel.

Billy was confused. Why would Miss Trudy be up at the tollhouse, and why would she need his help? He could walk up there in about an hour. He'd done it before. It was just shy of three miles. But he had been given this dollar to find a ride. A whole dollar! You could ride all the way to Catonsville on the electric car for ten cents—all the way to Baltimore for fifteen. So Billy figured he should probably do what Miss Trudy said and...

"You 'bout done with 'at now?" The farmer from Clarksville had returned from the saloon and appeared anxious to go.

"Yes sir, all ready, but hey mister—a friend of mine, a white lady, say she need my help and I gotta get up to the tollhouse on the turnpike to help her right away. Seein' how your wagon ain't but half full, you mind if I ride along?"

"Go away. I ain't got time for 'at foolishness," said the man, spitting tobacco juice to the side.

"Please, mister. It's for a white lady. She say she need my help and says it's real important. I can give you a whole dollar for the ride." He showed Hill the coin.

"Where'd you get a hoe dowar?"

In the end, Charley Hill agreed to give Billy a ride, but that he'd have to ride in the back on top of the grain sacks. Billy ran to the livery to tell Mr. Dorsey that he needed to ride up to the Columbia tollhouse and that he'd be back later in the afternoon.

The farmer didn't wait for him to return. He started his horses and set off through the busy plaza. Billy ran after him and hopped onto the back of the moving wagon.

The wagon rolled slowly up Columbia Pike. After about a half-mile they passed Kraft's slaughterhouse on the left. It must have been hog-killing day because Billy could hear them squealing in the shed out back. They continued up the winding road.

After a mile the grade leveled out, and they started to make better time. They passed very few people on the road. The cold air was laden with wood smoke, which puffed from every chimney.

They rode in silence. When at last they came to the tollhouse, the farmer stopped his horses and said, "Get on off 'n open 'at gate now."

Billy did what he was told. He undid the rope from one post and held it while the wagon passed through. Then he retied it. He expected that the wagon would stop and wait for the toll man, but it didn't. As the farmer from Clarksville drove off, he called back, "You don' mind payin' ma toll too, do ya?" Billy heard him laugh as the wagon receded into the distance, finally disappearing around a bend in the road.

Billy looked around but saw no sign of Trudy. The wind up here on the ridge was more biting than it had been in town. Billy figured that maybe Trudy had taken refuge in the tollhouse a little way back from the road. He walked down the path to the door and knocked.

He waited, but nobody came. He could see smoke rising from the chimney so it was likely someone was inside. He knocked again and called out, "Miss Trudy—You in there?"

After another moment, he heard a bolt being thrown back, and the door opened. A very large white man stood in the doorway with an angry expression. "Quit your bangin' on my door. Hey, you must be that crazy negro folks around here are always talkin' 'bout. What're you doin' way out here? You lost your way?"

Billy bowed his head in deference. "Mister, is Miss Trudy—Miss O'Flynn in there waitin' for me? I gotta message tellin' me to come up here 'cause she need some help with something."

"Miss who? Ain't nobody here, boy. Get you gone now." He started to close the door.

Billy reached out and held the door with his hand. "Please sir. Miss Trudy say it's important that I meet her here. I think she in trouble or somethin'. You sure you ain't seen her?"

The toll man eyed Billy's hand on the door with alarm. "I done told you I ain't seen Miss Nobody up here all day. Mind yourself, boy, I got a pistol and I know how to use it. Get you on back to town now." He pushed Billy's hand away and slammed the door. Billy heard the bolt being thrown into place.

Billy walked the short way back to the road. He was horribly conflicted. Miss Trudy was just about the only white person who was always kind to him. He trusted her and wanted to do whatever he could to help her. But she wasn't here, and, according to the toll man, she hadn't been here all day. Maybe Ninah-Lou got the message wrong. Maybe she meant the tollhouse on Frederick Road. Billy tried to remember Ninah-Lou's exact words. He was pretty sure she said Columbia.

Billy decided to wait. Maybe Miss Trudy would show up soon.

After a half hour he was freezing. The wind was going right through his coat and trousers. He decided the best thing to do would be to walk back to town. The exercise would warm him up, and maybe he would even catch a ride. Maybe Miss Trudy would be coming from town and would meet him on the way.

He took a last, forlorn look at the tollhouse and then started on his hike. One thing was for sure—he wouldn't make it back to Dorsey's before quitting time.

ASSAULTED AND ROBBED
C. E. Hill, A Montgomery Farmer,
Victim Of Negro Highwayman

Ellicott City, Md., Dec. 15.–Charles E. Hill, a farmer, residing at Brookville, Montgomery county, while returning from a marketing trip to Baltimore was assaulted this afternoon by an unknown negro near Columbia, Howard county, and robbed of a pocketbook containing a large amount of money.

Mr. Hill recognized his assailant as a negro who had asked him for a ride on his wagon at Ellicott City. His request was granted and in the vicinity of Columbia the negro left the team, cut across the country and waited for Hill's approach.

The negro concealed himself along the road and threw a large rock, which hit Mr. Hill squarely in the upper part of the face, knocking him unconscious. The negro made his escape after the assault and robbery. Mr. Hill was brought to Ellicott City, where his wounds were dressed. It is thought that his nose and skull are fractured.

[Baltimore Sun, December 16, 1908]

ASSAILANT ON THE LAM

Tuesday Evening, December 15, 1908

It was near closing time at the courthouse when Trudy finished going through a second box of land records. Edward Powell had assigned her to determine if there were any actual property liens in the name of A. H. Crawford, or Cullen, or any of his other known aliases. It was slow, tedious work. Trudy suspected that the advertisements for loans were purely a scam—that there never were any actual loans. If so, she was now wasting her time—but the paper needed to be able to say it had left no stone unturned.

The only other person in the records room was Johanna Ray. The older woman sat at the other end of the long table from Trudy. She had an open box of court records in front of her and was intently examining the contents of one folder with a magnifying glass. Johanna was a fixture in the records room. Trudy couldn't remember a time she had been here when Johanna wasn't. Johanna had no official purpose in examining the old records—as far as anyone knew it was simply her hobby.

Trudy sighed and was about to open the third box when she heard a commotion in the hallway. Someone was shouting her name. She put down the paper she had been examining and rounded the tall row of shelves. She saw her friend, Viola Snowden, trying to push past a guard to gain admittance. The guard was insisting, loudly, that no coloreds were allowed in here.

Trudy came forward. "It's all right Mike, she's a friend. Come, Viola, let's talk out in the hall."

They sat on a stone bench in the echoing marble corridor. Viola was very upset. "Trudy, you haven't heard? Everybody in town is looking for Billy. They're saying he killed a white man."

"What?" exclaimed Trudy. "That's absurd. Who would say such a thing?"

Viola dabbed at her eyes with a handkerchief. "It's all over town. The police are looking for Billy. I already went to Dorsey's livery, but Billy has been gone all afternoon. Lots of folks are saying they saw him riding on the back of a wagon up Columbia Pike, and now a farmer's been killed, and they say Billy did it. Trudy, we have to find Billy and find out what happened."

Trudy frowned, "This all has to be a big mistake. Have you spoken to Wosch?"

Viola nodded. "He's the one who told me. He came to the diner to ask me if I knew where Billy was. They're looking for him everywhere."

"But ... why would Billy ride off with a farmer? Did Mr. Dorsey send him?"

"I don't think so," said Viola. "I talked to Hank at the livery. He said Billy rode off in the back of the wagon and said he'd be back by quitting time. But he never came back."

They began walking toward the front door, Trudy's work in the records room forgotten. "Have they gone to his home—up in Oella?"

"I don't think so. The police I saw wouldn't cross the river. They're just looking in town."

"Hah," said Trudy. "It's this Crawford thing. They're all uneasy about jurisdiction now. They won't cross the river into Baltimore County. They almost arrested Daniel Easton on Saturday. But you can bet they've telephoned the Catonsville police. We'll have to hurry."

They practically ran through town, crossed the bridge, and ascended the hill to the colored section of Oella. They came to the house that Katie and Billy shared with another family and rapped on the door. Viola called out "Katie—you in there?"

Billy answered right away. "Hey, Aunt Viola, Miss Trudy. You look like you been runnin'. Come on in outta the cold." He led them into the kitchen where he and his mother had been eating hot stew. "I hope you ain't mad, Miss Trudy, but I waited for you long as I could. How come you never..."

"Billy," interrupted Viola breathlessly. "Where have you been all afternoon? Do you know what folks are saying in town?"

Billy tended to clam up when he was scolded, which he thought was what Viola was doing, judging by her reproachful tone.

Katie stood up and wiped her hands on a small towel. "What they saying 'bout my boy?"

Viola came to her and took her hands. "Oh, honey, you better sit back down. They're saying he killed a white man. The police are looking for him everywhere."

Katie did indeed sit. She was having trouble understanding what she had just heard. First she covered her mouth with her hands while her eyes darted about the room. Then she said, "What ... killed ... who? Billy, what you got yourself into now?"

It was as if Billy hadn't heard what Viola said. "I ain't done nothin', Ma. Who say I did what? I ain't done nothin'. I rode up the tollhouse way with that farmer, just like you said, Miss Trudy. I gave him the dollar and e'rything. I waited, but it was too cold. My fingers was freezin' so I came on home."

Now everyone looked quizzically to Trudy. It was her turn to be confused. "Like *I* said? When did I tell you to go to the tollhouse?"

"Ninah-Lou give me the message. She say 'here Billy, here a nice shiny dollar. Now you get on up to the tollhouse right away 'cause Miss Trudy say she need you.'" Billy thought for a moment while he appeared to be counting on his fingers. He continued, "So I was helpin' that farmer from Clarksville—and he wasn't no nice man, Ma, but I ask him can I ride with him up the tollhouse way and he say okay, but that I gotta give him the dollar. He made me ride in the back with the sacks. So I jump off at the tollhouse and he rode off. He ain't even stop to pay the man."

Trudy was puzzled. "I never told anybody I needed to meet you anywhere, Billy. Now listen carefully. They're saying you killed that farmer. So, you say you saw him ride off from the tollhouse, right?"

Now Billy was shocked. "Kilt! I ain't kilt nobody. Ma, tell 'em I ain't kilt nobody! I ain't got no cause to..."

Viola put her hand on his shoulder and guided him to a chair, "Billy, we believe you. Here—sit down. This is all a mistake. Are you sure there's nothing else you can remember about what happened?"

Billy thought hard. "I remember—Ninah-Lou say that Mr. Fate give her the dollar. You know—to pay for a ride—a whole dollar.

Then she kissed me right here." He grinned and pointed to his cheek. He was relieved that no one seemed to be scolding him anymore, and that Aunt Viola and Miss Trudy were going to figure things out.

The three women and Billy sat around the table, talking in hushed tones about what they should do next. They realized that they had very little time. The Baltimore County police were probably already on their way here from Catonsville.

Trudy advocated that they wait for the police and then try to sort it out. She said that Wosch was a good man and would find out what really happened.

Katie thought that was naive. "Honey, I been 'round a long time, and I ain't never seen a black man get a fair shake in the white man's court. Billy's lucky it was a man and not a white woman; else they'd already have him swinging from a tree. No, Billy, dear, you gotta run."

Viola agreed, "Your Ma is right, hon, you have to run. Chief Wosch is a damn sight better than most police, and maybe he will get to the bottom of this, but maybe he won't. Either way, if you run, you'll still be alive. White folks get scary when they think a negro attacked one of them."

It was all quickly concluded. Trudy was overruled. They decided that Billy should go to Catonsville. They had a cousin there who would probably let Billy hide out in the barn where he worked. Katie warned him sternly not to take the electric car even though it was bitterly cold outside. The police would have his description out by now, and everybody would be looking for him. Before he left, she hastily shaved off his mustache. It was not much of a disguise but better than nothing.

BEATEN AND ROBBED

Charles Hill Attacked by a Negro Near Ellicott City

William Hatwood, colored, is alleged to have perpetrated one of the boldest holdups in the history of Howard county, and is still at large. On Tuesday afternoon last, about two miles from Ellicott City, he is alleged to have brutally assaulted Mr. Charles Hill, who resides near Clarksville, on the Columbia turnpike, robbed him of about $40 and then left his victim bleeding and helpless in his wagon. Every effort has been made to locate Hatwood since that time by the police authorities, not only of Ellicott City and the neighboring towns, but of this city and Washington. It was reported yesterday that he had been seen here, but up to the present time he has not been definitely located. The victim of the assault is lying at his home in a serious condition.

Mr. Hill had been to Baltimore Tuesday attending to some matters of business and was on his way home at the time of the assault. When he reached Ellicott City he stopped at several places, and in making purchases displayed in the presence of Hatwood a roll of money. Before starting off again on his journey Hatwood approached him and asked if he would take him with him as far as Columbia. The request was granted and the two rode for some time together. Before reaching Columbia, however, Hatwood is alleged to have dismounted and before Hill could defend himself struck him in the face with a rock, breaking his nose, cutting a couple of deep gashes in his face and causing a probable fracture of the skull over his left eye.

After robbing his victim the negro made his escape to Catonsville, where he was seen afterward, and then he disappeared entirely. Hill, upon regaining consciousness, managed to drive about a mile to the home of Mr. Caleb Rogers, where he was given medical attention. Later he was removed to his home.

[Baltimore American, December 18, 1908]

CONFIDENTIAL SOURCES

Thursday Morning, December 17, 1908

Always punctual, Chief Julius Wosch arrived at exactly ten o'clock for his appointment at the offices of the Ellicott City Times. Without delay, the secretary ushered him to a small meeting room near the back and offered him coffee. He declined with a wave of his hand.

Trudy entered two minutes later followed by Edward Powell. Wosch stood to greet them. He bowed to Trudy and then shook Powell's hand. "Edward—As I mentioned to Trudy, it is not necessary that you join us. This is an informal interview. I am merely gathering information for the Hatwood case."

Edward Powell exchanged a look with Trudy and then said, "Yes. Well, I assume you mean the case of the assault on the farmer, Charles Hill, for which, we hope, Mr. Hatwood is only one of several persons of interest?"

"Yes, yes, of course, but..."

"And as for why I am here, my father and I agreed that I should attend in my capacity as legal counsel for the newspaper, as well as a senior editor. So I will be representing the interests of the paper and our employees, including Mrs. O'Flynn, who is now working on our own story on the Hill case."

Wosch looked to Trudy and then back to Edward. "Very well. Then, shall we begin?"

The three took seats at the table—Wosch on one side, Trudy and Edward on the other. Edward dropped a blank legal pad on the table and wrote the date at the top of the first sheet. Wosch pulled a small notebook from his pocket and flipped to a page in the middle. Trudy set a folder in front of her and folded her hands primly on top.

Wosch cleared his throat and licked the end of his pencil. "Very good. Uh, Trudy ... or am I now required to address you as Mrs. O'Flynn?"

Trudy smiled, "Trudy is fine, Julius."

Wosch relaxed somewhat. "Trudy—so, I assume you are aware that, contrary to a rumor circulated in town since the incident, Mr. Charles E. Hill was seriously injured, not killed, in the attack on Tuesday afternoon."

Trudy nodded. She had learned this immediately upon entering town the previous morning. It was a great relief.

Wosch proceeded, "This is good, because, although assault and robbery are very serious crimes, Mr. Hatwood will not be facing the prospect of a hanging."

Trudy interrupted, "Julius, if you knew him as I do, you would know that Billy Hatwood is not your man. I do hope you are..."

Edward patted Trudy on the hand and shook his head. They had talked before the meeting about avoiding arguments with the police, including Chief Wosch.

Wosch continued, "Yes, of course, Trudy, I shall try to speak more carefully. I know that you have a fondness for Mr. Hatwood, and this must be difficult for you. So allow me to get the obvious questions out of the way. Have you seen Mr. Hatwood since the incident?"

Before speaking, Trudy glanced at Edward, who nodded. "Julius, what evidence do you have that Billy Hatwood was involved in this assault?"

"What evidence?" Wosch was surprised at the question. "Many people saw him loading Mr. Hill's wagon at the depot. Half the town saw him ride up Main Street on the back of Mr. Hill's wagon. He even told his boss, Mr. Dorsey, that he was going up to the tollhouse."

Trudy took a sheet of paper from her folder and began writing as she said, "So, no one actually witnessed the attack?"

"Well, Mr. Hill witnessed the attack," countered Wosch. "I have not had the opportunity to speak with him directly, but he told Judge Renn that the negro did it."

"Ah," said Trudy. "So no identification has been made other than by Mr. Hill, who, I understand, had just had his skull fractured? And his only description is that a negro did it. So where is Mr. Hill now?"

Wosch said evenly, "Trudy, you have not answered my question. I must warn you that this is a police matter. It is your civic duty to share any information you have. Do you know where Mr. Hatwood is?"

"At this moment, no. But I can tell you that Billy—Mr. Hatwood—received an urgent message telling him to meet someone at the tollhouse. A girl by the name of Ninah-Lou delivered this message to Billy. I am told that she sells roasted nuts in front of Rodey's. Have you looked into this?"

Wosch shook his head as he wrote a note in his pad. "Thank you. This is the first I am hearing of this. You said Ninah-Lou. Do you have a last name?"

"No—I wish I did," said Trudy. "I looked for her yesterday and again this morning. She has not been seen since Tuesday. I do hope you can find her."

Wosch said, "So then, you *have* seen Hatwood since the attack? He told you this?"

"I believe this is a very important clue," said Trudy, ignoring the question. "This Ninah-Lou told Billy that the message was given to her by someone named Mr. Fate."

Wosch looked up from his writing. "Fate? Is that some kind of joke?"

Trudy frowned. "Julius, my friend's life is at stake. I suggest you follow up on this."

Wosch nodded, "Of course." He wrote in his book. "Do you know Mr. Hill?"

Trudy looked up quizzically. "No. I've never met the man."

"Have you ever been to Clarksville?"

"No."

"Did you have any knowledge of, or were you complicit in any way in the attack on Mr. Hill yesterday?"

"Me? Of course not, Julius. Why would you..."

Edward Powell interjected, "Julius, is Trudy a suspect in this matter? Because if she is, we're going to have to end this..."

Wosch shook his head, "You needn't worry. I'm just ... touching all the bases. So Trudy, where did you get the information about this Ninah-Lou and her message?"

Edward said, "This is a newspaper. We have the right to keep our sources confidential."

"Julius," asked Trudy. "Have you been up to the scene of the crime? I've spoken to several folks that go up that way regularly, and they all say that the theory in The Sun—that the assailant ran through some field to get ahead of the horse-drawn wagon—doesn't make a lot of sense."

Wosch nodded. "I rode up there yesterday morning, and I would have to agree. I do not know where The Sun got that bit—perhaps from a 'confidential source' of their own. Also, we do not think the stone was thrown, but rather it was used to repeatedly strike Mr. Hill in the face. The doctor said he was hit at least three times."

Trudy wrote as she asked, "Did you speak to the toll man?"

Wosch nodded. "I did. Wallers is his name. He remembers being disturbed by Hatwood." He held his hand up before Trudy could object. "I mean ... by an anonymous negro—he never got a name. Nor did he ever see Charles Hill or the wagon. He said simply that a large colored man banged on his door, threatened him, and tried to force his way in. He said he was afraid for his life. He got his pistol out after Hatwood ... I mean, the unnamed negro, left."

"Ah, so don't you see?" asked Trudy. "That corroborates Billy's version of the events. He got off at the tollhouse and then Hill drove off without ever paying the toll. And I would hardly call Billy large. He's five feet eight, if that."

Wosch eyed Trudy sternly. "So, it is apparent that you have indeed been in contact with Mr. Hatwood. I must warn you, as a friend, that you could be in legal jeopardy if you have been complicit in Mr. Hatwood's escape. He is now a fugitive from the law."

"And that," said Edward, "is where we will have to close this meeting."

"Just a couple more questions," said Wosch. "And I promise these are easy ones. Trudy, have you ever met any of the Hill family from Clarksville?"

"No," said Trudy. "As I said before, I've never met Charles Hill or any of his family."

"Have you ever heard of an August Harriman? Perhaps he goes by the name Gus."

Trudy was perplexed. "No, who is..."

"You never discussed an old juvenile case with Justice Wallenhorst involving August Harriman?"

"Julius, honestly, I don't know what you're talking about. How is this related to this case?"

Wosch smiled coyly as he stood. "Thank you Trudy ... Edward. I too have to keep some information and sources confidential. Now Trudy, remember what I said. If you hear of Mr. Hatwood's whereabouts, it is your duty to come forward."

A DASTARDLY ASSAULT

As Chas. E. Hill, from up Dayton way was going home from Baltimore, with a heavily loaded wagon, last Tuesday, a negro asked for a lift, which was willingly given. Things went smoothly until the Leishear hill on the Clarksville pike was reached, when Mr. Hill's passenger said he would get out, as soon as he reached the ground, he grabbed two stones and attacked Mr. Hill. With the first stone he shattered his forehead, and with the second he broke his nose. Seeing that Hill was out of commission, the negro again jumped into the wagon, tore open his clothes and took his pocket book, containing about thirty dollars and made off. Hill, recognizing the fact that he was seriously injured and about to bleed to death, drove to Mr. Dorsey Rogers' house, where attention was given him, a physician was summoned and the Ellicott City police notified to look out for the miscreant. Judge Renn, on his way home, hearing of the assault, brought Hill back to Ellicott City, where he laid a complaint before Justice Wallenhorst. As the negro's name was unknown, the warrant was issued in the name of John Doe, and the officers expect to pick him up soon when he will be severely dealt with.

[Ellicott City Times, Saturday December 19, 1908]

CAN SEPARATE NEGRO PATRONS
Washington Council Modifies Decision Regarding Restaurants

Washington, Dec. 19.–Corporation Counsel Thomas today modified his opinion, given about a month ago, that the Union Station restaurant would have to serve negroes in the same manner as they served whites. This order has been followed by a tendency among the negroes of Washington to assert their "rights" and force their way into restaurants patronized exclusively by whites, and into the cheaper theatres in the sections of the house where white people are seated.

The modification of the opinion today consists of a decision by the corporation counsel that the Union Station restaurant managers were entirely within their rights in insisting that the negroes be served at a secluded table.

[Baltimore Sun, December 20, 1908]

A RIDE IN THE FRINGED SURREY

Monday Morning, December 21, 1908

The weekend had gone by with agonizing slowness. Trudy had divided her time between Christmas preparations with her own family, and spending time with Viola in an attempt to comfort an increasingly frantic Katie Hatwood. There had been no word from Julius Wosch on the progress of the police investigation. Trudy's encouraging words to Katie that he would find the actual perpetrator were starting to ring hollow even to her.

Billy had stayed away since the night of the incident—now almost a week ago. Katie had received word only once, late on Friday night. Billy was staying in the loft of a barn in Catonsville. He said he missed being home and it was very cold at night. He wanted his banjo but he didn't think he'd be able to play it because his fingers were stiff. This message had come to them indirectly—via a friend of their cousin. Katie wanted to leave at once to visit him, but Viola convinced her it would be unwise to do so. They had good reason to believe that Katie's movements were being watched.

Trudy decided that simply waiting for the police to solve the crime was not enough, and that there would be no harm in doing a little investigating on her own. She might turn up loose ends that the police had missed.

On the way into town this morning, she had chatted with Daniel Easton on the street. Trudy had been at the Eastons' home many times in the past months helping Ella with their colicky infant. Trudy told Daniel about her concerns for Billy Hatwood and her plans to visit the scene of the crime herself. Daniel insisted that he give her a ride in his famous fringed surrey.

Thus at ten o'clock sharp she left The Times and walked the short distance down the hill to the Easton Sons' building. Daniel was waiting in the surrey, and they departed immediately. The weather was mild—much warmer than the previous week, and the ride was pleasant.

They arrived at the tollgate a half-hour later. They walked the short path to the tollhouse and knocked. Mr. Wallers, a large, rotund, and malodorous man admitted them into the dim interior. Evidently, the electricity wasn't working because he had hung kerosene lamps from the ceiling in three places. The house consisted of a single room with a table and wooden chair on one side and a cot on the other. The heat from the potbelly stove in the corner added to the stifling atmosphere.

Trudy wanted to get this interview done and be on their way as soon as possible. "Good day, Mr. Wallers. We can see that you're busy, so we'll only take up a moment of your time."

Wallers grunted in reply. He left them standing by the door as he went to the table. He sat in the only chair and retrieved a whiskey flask. He drank and smacked his lips before speaking. "So what's this about then?"

Trudy went on, "Yes—my name is Mrs. O'Flynn and this is Mr. Easton. I work at The Ellicott City Times and I'm writing an article about the attack that occurred last week."

"I already said my piece to the police." He sipped again from his flask.

"Yes, Mr. Wallers, I know you've already spoken to Chief Wosch, but I am hoping to find a few details that perhaps have not yet been printed. So..."

Mr. Wallers had been eying Trudy suspiciously before he interrupted. "If you're gonna put my name in the paper, make sure you spell it proper—Bertram Elias Wallers. That's Wallers without no 'T.' Now go ahead and axe what you're gonna axe me." He leaned back on the chair, resting his flask on his ample belly.

Trudy wrote the man's name on her pad and showed it to him. He nodded.

"Very good, Mr. Wallers. Did you see Charles Hill, the farmer from Clarksville, this Tuesday last?"

Wallers sighed. "I told a police I didn't. But the more I come to think on it, I'm pretty sure I did. A lotta folk stop in to pay the toll, you know? I can't keep track of 'em all. Speaking a which, that'll be ten cents."

Trudy looked at Daniel, who shrugged his shoulders, reached into his pocket, and handed a coin to Mr. Wallers.

"So, now you say you *did* see Mr. Hill. What did he look like when you saw him?"

This question seemed to annoy Wallers. "I dunno, about average. Like what they say in the papers. Normal feller. Nothing special."

Trudy wrote down the response word for word. "And did you see anyone else that afternoon?"

"Yes'm. I saw that colored man. Banged on my door and said his name was William Hatwood. Pretty near broke the door in."

"Hm. He said his first name was William? Are you sure you didn't read that in the papers, Mr. Wallers?"

The rotund man feigned offence. "Hey lady, you axed the question. I'm just telling you what I know. If you don't believe me, well, that's your problem."

"Fair enough—William, then. And how would you describe this man?"

"Big feller. Tall. Colored, like I say. Now, this was some time after that other feller, Hill, came by. So, this William Hatwood ... he said he'd just kilt a man, and I better let him in or he's gonna kill me too. He had him a big stick. Waving it around all over the place—big as my arm. Look like it might a had blood on it or something."

"I see. You must have been frightened. And where do you buy your whiskey, Mr. Waller?"

"Eh? My ... Whaddaya? I buy it in town—legal and everything. Gotta stamp on the bottle."

"I imagine it can be nippy in here on cold days. So how much of your whiskey did you have to drink last Tuesday?"

That question put an abrupt end to the interview. They had established that Wallers was unreliable, probably drunk last Tuesday, and had no compunction about lying. Trudy was glad that Daniel Easton was there so that he could corroborate when she described this encounter to Chief Wosch.

They got back in the surrey and drove on. The next stop was the location of the assault—only a short distance from the tollhouse. They came to a clearing just past a wooden bridge over a small stream. When they arrived, it reminded Trudy of the man-on-the-tracks crime scene she had viewed from the electric car back in March. Many people, horses, and carts of various sizes had been through here since last Tuesday, leaving little to be discerned. Nevertheless, they got out and walked the muddy ground.

Daniel tried to determine where the attack had taken place while Trudy walked the perimeter of the clearing. She stopped at the point farthest from the road, at the edge of a cornfield, and was about to turn back to join Daniel when something caught her eye. She almost missed it because it was the same color as the dry winter grass—a small cylinder of polished wood, closed on one end. She picked it up and returned to the center of the clearing.

"Daniel, What do you suppose this is?"

Daniel took the proffered object and examined it for a brief moment. "Ah, yes. I know exactly what it is." He went to his surrey and held the cylinder against the end of the rear axle. "You see? It is very similar to mine—a decorative axle cap—some kind of hard wood—oak or hickory. It covers the metal bolt. They put them only on the more expensive models."

Trudy pondered this. "Do you think this could be a clue?"

Daniel shrugged. "It could have been lying there for months. Although, I must say, it looks practically new. I think you should show it to Chief Wosch."

TO DANCE AT ELLICOTT CITY

A large subscription dance has been arranged by Mr. Caleb D. Rogers and Mr. Edward Burr Powell, which will take place at Rodey's Hall, Ellicott City, on Wednesday evening, December 23, at 8 o'clock and will attract a large and fashionable gathering from the surrounding country, as well as many from Baltimore.

Among the ladies who will act as chaperones are:

Mrs.–

R. Dorsey Rogers,	William R. Dorsey,
Arthur Pue,	G. R. Gaither Smith,
William S. Powell,	Edward M. Hammond,
Charles T. Matthews,	Gustavus Delcour,
John G. Rogers, Jr.,	Hammond Cromwell.

Arrangements have been made to have the 1 o'clock A. M. car from Ellicott City run through to Charles street the night of the dance.

[Baltimore Sun, December 19, 1908]

DANCE PREPARATIONS UNDERWAY

Tuesday Morning, December 22, 1908

As she had every morning since the incident, Trudy stopped at Rodey's Emporium on her way into town. It took her a while to find Martin Rodey. He was on the fourth floor directing a crew of workmen in setting up for the dance to be held the following night. She approached Martin from behind and tapped him on the shoulder.

"Oh, Trudy, why am I not surprised to see you again?"

"What is all of this for?" asked Trudy. The workmen were hammering together risers that looked like they would cover a third of the space.

"We just found out yesterday. As you know, the esteemed Miss Elizabeth Starr will be conducting our orchestra. She informed us that the ensemble will have forty-two musicians, including a small chorus—most of them recruited from the Peabody Institute. I believe it may be the largest group we've ever hosted."

Trudy shook her head. "Will there be ample room for dancing?"

"We will do our best. We're going to take down that partition. Then we have to get the decorations up. There is much to do and little time." Martin stopped and looked at Trudy sympathetically. "I'm sorry to disappoint you, but I still have not seen Ninah-Lou or her father, nor have any of my clerks downstairs."

Trudy frowned. "Is it unusual for them to disappear like this?"

Martin Rodey shrugged his compact shoulders. "They come and go. I can't say I miss them. I'd prefer they didn't sell their nuts and trinkets right in front of my store, but Officer Wosch says I have no legal reason to object as long as they're not on my property."

"Well ... please send word if you see them. Or, tell them to stop up at The Times and see me. Tell them I'll have a reward. Please, Martin—it's important. Billy's life is at stake."

Martin nodded and went back to his supervising. He yelled to two men who were moving a life-size cigar-store Indian. "You there—put that out on the sidewalk, in front of the store for now."

REPORTER IS RELUCTANT INTERVIEW SUBJECT

Wednesday Afternoon, December 23, 1908

Trudy would rather have been anywhere but where she was now—sitting in the same small meeting room where she had been interviewed by Julius Wosch the previous week. But William Powell had insisted, and the boss always got his way at The Times. Everyone seemed to expect that she had an inside track on Billy's current condition and whereabouts, which she of course did—but she had been sworn to secrecy by Katie Hatwood.

Joe Bach, one of the younger writers on the staff, backed into the office, pushing the door open with his shoulder as he held a cup of coffee in one hand and a sheaf of loose papers in the other. When he turned and pushed the door closed with his elbow, he dropped the papers all over the floor.

"Oh, sorry," he said. He set his half-spilled coffee cup on the table and knelt to gather the sheets. It took him several minutes before he was finally seated. He pushed his heavy spectacles high on the bridge of his nose and examined the first paper in the stack. Trudy waited patiently.

"Okay, so, Col. Powell says he wants me to write a short piece on the latest news on Hatwood for this week's edition, and that I should talk to you because you're ... friendly with him, or a neighbor, or something. I'm not sure what the connection is exactly."

Trudy waited and then said, "I was taught that when you interview someone for a story, you should ask short, clear questions. Are you asking me how I know Billy Hatwood?"

"Okay, thanks. Yeah. That is my question. How do you know Hatwood?" His eyes were set on his paper, never looking up.

Trudy spoke slowly while Joe Bach wrote what she said verbatim. "I live in Oella, across the river. We live in a tenement house not far from the colored section at the top of the hill. My friend, Viola Snowden—please don't put her name in your piece, she wouldn't like it—has introduced me to many of her kin and neighbors in that area. Billy lives with his mother off of Oella Avenue, not far from the old Banneker place."

When he finished writing, Joe Bach retrieved a small photograph from among his papers and handed it to Trudy. "So, this is he? Mr. Hatwood, I mean."

"Oh, I haven't seen that in years." Trudy took a moment to admire the picture. "His mother had him sit for a portrait shortly after they arrived in Ellicott City. Where did you get it?"

"Oh, um, I guess it's all right to say. Mr. Nussbaumer brought it in. He thought it would be helpful. He still had the negative. He's the one that took the portrait. He has a studio up on..."

"Second house on Tonge Row. Yes, I know."

"Right. Okay, so ... good likeness?"

"What?"

"The photograph ... it's a good likeness of him? I wouldn't know, I've never met..."

"I suppose it's a good likeness—other than that it's one of the rare times that he isn't grinning. His mother told him not to. I think it's about five years old, though. But he hasn't aged."

"Good, okay, yeah. Then I'll use it for my description of the suspect. I won't have to bother you with that. Col. Powell says he wants to print the photograph with the piece. So, um, next question. The Sun's piece on him says he's thirty-five. Is that about right?"

"Hmm, I don't think he's that old—thirty at the most. You know, you really should hike up to Oella and interview his mother, Katie Hatwood. She would know better than I."

Joe Bach laughed nervously, assuming the suggestion was meant as some sort of jest. "So, yeah, okay, I was told that Hatwood works as a coachman. Is that right?"

"He works at Dorsey's livery—odd jobs, stable hand, groom, unloading freight. I suppose he occasionally drives a coach."

Joe Bach continued writing, "Okay, so, coachman is right. I was told he is also a waiter?"

"A waiter? I don't ... well, he does occasionally work at Howard House when they have large gatherings and need extra help."

"Okay, okay, so waiter is right, too." Joe Bach finished writing. "I'm also going to mention the reward. What do you..."

"What reward?" Trudy asked with some shock.

"Oh, you haven't heard about the reward? Well, okay, all I know is that Sheriff Howard has been pushing the idea to the county commissioners and it looks like they're going to approve it. They really want to find this guy."

"I was really hoping it wouldn't come to that," said Trudy. "It will just lead to more hooligans searching the hills for any negro they can find. Did you see that poor man they dragged into town two nights ago?"

Joe Bach shrugged, "At least they didn't kill him. Sheriff Howard is afraid that without the reward, those same hooligans will perpetrate a lynching somewhere, and he won't find out about it until somebody finds a body hanging from a tree. He figures this way they'll bring him in, hopefully in one piece."

Seeing Trudy's distraught expression, he added. "Maybe they won't find him. Some say he's long gone. Do you think he'll ever come back?"

Trudy ignored the question. "Will that be all, Mr. Bach? I have my own stories to work on."

GIFT TO MARYLAND SCHOOL BOYS

Gen. Lawrason Riggs, president of the board of directors of the Maryland School for Boys, and Mr. G. W. Baker, Jr., secretary of the board, visited the school yesterday and presented to the boys a phonograph and a number of musical records. The inmates are looking forward eagerly to their Christmas dinner.

[Baltimore Sun, December 25, 1908]

LOOK OUT FOR HIM

William Hatwood, colored, supposed to have committed a murderous assault, and highway robbery, on Charles E. Hill, last week. The County Commissioners, of Howard county, Maryland have offered $50.00 reward for arrest of this man. He is about 35 years old, about 5 feet 8 or 9 inches tall, weighs about 160 pounds, broad shouldered, generally well dressed, is coachman or waiter, occasionally doing laboring work. Notify Sheriff or Chief of Police, Ellicott City. We want him caught.

[Ellicott City Times, December 26, 1908]

A MOTHER'S LOVE AT CHRISTMAS

Friday, December 25, 1908

The Christmas celebration at the O'Flynn household held to the usual yearly traditions. In the morning, they all attended mass at St. Paul's church. For their midday feast, Niall purchased a rib roast from Treuth's butcher shop, which he cooked on a spit over an open fire behind the house. Side dishes included canned yams, sauerkraut, black-eyed peas and fresh asparagus shipped from Florida. For dessert, Trudy and her niece baked a fresh fruitcake from citron, cocoanuts, walnuts, almonds, currants, figs, and spices, all purchased from James Steward's grocery.

Following the feast, the children opened presents. Trudy had done her shopping at Wallenhorst & Son's dry goods store, which always carried a large selection of toys this time of year. Justice Wallenhorst himself often strolled the aisles of the store dressed as Saint Nicklaus, handing out candies to the children. For her eight year old, Sean, Trudy had purchased a toy train. For her niece, she had bought an elaborate doll with a huge feather hat, frilly dress, and shiny red shoes. Finding a gift for her older son, Colin, was more difficult. He was at that awkward age of wanting to be treated as an adult—he was now working at the mill in the dyeing room—but still wanting to play with toys. Trudy had brought him some woodworking tools.

In the evening, they attended the annual Christmas party at the large hall over the Oella Mill company store. It was one of the four times in the year when the mill completely shut down so that they could do maintenance on the millrace. Consequently, most of the employees were able to attend. The Dickey brothers, the owners of the mill, held court, greeting the workers as they arrived. Music was an impromptu competition between Irish reels, German polkas, Christmas Carols, and occasional performances of popular songs by the Oella brass marching band. "Hot Time in the Old Town Tonight" was always a favorite.

Trudy tried to enjoy the time with her family and friends, but thoughts of Billy in a cold shed in Catonsville, and of Katie

Hatwood pining for her son kept nagging at her. So early in the evening, she quietly slipped out the door. She walked the mile up the hill to the colored neighborhood and knocked on Katie's door.

Trudy was admitted in silence. Viola was there with her daughter. They had eaten a meager meal of beans, smoked sausages, and canned collards. The plate of food in front of Katie remained untouched.

Katie stood when Trudy entered the room and came forward to embrace her. The older woman began weeping. "Trudy, when am I going to see my boy again? Sleeping in that cold barn all alone on Christmas night? This the first Christmas he's ever been away from his Momma. It ain't right."

Trudy struggled to come up with something optimistic to say—something about how the truth will come out and all will be well again. But it fell flat.

"Thank you for your kind words," said Katie, "but I was a slave in North Carolina until I was twelve years old. I seen my daddy whipped and my sister sold away. We colored folk have all seen how this goes a hundred times. Did you see that gang of white hooligans sitting on crates over by the trolley tracks? They had a fire going all day—having a grand old time passing around a bottle."

"Um, no. They weren't there when I walked by just now," said Trudy.

"Maybe they took Christmas night off," said Viola. "They've been out there all week, stopping every colored man that happens by. A couple of unlucky men got themselves hogtied and carted into town. It will only get worse now that your paper advertised that damned reward."

"I tried to stop them," said Trudy. "It was out of my hands."

"Reverend Mosby tried to get the police to shoo them off. But it ain't done no good," said Katie. She paused for a moment, thinking about what Trudy had said. "So, you say those men ain't there now? You think we could sneak down the hill and hop onto the electric car to Catonsville? Surprise my boy, bring him some supper—maybe a dry blanket?"

It was Viola who answered. "I thought about that. Maybe they let their guard down since it's Christmas. But I wouldn't count on it. The police probably have spies on all the cars. I heard they're even paying black folks to keep a watch out. You'd be leading them right to Billy."

A lengthy silence passed before Katie sighed heavily and said, "Well, I guess we are just going to have to wait until my fool cousin thinks he can ride Billy down to Washington."

"Washington?" asked Trudy.

Katie and Viola exchanged a long hard look, weighing whether they should bring Trudy into their confidence. After Katie nodded, Viola said, "Hon, we'll tell you the plan. But you have to promise that it doesn't leave this room. Don't tell your family. Don't tell anyone at the newspaper, and especially don't tell any police."

Trudy was hurt. "You know I would never ..."

Katie interrupted with a wave of her hand. "I know, I know. You've been real good to us considering you're white and don't have any reason to be. So here's what we're thinking ..."

Katie told her about the plan they had hatched with the cousin in Catonsville. It had been slow in the making because indirect communication through a mutual friend had been necessary, and this friend wasn't keen on making the trip between Catonsville and Oella too often for fear of arousing suspicion.

Katie had decided that coming to Maryland had been a huge mistake, and that she and Billy would be better off back in North Carolina. They still had many kin in their home town. She thought the two of them could blend in easily. Maybe the police wouldn't think to look for Billy there.

The trick was how to get there. The cousin had come up with the idea. He made trips to Washington from time to time for his employer. He thought he could hide Billy in the back of his wagon under some blankets until they were well away from here. When the time came, Katie would take the electric car to Baltimore and get on a southbound train. They would meet at Union Station, switch to a Southern Railway Line train, and then be on their way to North Carolina.

EXPECT "MESSIAH" TO RISE
Koreshans Believe Their Chief Will Come To Life Again

Tampa, Fla., Dec. 26.—All Christmas Day, devoted followers of the Koresh leader, Dr. Cyrus R. Teed, kept a close watch upon the body of their fancied Messiah, expecting a miracle, but he did not rise from the dead.

Now some of the bolder members of the colony are expressing a doubt and advocating immediate burial, but Victoria Gratia, successor to "The Headship," as chief officer of the sect is called, insisted upon another day's delay.

Since Teed's death no stranger has been admitted within the limits of the colony. Teed leaves a considerable estate, which, according to the law of the Koreshans, will be divided among his followers.

"Koresh I" died last Tuesday. He claimed absolute immortality for himself and for 100,000 others who would accept his doctrines. Christmas was the day designated for his reappearance on earth. His followers gathered around his bier and watched for signs of recurring life. But they watched in vain. Their prophet and leader was irrevocably dead, like any other human being. His divinity availed him naught.

Teed was born in New York State and early in life claimed to be of divine origin. In 1892 he created considerable interest in Chicago, where he preached his peculiar doctrine. Later he and his converts went to Florida. The "divinity" exploded through his death, and it is likely the colony will disintegrate.

There is, or was, a small colony of the faithful in Baltimore, the "Messiah" having visited this city several times.

[Baltimore Sun, December 27, 1908]

MISCREANT RECOLLECTS HIS HANDIWORK

Sunday Afternoon, December 27, 1908

Everett Hardin rode comfortably in his buggy along River Road. He was returning to town after having traveled two miles east to deliver a package of cocaine powder, and to receive payment from one of the foremen at Thistle Cotton Mill. It had been a lucrative trip. The sky was clear and bright. The air was brisk. Other than a few cold days it had been a mild winter. The rushing Patapsco River on his left was unseasonably ice-free.

His mind returned with satisfaction to the events of that frigid day, almost two weeks ago, when he had taken his revenge upon the hated Charley Hill. As he rode along the river, he indulged himself by reliving each moment of the attack.

The plan had worked perfectly. He had to wait in the clearing for only a brief time when, as expected, Charley drove his wagon around the bend. The man was alone, having dropped Hatwood off at the tollhouse. When the wagon drew close, Hardin whipped his horse. His buggy lurched forward onto the road, blocking the way. Charley shouted in anger and pulled the reins, attempting to veer off. The horses on both carts drew parallel to each other and had no trouble avoiding a collision, but Charley's wagon scraped the rear wheel of Hardin's buggy when it came alongside.

After bringing his wagon to a stop, Charley let loose a tirade of profanity that brought Hardin back to his youth. Age had not tempered the man's tongue one bit. Hardin sat in his buggy, smiling, and waiting for any sign of recognition from the Clarksville farmer.

At length, the man paused in his fulmination and said, "Hey, ain't you 'at feller from yesterday? Where'd I see you at?"

"Yes, Charley, it is me," Hardin said as he descended from his buggy and walked toward the farmer. "I see you're still as dumb as a turd. You still don't recognize me? I heard that your Pa croaked some ten years ago. I was glad about that—saved me some trouble. So I reckon you and Little John can drink and smoke in the house now. Hey, how is Mahalie? I bet *she'd* remember me."

Charley was dumfounded. "Mahalie? What in? Who are ..." He squinted his brown eyes and furrowed his forehead. Recognition came gradually. "Emmett?" he muttered weakly.

Hardin had reached the side of the wagon by then and had stepped up eye-to-eye with his childhood betrayer.

Charley had trouble believing his own eyes. "Emmett ... it is you ... ain't you...?"

The Chemist had been aiming for the soft bones of the temple, but Charley saw movement out of the corner of his eye and turned his head into the oncoming rock. It hit him square on the nose. After this, Charley began thrashing about wildly, ineffectually trying to fight back. Hardin swung again, hitting Charley above his right eye. This blow made good contact. Hill fell silent and slumped across the wagon's bench.

Hardin thought he heard a sound on the road to the north—a horse neighing? It was dangerous to tarry here. Believing that the job was done, he mounted his buggy and drove south.

He had been disappointed the next day to find out that Charley had survived the assault. He realized then that it had been folly to allow Charley to recognize him. Luckily, none of the newspaper accounts of the attack mentioned his former name. He had read somewhere that victims of head injuries often had trouble remembering the moments immediately before the event. He hoped that would be the case with Charley.

He had briefly considered riding to Clarksville to finish the job. It would be intriguing to see his boyhood town again. But no—it was too risky. Hill might yet die. He decided that the best course would be to quietly go on with his life and see how things play out.

The last minute improvisation to provide a scapegoat had been a huge success. Hatwood had been blamed and would be caught sooner or later. If the negro had any luck, he'd be apprehended by the police and would spend a long time in jail. Otherwise ... well, Ellicott City hadn't had a good lynching since Jacob Henson had been dragged from the jailhouse some thirteen years ago.

He drove his buggy through the covered bridge and started up Main Street. He noticed many strangers in town, mostly unwashed young men. Small groups congregated outside of the town's numerous saloons. He had heard that several negro men had been dragged into town and presented to the police since the incident, but none had turned out to be Hatwood.

Mayor Leishear had called a town meeting the previous night in Easton's Hall, and Hardin had attended. Evidently, the city's most prominent citizens were perturbed by the number and appearance of interlopers. They wanted the authorities to do something about it. The Chemist marveled at his own actions that had set all of this in motion.

"Mr. Hardin!"

Hardin looked to his right to see Officer Wosch coming out of his home and walking toward him. His arm was up—hand out. He was being halted. He pulled the reins to stop his horse in front of the policeman.

"Chief Wosch—Good day. What can I do for you?"

"Mr. Hardin, we have not been formally introduced. I know of your pharmacy up on Mercer." He held out his hand. Hardin shook it.

The policeman began idly pacing around the buggy. "It is a fine afternoon to be out and about. Have you been out Catonsville way?"

Hardin seemed confused by the question. "Catonsville?" He looked behind him. "Oh. No. Just over in Oella."

"Ah, Oella," echoed Wosch. "And this is a fine piece of equipment," he said, running his hand over the side of the buggy's frame. "Is it new?"

"Well ... I bought it in June. So ... fairly new. It's a bit dirty now with the winter mud."

"Fine piece of equipment," repeated Wosch as he circled around the back of the vehicle. "Where are you from, Mr. Hardin?"

Hardin was beginning to worry that this was more than a friendly chat. "Uh, I just told you. I was out in Oella." He grasped for something innocent-sounding to add. "Um, looking for that negro fugitive ... like everyone else." He smiled in what he hoped was a casual manner.

"Ah," said Wosch. "Good, good—I do hope he is found soon, and by a local citizen such as yourself. But what I meant, Mr. Hardin, is where are you from *originally*? I do not believe you grew up here in town, yes?"

Hardin paused before answering. He didn't want to admit to being from Clarksville, but the policeman would probably be able to find that out if he did a little digging. Perhaps he already knew. "Look, Chief Wosch, am I being suspected of some...?"

Wosch waved his hands dismissively. "Oh, no. My apologies. It is only my natural curiosity. My wife tells me that I often come on a bit strong. Can I ask you though, have you been up Columbia way recently?"

Hardin became alarmed. "Columbia ... you mean up the turnpike?" He pointed up the hill as if it required clarification.

Wosch nodded and smiled, waiting for an answer.

Hardin's instinct told him it would be unwise to deny it outright. Wosch knew something. "Um, depends on what you mean by recent. I was up that way about a month ago. I..."

"Oh, look. You have damaged your buggy." Wosch gestured toward the left rear wheel.

Hardin dismounted to examine the wheel. "Damaged? Really?"

"Yes. Look, the spokes are scratched here and here, and ... look. A piece is broken off. The axle cap, I believe it is called."

"I never noticed that," said Hardin, running his fingers over the place where the wood had sheared off.

"Maybe this will help." Wosch reached into his coat pocket and retrieved a small cylinder of wood. He held it to the uneven break on the axle. It fit perfectly.

Hardin was dumbfounded. "Oh, but where did you...?"

"It was found up near Columbia, Mr. Hardin. That is why I asked. Here." He handed the piece of wood to Hardin. "Perhaps your livery could glue it back on. Curious thing—It was found in the very clearing where Mr. Hill was attacked two weeks ago. Do you know Mr. Hill?"

"Mr. Hill? Why, no, I don't believe I..."

"Chief Wosch! Chief Wosch!" A boy was running up from lower Main Street. "They's a fight in O'Brian's," he said breathlessly. "They's goin' at each other with knives. Somebody's gonna get kilt!"

"Who is, Teddy?" asked the policeman.

"I dunno. I think they's from outta town."

Wosch sighed heavily. "Happening every day now." He tipped his hat to Hardin. "If you will excuse me, we can finish our conversation another time." He hurried down the street.

FUGITIVE CAPTURED AT LAST

Monday Morning, December 28, 1908

Trudy sat at her desk collecting information for this week's Personals section when the news arrived. A commotion in the front receptionist's area drew her and several of her coworkers from their desks. A newsboy had run in, and was now breathlessly relating a conversation he had overheard while standing down the street in front of Chief Wosch's house, which doubled as the town's police station.

Hatwood had been caught.

Trudy grabbed her coat and hat and ran down the street. She entered the station to find Deputy Sheriff James Hobbs sitting at the desk in the front room. He was just setting the candlestick telephone down when she burst in.

"Jim—I just heard. What can you tell me?"

"Well, good morning to you too, Mrs. O'Flynn. To what might you be referring?"

"Come on, Jim, don't play dumb. The word is that somebody found Billy?"

Jim Hobbs was second in command to George Howard, sheriff of the seemingly eponymous Howard County. They both often worked closely with Chief Wosch of Ellicott City's nascent municipal police force. Hobbs was a portly man in his mid fifties. He was mostly bald with an unfortunate, graying comb-over that fooled no one. He relished his authority and sometimes came across as overly formal when dealing with the public.

Hobbs took his time shuffling and sorting papers on the desk before clearing his throat and speaking. "I was just communicating by telephone with Chief Wosch. No doubt one of your operators was listening in?" Trudy did not react, so he continued. "The chief is currently located at the Catonsville jail. He related to me several details concerning this case and authorized me to release them." He adjusted his reading spectacles and examined the notes he had just taken during his call. He adopted the officious tone that he used when speaking to reporters.

"The fugitive, a Mr. ..."—he looked at his notes—"William Hatwood, was apprehended this morning by Officer Stevens of the Catonsville Police. The police telephone operator received a tip early in the a. m. from an anonymous informant, colored, which turned out to contain accurate information. Forthwith, Officer Stevens, with a cadre of Baltimore County police, proceeded to the indicated farm adjacent to the Frederick Turnpike on the eastern outskirts of Catonsville, where they encountered said suspect. The officers discovered him sleeping on horse blankets in the harness room behind the stable. From his disheveled appearance, they deduced that the suspect had evidently been in hiding at that location for some time. The suspect was subsequently transported to the Catonsville jail where he is currently being processed. Following the completion of all appropriate paperwork, it is expected that he will be transferred here to Ellicott City later this afternoon."

Trudy looked behind her. She was indeed the only one in the room. "Uh, thanks Jim. Say, do you mind telephoning the Times and giving them that statement so they can get the word out."

Jim looked bemused. "I assumed that, in speaking to you, I *was* speaking to the Times."

"Well, yes, but, as you probably know, Billy—Mr. Hatwood, is a friend of my family's. I have to run up to Oella right away to tell his mother this news."

"Very well," said the policeman with a dismissive wave of his hand.

"Thanks, Jim. You're great. When you call, ask for Joe Bach. He'll be eager to hear from you."

Trudy hurried toward Oella. She did make one stop—in Kraft's diner. She had to push past people waiting in line to enter the restaurant—many more than the normal lunch crowd. Once inside, she elbowed her way to the counter and spoke to Viola. She related the news about Billy and asked Viola to come with her to give the news to Katie Hatwood. Viola subsequently spoke to her boss, who said that she shouldn't bother coming back if she left now, what with all the customers at the counter, and new ones waiting to get in. Viola wanted to accompany Trudy, but she really needed to keep her job.

So Trudy would have to do this on her own. She hurried across the covered bridge and started up Westchester Avenue. Near the crest of the hill she came across Katie in her Sunday finery, slowly and determinedly walking into town. At her side strode Johnzie Meyers, Katie's seventy-year-old neighbor.

"Katie—I was just coming to tell you the news."

Katie and Johnzie barely reacted. They continued their slow, determined pace. Katie's face was stoic. "No need. Word travels fast 'round here." Johnzie grunted in agreement.

Trudy took her place at the older woman's side. "What did you hear?" she asked.

Katie gave a disgusted sideways glance as they walked. "Same as you, I expect. They found my Billy. They're gonna fetch him here and throw him in jail. Ain't gonna be no justice." Again, Johnzie grunted his assent.

"I hope you're wrong. You know, Officer Wosch is working on a new angle. Some new evidence has been found that may be important. He is supposed to..."

Katie uttered a mirthless laugh—more of an abrupt exhalation. "I was *supposed* to go to Union Station tomorrow. Had my bags all packed and e'rything. That no good cousin of mine was *supposed* to get Billy there on the back of a grain wagon. Probably turned him in for that damned reward your paper offered, excuse my language. Might as well be thirty pieces of silver. Worth more than his own flesh and blood." She shook her head ruefully.

The three entered town and began a slow walk up Main Street. The town was swelling with outsiders by the minute. It had become a carnival atmosphere. They had to step well out into the street to get around an unruly group in front of Curran's Saloon.

The excitement in the town was palpable. Everyone seemed to know that "the negro" had been caught and would be brought to the jailhouse this afternoon. Trudy wished that the police had been more discreet in letting this information out. Perhaps it would have been better if they had held Billy in Catonsville. But the crime had occurred here in Howard County, and everyone was a stickler for proper jurisdiction these days.

They entered the police station and found Jim Hobbs still at the desk. He was currently addressing a small group of local men. Trudy recognized most of them. They all wore blue armbands and had their right hands in the air. Hobbs was having them recite an oath as he swore them in as deputies to help keep the peace.

When they had all finished the oath, Hobbs said, "Listen up, men! I received word from Chief Wosch that they expect to leave Catonsville on the first electric car after three o'clock. The car has been commandeered solely for this purpose and will not be making any other stops. They should arrive at the turn-around at Church Road at approximately three twenty. Officer Stevens and other Baltimore County police will assist Officer Wosch and Sheriff Howard in escorting the prisoner. Please pass this word to the other deputies, but for now, refrain from telling the public. You are to assemble at three o'clock at Main and Church to wait for the car. Do not let anyone without an armband anywhere near the prisoner. Be advised that there are many men from Clarksville in town looking for retribution. Our job is to ensure that this remains an orderly affair. Justice must be done. That's all for now, men. Hop to it!"

The men dispersed. Trudy and Katie came forward as Hobbs began sorting papers on the desk. Johnzie waited by the door.

Trudy cleared her throat and Hobbs looked up. "Oh, Mrs. O'Flynn—I did as you asked. I called The Times and spoke with Mr. Bach. Not such a bright lad, is he? Is there anything else I can do for you at this time?"

"Thank you. Uh, Jim, this is Mrs. Hatwood."

Katie had been waiting deferentially a few steps behind with her head down and her gloved hands on her pocketbook. She now came forward.

Jim Hobbs nodded but did not offer to take her hand. "Hatwood? Oh, so she's some relation to the prisoner?"

"Yes, Jim," said Trudy, "Katie is Billy's mother. As you can imagine, she is very concerned about her son's safety."

Hobbs nodded, "Yes, yes. I imagine you overheard what I said to our new deputies. Ma'am, I can promise you that we will do our best to make sure there is no lynching in Ellicott City. I have been instructed to deputize as many men as I need."

Katie flinched at the word "lynching." She recovered and said, "Thank you, officer. Can you tell me, what's gonna happen to my Billy?"

Hobbs looked at her for a long moment, choosing his words. "Mrs. Hatwood, your son stands accused of a serious crime. The wheels of justice are turning. A preliminary arraignment hearing is scheduled for this afternoon at five o'clock with Magistrate Wallenhorst. After that, your son will either make bail, which is unlikely, or will stay in the city's jail until trial. The trial will be scheduled at the hearing, but it could be as late as March."

Katie's worried expression intensified, but she said nothing.

"Jim," said Trudy, "I'm going to take Mrs. Hatwood to wait up at the Times. Could you telephone me there in case anything changes?"

Hobbs agreed. As the two women were leaving with Johnzie, he called out. "And Mrs. O'Flynn—I fully expect the news of the arrival time to leak to the public, but if you could, do try to keep it confidential. And do be careful. There are quite a number of unsavory characters roaming about the streets."

The two women and Johnzie walked to the Times building and began their vigil in a third story meeting room overlooking Main Street. Trudy might have preferred to wait in one of the many lunch counters in town, but none of them served negro patrons.

POSITIVE IDENTIFICATION

Monday Afternoon, December 28, 1908

Trudy, Katie, and Johnzie waited for almost two hours. Trudy offered to have coffee and sandwiches brought in, but neither of her guests was hungry. At three o'clock, the three left the Times building and walked the short way up to Church Road. A huge crowd had gathered, preventing them from getting anywhere near to the trolley turn-around.

Jim Hobbs had been true to his word about recruiting deputies. Most of the men near the spot where the electric car would stop wore blue armbands. They formed a line and weren't letting anyone else near.

Trudy led her companions back down the hill. They entered Howard House Hotel, ascended the stairs, and came out of the rear door onto Church Road. They were now across from Easton's Hall, just up from Main Street. The crowd was thinner here. They planted themselves along the street in hopes of seeing Billy as he was marched to the jail.

At precisely three eighteen, the electric car could be heard crossing the trellis bridge and then merging onto the track at the base of Main Street. A roar went through the crowd when the car became visible as it rounded the bend in front of Caplan's Dry Goods. It pulled into the turn-around and halted abruptly. Men with blue armbands quickly surrounded the car three deep.

The shouting grew deafening even from where Trudy stood half a block away. A few ornery men wielding baseball bats rushed the car, but the police and deputies fended them off. There were at least a dozen uniformed policemen on the car. Trudy caught fleeting glimpses of a colored man in their midst.

All at once, the policeman burst from the car and formed a circle around the prisoner. Deputies immediately surrounded them as they hurried up Church Road toward where Trudy and her companions stood. It happened so fast that the onlookers had little time to react.

When they drew near, Trudy could finally see Billy. His clothes were filthy. His hands were tied behind his back. He was having trouble walking and stumbled more than once. His hair was caked with dirt and grease. His lower lip and left eye were noticeably swollen. It was evident that the police had treated him none too kindly. Billy's eyes darted here and there through the crowd, projecting a look of raw fear. She heard him call out to anyone who would listen that he ain't done nothin'.

Just as Billy was passing them, he tripped on the uneven cobblestones. With his hands bound he was unable to break his fall, and he landed hard on his shoulder. Katie ran forward and knelt to comfort him. She cradled his head in her arms and kissed him on the forehead. She was quickly pulled away as the uneasy guards yanked Billy to his feet and pushed him forward. He tried to break free again and move toward his mother, calling, "Momma! I'm sorry, Momma. I ain't..." He was hauled away.

After being roughly shoved away from the prisoner, Katie managed to make her way back to the side of the road where Trudy and Johnzie stood. An older woman who had been standing behind Trudy now came forward and slapped Katie full on the face.

They were dumbfounded by the gesture. The woman came very close to Katie and yelled, "How dare you! We all heard what he said to you. He's sorry, indeed. That's as close to a confession as they're likely to get. What's wrong with you people? Lies and violence! He'll get what's coming..."

Trudy inserted herself between the woman and Katie. She put her arm around Katie and steered her down the hill, away from the crowd. She had seen this woman before: a regular at St. Paul's Church—always sitting in the front pew, impeccably dressed, usually with an absurdly ornate hat. The woman spoke regularly at church meetings and was always the first to volunteer for this or that committee, especially if it involved being able to exercise authority over others.

Trudy now remembered that this woman had been one of the organizers of the passion play that the church had held last Easter. Colin and Sean had been recruited to be part of the crowd in a reenactment of the Stations of the Cross. This woman had coached the children on angry things to yell as the boy playing Jesus—her own son, of course—was marched by with his papier mâché cross. Apparently the woman had no sense of irony.

Trudy and Katie watched as the mob proceeded up the street—the prisoner surrounded by police, surrounded by deputies, and followed by a hundred or more unruly men. They lost sight of them as they rounded the corner on Emory Street and rushed toward the jailhouse.

Viola's shift at Kraft's diner ended at three. She took charge of Katie and Johnzie and brought them to a house in town where she knew they would be welcome as they waited for news.

Trudy decided she would try to attend the hearing that Jim Hobbs had mentioned. It was to be held in one of the smaller rooms in the courthouse on the hill. She arrived at four o'clock and took a seat behind the defense table. She hadn't waited long before men with blue armbands began arriving. The deputies included Daniel Easton and Edward Powell, who both took places near the front. Trudy discerned that the strategy was to fill the room early with deputies and other locals, leaving little room for out-of-town troublemakers.

Edward Hammond, a young, court-appointed attorney entered the room through a side door and sat at the defense table. He took out three freshly typed sheets of paper and began studying them. Trudy got his attention and began speaking to him in hushed tones. She wanted to make sure he was as informed as possible.

A moment later, Martin Burke, the state's attorney, entered through the same door, followed by a man with the appearance of the prototypical farmer, replete with overalls, patched coat, and dusty slouch hat. He was rail-thin with sunken cheeks and a thin gray beard that tapered to nothing over his chest. The two sat at the prosecutor's table. The farmer removed his hat and began fingering a Bible.

The room quickly filled, leaving many angry men in the hall outside. At five o'clock the main doors were closed. Then, through the side door, strode the fastidious Justice Wallenhorst. He took his seat at the judge's bench and banged his gavel repeatedly for quiet.

After the room settled, Wallenhorst nodded to the bailiff. The door opened again and Billy Hatwood was ushered in. His face and hair had been cleaned, but he still wore the filthy rags Trudy had seen on him in the street. He took his place at the defense table alongside his attorney, whom he was now meeting for the first time.

The hearing did not last long. The state's attorney gave an opening statement announcing the charges of robbery and assault. Justice Wallenhorst asked if there was a witness present who could identify the defendant. Burke said that the victim's brother, a Mr. Benjamin Hill, was present and could do so.

The farmer stood. He held the Bible over his heart and raised his right hand, expecting to be sworn in.

"That will not be necessary today, Mr. Hill," said Justice Wallenhorst. "So, am I to understand that you were present when the assault was committed?"

It took Benjamin Hill a moment to understand the question. "Well, no, your honor, I wasn't there myself."

"So if you were not present, on what basis can you identify this or any other suspect in the crime?"

Again, after a pause, Benjamin said, "Well, your honor—he's sittin' right there!"

"I understand that we have an accused man sitting here, Mr. Hill. My question is how *you* can identify him."

"How? Your honor, he's a ... a *negro*, your honor. Charley said the man that walloped him was a negro about that feller's size right there." He pointed angrily toward Billy.

Billy flinched. "I ain't done nothin'," he insisted.

This caused a commotion in the room. Wallenhorst banged his gavel for silence.

"So, Mr. Hill, is that the extent of the description given by your brother, whom you call Charley, that he was attacked a negro?"

"Well, of course, your honor. That's him right there. God as my witness." He pointed toward the ceiling for emphasis.

Wallenhorst paused and wrote something on the pad in front of him. "Thank you Mr. Hill. You may sit down."

Benjamin Hill seemed bewildered and annoyed that his testimony was being treated with such little gravity. He looked around the room for support and, seeing none, eventually did sit down.

Wallenhorst addressed the state's attorney. "Mr. Burke, I believe that the description provided by Mr. Hill here could easily apply to several hundred men in this area. I find it inadequate. Do you have anyone else who can provide a positive identification?"

Martin Burke stood. "Well, your honor, only the victim himself. My understanding is that he is still recuperating in Clarksville."

"I see." Wallenhorst again addressed Benjamin Hill. "Mr. Hill, is your brother well enough to travel? Can he be here, say ... tomorrow?"

Benjamin Hill, still sulking, remained seated as he mumbled, "I reckon we can get him here."

Wallenhorst said, "Then please do so. We cannot indict a man for such serious crimes without a more compelling identification. Mr. Burke, do you have any thoughts about bail?"

"Uh, clearly your honor, Mr. Hatwood is a flight risk. He's been a fugitive for two weeks already."

Wallenhorst continued writing and then looked up. "Mr. Hammond?"

The young attorney looked surprised at being called upon. He looked briefly at his client. He stood and addressed the judge. "Um, your honor, my client is innocent of these accusations. He is a long-time resident of Oella and lives with family. We request no bail."

Wallenhorst, seeing that nothing further would be offered, said, "Very well. Set bail at one thousand dollars for each of the two offenses. This hearing is adjourned until tomorrow, December twenty ninth, at ... two-thirty in the afternoon."

The noise out in the hall had been audible throughout the brief hearing. The judge was about to bang his gavel when a thought occurred to him. "Sheriff Howard?"

The sheriff, who had been sitting near the back stood. "Yes, your honor?"

"Sheriff, this room is not large enough. Will the main courtroom be available tomorrow?"

Sheriff Howard glanced at the bailiff in the back of the room, who shook his head. "I don't think so, your honor. They only started paintin' this mornin'. Took 'em two days to put up the scaffolds, I doubt if they'd..."

"Mr. Easton," Wallenhorst called to Daniel Easton, who, as one of the deputies, had been standing against the window on the side of the room. "Would it be possible for the county to have the use of your hall on Church Road for our hearing tomorrow?"

"Oh, certainly, your honor," Daniel Easton answered in his sonorous baritone. "I can assure you that the venue is available and will be put at your complete disposal." He bowed.

"Very well," said the judge. "This hearing is adjourned until tomorrow afternoon, two-thirty, at Easton's Hall on Church Road." He banged the gavel.

COUNTLESS LOVERS

Monday Evening, December 28, 1908

Hardin departed Angelo Cottage at ten p. m. to make one of his nocturnal deliveries to Thistle Mills. He had arranged with Gaither's livery to have a horse ready. His cargo was light this time, and his plan was to simply saddle and ride the horse rather than hitch it to his buggy. It was a pleasant, cool night. Stars shown brightly over the hills of Ellicott City.

He had not been overly concerned about the capture of Hatwood. The negro would of course deny having anything to do with the attack, but no one would listen to him—at least no one of consequence. If all went according to plan, he would be convicted and sent to the penitentiary in Baltimore for many years.

The unwelcome inquiry by Chief Wosch was another matter. Where had this come from? Did that fool, Charley Hill, finally regain some memory of the actual attack? Hardin would now need to come up with a story about how his buggy's wheel might have become damaged near Columbia. He didn't want his childhood connection to Clarksville to become known. If the worst happened, he should also have a plan ready for fleeing town.

Fortunately, he had some time. Wosch would be tied up with the Hatwood affair for the present.

He strode down Church Road and came to the intersection where Emory Street forked off to the right. The Ellicott City jailhouse was just a short way up. He stood and beheld a strange sight.

Many men milled about the open area in front of the jail. Hardin approached. Off to the left he saw fifty or so, some with hoods, presumably all white. They held torches and a variety of farm implements—forks, rakes, hoes. A thin elderly man stood on a soapbox before them shouting in a hoarse voice. His left hand clutched a book, which Hardin presumed to be a Bible. His right hand waved about, punctuating his fiery sermon.

Directly in front of the jailhouse stood another group. These men included negroes and whites in roughly equal numbers. The whites appeared to be wearing dark armbands. Many in this group also held torches. They stood grim faced, holding a variety of makeshift weapons—mostly clubs and baseball bats.

The uneasy truce between the opposing groups appeared to be holding for now.

Hardin returned to Church Road and continued down the hill. He came to Easton's Hall. This had been the site of frantic activity earlier in the evening with preparation for the hearing to be held tomorrow afternoon. The sliding door of the carriage house below the hall had been left open and the electric light within was illuminated.

This concerned him because of many reports of vandalism of late. He thought it prudent to check on his buggy despite the fact that he didn't anticipate needing it tonight. There was no one about, which was odd. The door should have been secured and the light extinguished. Perhaps it was an oversight, or perhaps someone was still working here but had to step out for a minute.

He made his way toward the center of the space where he had left his buggy. He circled around it and lingered at the left rear wheel where Gaither's had glued the wooden axle cap. How could he have missed that? Hopefully, it would come to nothing.

The front of the buggy abutted the post in the center of the room. He noticed the surface of the post now for the first time. Countless lovers had carved their initials into it over past decades. He felt a wave of bitterness—he, himself had never had an occasion to have his initials thus inscribed, and likely never would. The carvings went from the top of the post where it supported the center beam of the hall, all the way to the bottom, where it rested on a concrete footer.

Satisfied that his buggy was unvandalized, he switched off the electric light, slid the door shut, and continued down the hill toward the livery. It would be an easy errand. He would be home by midnight.

He was crossing Main Street when inspiration struck. He halted in the middle of the street between the trolley tracks. He quickly thought through the ramifications and contingencies. The idea was good. It felt just like the moment of inspiration he had had two weeks ago to provide Hatwood as a sacrificial lamb. He suspected that this was how genius worked—in flashes of sudden insight.

This new plan would likely work, and it had very little risk. It was satisfying on many levels. It would at last make his revenge complete on *all* of those who had wronged him. It would also solve his problem with Wosch.

He continued to the livery. When he got there, he asked if that, in addition to the horse, he could borrow a farm wagon for a brief period, and perhaps a sledgehammer.

EXPECT LYNCHING AT ELLICOTT CITY

A GATHERING OF STRANGERS AT MIDNIGHT

A COLORED MAN IN DANGER

Officials Fear That William Hatwood May Be Killed by Mob for Assault on Mr. Charles E. Hill

Determined-Looking Men Seen in Town at Late Hour

At midnight it was expected at Ellicott City that an attempt would be made before morning to lynch William Hatwood, colored, who was arrested by Patrolman William Stevens, of Catonsville, at the point of a pistol, on the charge of having assaulted Mr. Charles E. Hill, a well-known farmer of Howard county, on Columbia avenue, about two and one-half miles from Ellicott City, on December 15.

Rumors of a possible lynching were rife throughout Ellicott city yesterday, but after the colored man had been remanded to jail, the excitement subsided, and during the early part of the night there was no evidence of any possible violence to the prisoner.

Shortly after 10 o'clock, however, some strangers arrived in the town who moved about the streets in a manner that indicated to the town officials that a lynching might be attempted during the night. There was no disorder, however, on the part of these men.

[Baltimore American, December 29, 1908]

PROMINENT OELLANS TO ATTEND HEARING

Tuesday Morning, December 29, 1908

Trudy and Katie Hatwood had tried to get into the jailhouse to see Billy the previous night, but because of the unruly mob, the jail wasn't allowing any visitors. Viola had spent the night with Katie. The older woman was overcome with fear for her son. At least the makeshift gangs of vigilantes that had been prowling around Oella for days had gone. Katie could finally get some peace in her own home.

The hearing was scheduled for this afternoon at two-thirty. They were expecting a huge crowd. Because of the fear of violence, word had gone out that no women would be allowed to attend. Mayor Leishear and Sheriff Howard had discussed the possibility of limiting attendance to Ellicott City residents but in the end they decided that was untenable. The Hills and their Clarksville friends would likely start a riot if they were excluded.

Many of the colored men who lived in Oella and who knew Billy had promised to be there. Johnzie Meyers, Sammy Scroggins, and even Mooney Queen, who was almost eighty, planned to attend. They all intended to raise a fuss if there was any hint that the proceeding was becoming a railroading. Trudy had tried to explain that this was simply an arraignment hearing, not a trial. Judge Wallenhorst only required that a proper identification by a witness be made. The result would be that Billy would be formally charged with the crime.

Trudy found herself hoping that Charles Hill's injuries would be too severe to allow him to travel.

HATWOOD HEARING HELD

Tuesday Afternoon, December 29, 1908

Daniel Easton arrived early to make sure all arrangements were in place for the hearing. A few rows of chairs had been brought in from the Howard House, but most attendees would have to stand. When Justice Wallenhorst arrived, Daniel offered to light the potbelly stove in the corner, but the judge didn't think that would be necessary. It was a clear, sunny day with a temperature in the mid fifties, and with that many people in a confined space it would be plenty warm. They might even want to open a window or two.

As the appointed time drew near, the hall filled quickly. A line had formed in the street waiting to climb the doubling-back staircase on the uphill side of the building. Entry to the hall was slower than it could have been because the bailiff had been instructed to make sure no one brought firearms or any other type of weapon.

At ten minutes past two, the way was cleared and his brothers assisted Charles E. Hill up the staircase and into the hall. His head was wrapped in a bandage, and the parts of his face that were visible were yellowish and swollen. He took his place behind the state's attorney's table where he was greeted by Martin Burke.

Billy Hatwood, for the time being, was being kept in a prisoner transport wagon outside of the hall, surrounded by deputies.

It was nearly time to begin, and the hall was full. Many of the town's most prominent citizens had come and now occupied the rows of chairs near the front of the room. These included both of the Easton brothers, Martin Rodey, Edward and William Powell, and Dorsey Rogers from Columbia, at whose house Charles Hill first sought refuge after his attack. Chief Wosch and Sheriff Howard stood to the side between the potbelly stove and a stack of coffin boxes that were being stored by the Eastons. Three policemen from Catonsville were present along with reporters from The Ellicott City Times, The Baltimore Sun, and The Baltimore American.

At two-thirty, Justice Wallenhorst instructed the bailiff that no more should be admitted. The hall contained more than a hundred and twenty men—about equal numbers of local residents and out-of-towners. The men who had been left outside of the hall at first complained, but then dispersed.

Justice Wallenhorst banged his gavel and brought the hearing to order. "Gentlemen, I understand that passions are high in the matter of the attack on Mr. Hill. But I warn you that no disruptions or outbursts will be tolerated. This hearing will be conducted in an orderly and fair manner."

Wallenhorst turned toward Charles Hill and said, kindly, "Good afternoon Mr. Hill. We thank you for making the arduous journey from Clarksville in your condition. I promise that we will detain you no more than is necessary."

Charles Hill nodded but remained silent.

The judge continued, "I do not know if you remember, Mr. Hill, but this is not the first time you have sat before me in a hearing. I believe it was almost twenty years ago—a juvenile case of some sort. I believe you were witnessing for the state."

Charles Hill stared dumbly at the Judge. He did manage to shake his head, meaning that he had no recollection.

"No matter, no matter," Wallenhorst went on. "Bailiff," he called to the back of the room. "Please bring the accused."

After a momentary pause, the door at the back of the room opened, and in came Billy Hatwood led by two policemen. He had been cleaned up since yesterday and had been given a fresh suit of drab prison linens. He still had abundant bruises and a swollen left eye. He looked as if he hadn't slept at all the previous night.

As he was brought forward, his eyes fell on his two elderly neighbors. "Johnzie, Mooney—I ain't done nothin', All's I..."

Several in the hall began shouting insults and rebukes. Justice Wallenhorst banged his gavel. "We will have silence in this hearing room or I will clear the hall! Mr. Hatwood—please remain silent unless you are asked a question."

Billy was brought to the side of the room, where he was directed to sit in a chair between Wosch and Sheriff Howard.

Wosch had been given a tip earlier in the day that as soon as Charles Hill identified Hatwood, several ruffians from Clarksville planned to rush forward, grab the prisoner, and drag him into the hills for a lynching party. In addition to the two policemen, Hatwood was surrounded by deputies. They didn't want to take any chances.

Wallenhorst turned again to Charles Hill, "Mr. Hill—Is the man who attacked you now present in the courtroom."

Hill slowly turned his head and looked at Hatwood with his unbandaged eye. "He is, judge."

"Chief Wosch, Sheriff Howard, please direct the prisoner to stand," called the judge.

Hatwood stood of his own accord.

"Mr. Hill," asked Wallenhorst. "Is this man standing here the one who attacked you?"

Charles Hill turned again and gave Hatwood a long hard look. The room was silent, as if every man were holding his breath.

"Yep, judge, that's 'im," said Hill.

Several men in the crowd lurched forward. Chief Wosch pulled out his nightstick and stepped in front of Hatwood.

HAVOC BY QUAKE

THOUSANDS LIKELY DEAD

Rome, Dec. 28.–The three Provinces of Cosenza, Catanzaro and Reggia de Calabria, composing the Department of Calabria, which forms the southwestern extremity of Italy, or "the toe of the boot," were devastated today by an earthquake, the far-reaching effects of which were felt almost throughout the entire country.

The town of Messina, in Sicily, was partially destroyed, and Catania was inundated. In Messina hundreds of houses have fallen and many persons have been killed. Owing, however, to the fact that telegraphic and telephonic communications were almost completely destroyed, it is impossible to obtain even an approximate idea of the vast damage done.

[Baltimore Sun, December 29, 1908]

LADIES SAFELY AWAIT OUTCOME

Tuesday Afternoon, December 29, 1908

As the hearing was beginning, Trudy and Viola stood together in front of Dr. Mordecai Sykes' three-story French-style mansion. They were among a crowd of mostly women plus a few men who didn't make it into the hall before it reached capacity. Doctor Sykes would likely have shooed them all away had he been seeing patients today. But instead, he was attending the hearing in Easton's hall along with most of the city's prominent men.

"You talk to your judge friend about that toll man?" asked Viola.

Trudy nodded. "Yes. Chief Wosch was there when I spoke to him and he agreed. The toll man—Wallers is his name—he's off the witness list."

"Good," said Viola. She was glancing around warily, realizing now that she was the only negro in the group.

A young woman approached them. "Hey Trudy, gosh, they didn't even let *you* in?"

Trudy shook her head, "Hi Millie. No. Sheriff Howard said 'no ladies' and no amount of arguing would make him budge. Oh, this is my friend Viola. Viola, this is Millie. She works at the telephone exchange."

Viola nodded. Millie ignored her and continued speaking to Trudy. "It's exciting, isn't it? To think we might have a hanging?"

"Hanging?" said Trudy. "He's not even accused of a capital offense, even if he were guilty, which he most certainly is n..."

"Come on, Trudy," said Millie. "Did you get a look at the victim when they brought him in ... that Hill fellow? He looks half dead to me." She let out a short giggle. "Gosh, the trip here might kill him. Then it'll be murder for sure. Say, I'm trying to think. Do you remember when the last hanging was?"

"Oh Two," said Viola dryly. "Frank Jones and John Johnson. I knew them both."

Millie acknowledged Viola for the first time with a lengthy scowl. She said, primly, "Well, from what I heard, they got what they deserved. Robbery and murder, as I recall. They..."

"They were innocent," said Viola, her voice rising. "The only thing they were guilty of is being black in the wrong place at the wrong time. Just like Billy is today, he..."

"Viola," interrupted Trudy, "maybe this isn't a good place to discuss this." Several in the crowd had taken notice of Viola and had alarmed looks on their faces.

"Here, let's go down this way." Trudy took Viola by the arm and guided her down Forrest Street, away from the crowd. It was a narrow, cobblestone alley that circled behind the Sykes mansion and Gaither's livery.

They stopped at a low wooden railing overlooking the Tiber River. They idly gazed across the narrow stream at the backs of the stone houses known as Tonge Row. At length, Viola broke the silence. "You know as well as I do that whatever is going on up in that hearing ain't gonna be any kind of justice. Katie said she's been praying hard to Almighty God to put a stop to it."

Trudy nodded. "This time I have to agree with you. Wallenhorst is a fair man, but he's a stickler for the rules. The system is stacked against people like Billy. Nobody is going to speak up on his behalf. Our only hope is that the real attacker is found."

"Small chance of that when there ain't nobody looking," said Viola with disgust.

"Don't give up hope yet. I told you about..." Trudy stopped abruptly. She furrowed her brow looking down the embankment at the stream's edge. "That wasn't there yesterday."

"What? What are you looking at?" asked Viola, trying to follow Trudy's gaze.

"That." Trudy pointed. She turned and put her backside on the low rail, swinging her legs over the top—difficult in an ankle-length skirt. She began carefully descending the bank.

"Trudy, what are you doing? You're going to ruin those shoes and get mud all over your good clothes. Get out of there now," scolded Viola.

Trudy squatted at the water's edge and was examining a long wooden pole. One side of it was in the water. The other end was hidden among the brambles. She followed the length of the pole into the brush. About two-thirds of the way along the length she found it: "T.O. & G.L" carved inside a heart shape.

Trudy was dumbfounded. "Why would this be here? Would they have replaced it? When would that have...?" The realization hit her hard. She lost her balance and sat back in the mud on the embankment.

"Trudy, are you okay?" Viola had made it over the railing and was now coming toward her.

Trudy jumped up. She scrambled up the muddy bank, stumbling more than once. She was a mess by the time she reached the top. She practically threw herself over the railing and began running up the cobblestones. She didn't stop when she came to Main Street, but crossed over and started up Church Road. Easton's Hall was just a short way up on the left.

She was just even with the building when she heard a sound like a thunderclap. Her first thought was that a shotgun had been fired inside the hall. She stopped in her tracks and turned toward the building.

Then several things happened at once that she had difficulty understanding until later: The sliding door of the carriage house below the hall flew open from the bottom, suspended by the upper runner—like a hinge. The window on the lower left shattered, expelling glass out onto the street. A violent gust of air knocked her back, and she sat roughly onto the street. Something small and hard hit her left cheek. The building shook visibly but did not fall.

Almost immediately afterward, she heard the prolonged wailing of a hundred voices in shock and agony.

COULD IT HAVE BEEN ANARCHISTS?

Tuesday Afternoon, December 29, 1908

Chief Wosch had just stepped in front of Hatwood, preparing to ward off the angry out-of-town farmers, who, as had been expected, were now rushing toward him. A sound like a gunshot echoed through the hall. Wosch's first reaction was a feeling of annoyance that the bailiff had not been careful enough in disarming the hearing's attendees.

Then he had an inexplicable experience that reminded him of the one time in his life, in his early twenties, when he had gotten drunk. He became disoriented. He lost his balance and fell backward into the prisoner behind him. The men who had been rushing toward him were now receding. They, too, had looks of surprise on their faces at this unexpected state of affairs. They reached forward, grasping at air as they fell.

Wosch's wits returned and he realized in a flash what was happening. The entire floor of the hall had split open, from one end of the hall to the other, and was now forming a gigantic wedge in the center. The men who had been rushing toward him now fell into the carriage house below. The crash was deafening. Wosch, and Hatwood behind him, were now sliding into the widening pit on top of the others.

Even as he fell, his police mind was analyzing the situation. Had someone dynamited the hall? Was that the initial blast he had heard? Perhaps it was that anarchist who had killed himself earlier this month in Catonsville. No—that didn't make sense. He was dead. Perhaps, then, he had accomplices. Everyone knows how much anarchists love dynamite.

He hit the concrete floor. The impact knocked the wind out of him even though it was softened somewhat by the fact that he landed on top of other bodies that had fallen before him. He felt a stabbing pain in his back as someone or something landed on top of him.

Being near the perimeter of the hall, Wosch was one of the last to fall. He attempted to raise himself up but something heavy was resting on his back. He was able, with great pain, to twist himself and look. One of the coffin boxes that had been stacked against the wall had come down on top of him. He pushed it off, sat up, and was able to survey the scene. Writhing bodies were all around, groaning, screaming, thrashing. He looked up. The electric lights were still suspended from the ceiling, which was now far above them. They were still illuminated and swinging on their wires.

Something caught his eye that took him a moment to recognize. The small potbelly stove was swinging on its exhaust duct in a wide arc. Presently the duct gave way and the cast iron appliance fell. Fortunately it landed on unoccupied concrete with a deafening clang.

Wosch could see that someone now had the side door of the carriage house open. Those that could still walk were rushing toward the single exit, trampling anyone in their way. Someone stepped on his right ankle and he felt a searing pain that almost made him black out.

EASTON SON'S HALL COLLAPSES

HATWOOD'S CAPTURE FOLLOWED BY A TERRIBLE CATASTROPHE

On Monday last Wm. Stevens, the Baltimore county officer stationed at Catonsville, was informed that Wm. Hatwood, the colored man whom it is claimed assaulted and robbed Mr. Chas. E. Hill, of the Fifth district, on the Columbia pike, Dec. 15th last, was in the vicinity of Catonsville, and at a small place called Paradise. Officer Stevens followed this man and after arresting him at the point of his revolver, brought him to Ellicott City, and turned him over to the authorities. Hatwood was held for a preliminary hearing in default of $1,000.00 bail, on each of two charges, the first one of robbery, and the second, assault with intent to kill. The time of the hearing, Tuesday Dec. 29th, at 2:30 P. M. found the prisoner and a large crowd of people eager to hear the testimony of Mr. Hill, before Judge Wallenhorst in the court room at Easton's hall. The crowd inside numbered about one hundred and fifty, and the people from the country were still pushing through the door when the accident happened.

After Sheriff Howard had read the warrant to the prisoner, the judge asked Mr. Hill, "Is that the man?" Mr. Hill answered, "yes he is." The people naturally crowded toward the centre of the room to get a better view of the prisoner at this point, and without any notice or warning the centre of the whole length of the floor parted, precipitating all in the room into a struggling mass, mixed up with tables, benches, a stove, chairs, and other things in the room, in a narrow space on the concrete floor 15 ft. below. A stampede over the wounded began which added to the injuries, and one man rushed about brandishing a revolver, running over the helpless bodies, pinned against the hard floor with beams and splintered timbers. Luckily the negro Hatwood's foot was caught, in a way in which he could not extricate himself and he was helpless. All of the officers were more or less stunned and injured, and had not everyone been helping the wounded, it would have been a very convenient time for the much talked of lynching. The injured were carried temporarily to the nearby residences, and the engine room was turned into a temporary hospital together with the Howard House. The full force of physicians were on hand also Drs. Macgill and Mattfeldt, of Catonsville.

[Ellicott City Times, January 2, 1909]

THE VICTIMS EMERGE

Tuesday Afternoon, December 29, 1908

Trudy had been knocked backward and now sat splayed in an undignified manner on the hard cobblestones. Almost immediately after the building stopped its violent shaking, a sustained moaning and wailing could be heard from within. There were many people milling about outside of the hearing—women, and men who were denied entry because the hall was full. They now stood and gazed dumbfounded at the trembling structure.

Despite the noise and shaking, the building remained standing. From the outside, other than the burst window, it looked undamaged.

Recovering her wits, Trudy arose and ran to the uphill side of the building where a separate door to the lower level was located. She hoped that it would not be bolted from the inside, as it often was. She pulled on the door handle and, with difficulty, slowly pried it open. It was not bolted, but it appeared that the door no longer fit the frame.

She was thrown backward when several men rushed through the doorway to escape the mayhem within. She landed in the dirt underneath the stairway landing.

A man appeared and helped her to her feet. "Trudy—I'm surprised to find you here! I was working in the kitchen when we heard the most bizarre sound. Do you know what happened?"

Men were streaming from the open door, many limping or cradling injuries of various kinds. These were the lucky ones who could still walk.

"John! Thank God you're here. I think ... that the hall's upper floor collapsed. There will be many hurt. Can you send someone for help?"

John Reichenbecker was one of the chefs at the Howard House restaurant. The kitchen was at the back of the second floor of the hotel, just across Church Road. As they did preparatory cooking for the dinner hour, they would typically open windows to dissipate heat from the stoves. Many Howard House employees had heard the collapse and were now arriving. John began directing them.

Someone was ringing the bell of the engine house. Mayor Leishear, who had not attended the hearing, came running up the street with two large buckets, evidently thinking that fire had broken out.

The stream of wounded men coming from the building now slowed. Edward Mellor appeared at the door followed by William Powell. The men were leaning on each other, as both could barely walk. Trudy helped them clear of the building where they could sit on the grassy slope. Powell said that there were still many men in the building who were incapable of moving.

Men with stretchers arrived and went into the building. Trudy wanted to follow and assist with the wounded but she was told to stay clear.

Stretchers began to emerge from the hall carrying the more severely wounded. Daniel Easton was one of the first. He was awake, but clearly in great pain, his upper leg bent at an unnatural angle. They brought out Martin Burke, the states attorney, with his face and head covered in bloody rags. A reporter from the Baltimore American that Trudy knew, William Hall, was brought out next. His face was a mess. He looked like he had lost badly in a bare-knuckle boxing match.

Johnzie Meyers was carried out unconscious. Mooney Queen walked alongside him, holding a cloth to his bleeding head. Martin Rodey was chattering amiably when they brought him out. He said that he had tried to walk, but his left leg simply wasn't working. Sheriff Howard came next. His clothes were ripped in many places along the left side of his body. He appeared to be struggling for breath.

Charles Hill was also unconscious when they carried him out. His head was still wrapped in the bandage he had worn when he arrived for the hearing. Following him came Billy Hatwood, leaning heavily on John Reichenbecker as he hobbled through the door.

Billy's face spread into its characteristic wide grin. "Miss Trudy—did you see what happened? I knew Momma would be prayin' to God to stop this mess."

"Billy, you're hurt." She turned to Reichenbecker. "Isn't there a stretcher for him? Look at his twisted leg."

"Sorry, ma'am. Chief Wosch is still in there, pinned under a bench. He grabbed me and told me to get the prisoner back to the jail and to make sure it was secure. I think he's still worried there could be violence."

"You're going to need help getting him there," said Trudy. She glanced up Church Road in the direction of the jail and saw ... Everett Hardin. It took her a moment to recognize him. He was on the side of the road about a half-block away. He just stood there, observing the activity, calmly smoking a pipe.

Trudy waved to him and called his name. Eventually he saw her. He emptied his pipe and then jogged briskly down the hill.

"Good afternoon, Mrs. O'Flynn. The weather is fine today. I trust you are well?"

Trudy was taken aback by the casual pleasantries given the pandemonium surrounding them. "Mr. Hardin, we could use your help."

Hardin seemed surprised by this. "My help? Oh, you mean with all of the ... of course, madam. How can I be of assistance?"

"Mr. Reichenbecker here needs to get Billy back to the jail where he will be safe. They'll probably need men to keep watch until all of this is under control."

Hardin looked from Reichenbecker to Trudy, and then to Billy. He appeared to be trying to make up his mind. After a pause, he said, "Yes, of course." He took Billy's other arm and together they helped Billy up the hill. Trudy watched them round the corner on Emory toward the jailhouse.

The last two out of the building were Justice Wallenhorst and Chief Wosch. Wallenhorst looked badly hurt and was muttering incoherently. Wosch was his usual stoic self, gritting his teeth through what must have been intense pain.

The most severe cases were rushed to St. Joseph's Hospital in Baltimore. Others were taken to the Howard House, the engine house, and several nearby residences, which were all hastily converted into makeshift hospitals.

TALK OF LYNCHING AT NIGHT

Men Gather After Accident
And Threaten Violence to Negro

Ellicott City, December 29.–About 35 men, who were unable to get their trains out of Ellicott City to their homes, remained over night at the Howard House. Frequent conferences were held in and around the hotel at which plans to lynch Hatwood were discussed. Several efforts were made during the evening to get a rope to hang the negro with.

At 10:30 P. M., when it was learned that Deputy Sheriff Hobbs and his wife had retired for the night, the men seemed on the point of charging up the hill to the jail, but some held back and dissuaded the others from making the attempt. Round Sergeant Walker, of the Baltimore county police force, was sent to aid the Ellicott City police, who were worn out by the vigil of the night before and by their injuries.

When seen in his cell at the jail after the accident, Hatwood did not seem to realize what had happened. The excitement of the evening had made him almost dumb. He said his leg was paining him badly.

"I don't know nothing about it," was the only response he would make to all questions asked him.

There are nine negro prisoners in the jail, which is on a hill several hundred yards from the collapsed building. The prisoners said they could hear the crash and screams. The negroes were excited and it took considerable effort on the part of the employees about the jail to quiet them.

[Baltimore Sun, December 30, 1908]

FAILED ATTEMPTS

Wednesday, December 30, 1908

Trudy promised Katie Hatwood that she would try to get in to see Billy today. She had made two attempts in the morning, both of which failed. Protests were ongoing in the courtyard in front of the jailhouse. Angry men in white hoods chanted loudly for justice, by which they meant a lynching. Many women joined in from the perimeter. Trudy could not even get close to the heavily guarded door.

She decided to try again in the midafternoon. After trudging up the hill and turning the corner on Emory, she was gratified to find the area in front of the jail unoccupied. The protesters were finally gone. The courtyard was eerily quiet.

She knocked on the heavy door. It was answered a moment later by a tall, portly policeman that Trudy did not recognize. He wore a Howard County sheriff's office uniform.

"Oh, hello officer. I was hoping that Jim Hobbs would be here?"

"Uh, no ma'am. Jim twisted his shoulder pretty good yesterday. Doc told him to take it easy. My name's Officer Maynard from down Laurel way."

"Well, good afternoon, I was hoping to be able to see Billy ... uh, William Hatwood, the prisoner?"

"Oh, I'm sorry ma'am, you just missed him. They've been waiting since early morning for the wagon. It got here about half hour ago, it did. The prisoner's been transferred to the Baltimore City jail. They decided it was too dangerous to keep him here, what with all the protesters wanting to ... well, you know, take the law into their own hands."

Trudy lowered her head in disappointment. The police had, of course, kept the transfer a secret. "Oh ... I guess that was prudent. It's just that I was really hoping to see him. His mother is very worried."

Officer Maynard made no reply.

Trudy was unsure what to do next. Before leaving, she asked, "Baltimore City jail—when do you think it will be possible to visit him there?"

"Well, ma'am, I really don't know. I'd give it a day or two at least. They'll need to process him and get him all settled in, uh huh. I believe they're planning to keep him there until the grand jury meets here in March, so there's no hurry."

Trudy turned to go. "Well, thank you again, Officer ...?"

"Maynard ma'am. You have yourself a blessed day now." Trudy heard shouting from within the jail. "Ma'am, I don't mean to be rude but we kind of have our hands full here." He closed the door.

Trudy walked down the hill. As she rounded the corner, Mr. Hardin was riding up Church Road on his buggy. He tipped his hat to her as he passed, but did not stop. How fortunate for him, she thought, that his buggy was not in the carriage house when the upper floor collapsed.

HATWOOD IN JAIL HOSPITAL

Negro Charged With Murderous Assault Has Broken Bones.

With the bones of his left leg broken, William Hatwood, the negro who is charged with a murderous assault upon Mr. Charles E. Hill, a well-known farmer of Howard county, is in the hospital at the city jail. Hatwood does not complain much, but takes his injury and imprisonment like any other negro of his type.

The jail officials have no trouble with Hatwood. He is said to eat well. Jail Physician Wilkins believes he will soon recover from his injury.

The name of Rev. Vernon N. Ridgely, who aided in rescuing the injured, was inadvertently placed among the injured in THE SUN yesterday. He did not arrive at the scene until after the accident.

State's Attorney Martin F. Burke, Martin Rodey and Samuel Coggins, colored, at the University Hospital; Louis Koontz at the Maryland General Hospital, and Charles Jones, at the Union Protestant Infirmary, who were injured in the collapse of the temporary courtroom Tuesday afternoon, were reported to be in a favorable condition.

[Baltimore Sun, January 1, 1909]

BUREAUCRACY IN ACTION

Week of Monday, January 4, 1909

By Monday, Trudy felt that she had waited long enough for Billy to be "settled in," as Officer Maynard had put it. She picked up her telephone and asked Dot to connect her through to the main number for the Baltimore City Detention Center. It took several minutes to put the connection in place, as it had to go through the C&P offices at Catonsville and Central Baltimore, and then a smaller switchboard operated for the Baltimore City government.

Finally, a man answered, identifying himself as Officer Sullivan.

"Good morning officer, I want to make arrangements to visit a prisoner whom, I understand, is being detained at your facility."

"At my what? Hold on a minute." Trudy heard angry yelling in the background before the man came back. "Sorry, miss, things are a bit batty here today. You say you want to visit a prisoner? Which one?"

"His name is William Hatwood. He was transferred ..." Trudy paused as she heard more yelling. Officer Sullivan's was apparently in the midst of a heated argument with a coworker.

At length he came back. "Sorry again. Say, I'm going to have to take care of this tommyrot. Can you telephone again in say ... how about this afternoon? And what was the name of the prisoner? I'll look him up when I get a minute."

"Hatwood, first name is William. Thank you, I will ..." the officer had already hung up.

She tried again at around two o'clock in the afternoon. After the connections were in place, a gruff voice answered the telephone, "Mulholland."

"Good day. I called this morning and spoke to an Officer Sullivan about visiting one of your prisoners named..."

"Sullivan? He's not in today."

"Um ... the man I spoke with said that that was his name. But it is of no consequence. I wish to make arrangements to visit a prisoner by the name of William Hatwood."

"Hatwood? I don't think we have anyone by that name."

"Well, don't you have a list you could check or something? He was just transferred there on Wednesday last."

"Wednesday? Hang on. Let me check. Hatwood, Hatwood, Hatwood..." There was a lengthy pause. "Nope. No Hatwood here. You sure you got the name right?"

"Yes, officer, I'm quite certain. That's Hatwood with an 'H'."

"Yeah that's what I looked for. He ain't on the list. Maybe he ain't processed yet. It takes a day or two."

With utmost patience, Trudy said, "Yes, that is what I have been told. But he has been there now for five."

"Hatwood, Hatwood ... Okay lady, I looked twice. No Hatwood on my list. That's all I know. Tell you what. Call back tomorrow and talk to Officer Leitch. He'll know."

"Well, I could do that but..." Again, the line was already dead.

On Tuesday morning she called and asked for Officer Leitch and was told that he wouldn't be in until Thursday. Then the man summarily hung up.

She called back that same afternoon and, to her surprise, Officer Leitch answered the telephone. He checked the same list that Mulholland had the previous day, and declared that there was no Hatwood at the prison.

Trudy quickly interjected before Officer Leitch could hang up. "Sir, perhaps there is some mistake? He was transferred there from Ellicott City on Wednesday last."

"Ellicott City? Why didn't you say so? That's ... that's Howard County. He'd be in the jail there. You should call their sheriff's office."

It took Trudy a while to convince Officer Leitch that Hatwood wasn't in the Howard County jail. Eventually he gave her a different number to call, which she guessed was a step above him in the administrative chain.

She called that number and was told that the man she needed, a Mr. Lautenberger, had already gone for the day. The person insisted that there was no one else who could help her.

On Wednesday morning, she called again and spoke with Mr. Lautenberger. He recognized the prisoner's name. "Oh, you mean that colored fella who tried to kill the farmer but the courthouse fell down?"

Trudy saw no point in correcting the man. She just said, "Yes. That's the one."

Lautenberger insisted that, after a full week, the prisoner would definitely have been processed. He suggested that she call the main number again in an hour, and promised he would call them right away to straighten it out.

She had the call put through to the main number an hour later. "Baltimore Prison, McClung speaking."

"Good day, officer. I want to visit a prisoner named Hatwood and I believe a Mr. Lautenberger from your administrative office called ahead?" Trudy had learned to put all of the information for her inquiry in a single rapid-fire sentence so as not to be interrupted or hung-up upon.

"Lautenberger? Who's he?"

Trudy sighed. "From prison administration. He said he would call ahead. Apparently Mr. Hatwood is not on your list for some reason."

"Never heard of a Lautenberger and ain't nobody called here."

And so it went throughout the week. By Friday afternoon, she had resigned herself that she would simply have to take the electric car into Baltimore and show up at the prison. They'd have a harder time ignoring her if she stood in front of them.

But then, late on Friday, she finally spoke to an Officer Van Cleave who was able to help her. Evidently there was a separate list for transfers from other jurisdictions that nobody before had thought to check. Trudy was able to set up a visit for one o'clock in the afternoon on Tuesday the twelfth. She was warned not to be late.

DIES FROM ELLICOTT CITY CRASH

Mr. Johnzie Myers, one of the oldest residents of the First district, died early yesterday morning at his home, on the Old Frederick road, near Oella, as a the result of injuries received by the collapse of a floor in Easton's Hall, Ellicott City, several weeks ago, in which a large number of persons were seriously injured.

Mr. Myers previous to the accident suffered several paralytic strokes, and on the day of the accident went to Ellicott City with his friends to attend the hearing of Hatwood, the negro who is charged with murderous assault. When the crash came Mr. Myers was in the midst, receiving a badly fractured shoulder and other injuries. His condition became gradually worse.

Mr. Myers was for many years head machinist in the old mill at Grays, now occupied by the Patapsco Electric and Manufacturing Company, until it closed down and went out of the cotton goods business. He then became head machinist of the Thistle Manufacturing Company at the mill at Thistle, near Ilchester, remaining in that position until several years ago, when he resigned. He was about 80 years old and is survived by one daughter, Mrs. Warren Gaw, and two sons, Messrs. John and Samuel Myers.

[Baltimore Sun, January 11, 1909]

WHO BENEFITS?

Tuesday, January 12, 1909

Trudy climbed onto the eastbound electric car at the depot next to McDonald's general store. At this time of day, just after eleven o'clock in the morning, cars left every hour. She didn't want to be late for her appointment to see Billy.

The car ascended into the hills of Oella. The stops became more frequent as it made its way through Catonsville and west Baltimore. Trudy was beginning to think she should have left earlier. She arrived at the final stop at Park Avenue and Lexington Road a few minutes before noon. There would be time.

Having never before been to the Baltimore jail, she had studied a map before leaving. From the station to the jail was a little over a mile. She had intended to take a coach, but when she got to the street, none were available. There were, however, four automobiles parked in a row. A man stood aside the lead one beckoning to her.

"Taxicab, madam? Finest in the city."

Trudy was hesitant. She had never ridden in one of these contraptions. "Is it safe?" she asked doubtfully.

"Safe? Madam this is a brand new Pontiac Model E Roadster. Best in its class—rubber wheels, two-cylinder engine, leather seats, canvas top. Why, just look at her—not a scratch on her." He held the left side door open.

Trudy shrugged. She took the man's hand and climbed onto the high seat. The man went to the front of the automobile, blew on his hands, rubbed them together, and then began turning the crank. The engine sprang to life, vibrating the whole vehicle, violently at first and then more smoothly. The man climbed aboard on the right side and revved the engine a few times, which was directly below the bench on which they sat.

"Where to, madam?"

"Baltimore City Jail."

"Egad! A proper lady like you going to the jail? I'd bet money there's a story in that." Trudy remained silent. The man added, "Never you mind me. The boss is always telling me, Luigi, you talk too much. A chauffeur needs to mind his own business. Yes ma'am, we are now the Taxi Service Company of Baltimore. Incorporated last month. Boss says it's the wave of the future. He says no man will want to own his own automobile when they can pay to be driven. Sit back ma'am. I'll have you there in a jiffy."

The vehicle was more comfortable than Trudy would have expected—and faster. They must have been going thirty miles per hour at times. Trudy had to hold onto her hat as the chauffeur zipped by horse-drawn buggies and slower automobiles. They quickly made their way through many harrowing turns to the northeast.

They arrived at the jail at twelve fifteen. Trudy hoped this would leave enough time to get through any red tape.

The city jail was on Van Buren Street, just down from the railroad stables. It was a six hundred foot long stone building set a hundred feet back from the street. A forbidding fifteen-foot wall abutted the street, hiding all but the top two levels of barred cell windows.

The automobile came to a stop in front of the gatehouse. She could now see through the gate to the central structure that housed the administrative offices, towers, and a cupola that rose forty feet higher than the surrounding structures. A guard was perched atop each of the watchtowers holding a rifle at the ready.

In contrast to her experiences on the telephone, the admitting process for visitors ran very efficiently. After filling out and signing several forms, she was deprived of her handbag and her hat, and promised that these would be returned to her upon her departure. A guard brought her to a large visiting room containing several square tables. Each table had two chairs on opposite sides.

Billy was waiting for her at one of the tables against the far wall. He did not stand as she and her escort approached. She saw that his hands were manacled. One of his legs was heavily bandaged below the knee. He looked up and acknowledged her presence with a nod. She perceived that he was trying to grin, but it came off as a grimace. His face bore a dour, beaten look.

She took the seat opposite him. The guard recited a series of rules, including that she was not to attempt to touch the prisoner or give him anything. Nor was she to attempt to receive anything from him.

Trudy folded her hands in front of her on the table. "Billy, I'm so sorry that this is happening to you. Are you in pain?"

"Naw, Miss Trudy, it don't hurt much." He looked up briefly and made another attempt at his signature grin. "Doc says I be good as new in no time."

Trudy started to reach out to take his hand but stopped herself, remembering the guard's warning. "Billy, I'm afraid I have some bad news. Johnzie Myers died yesterday. He got sick after his injuries when the building fell. I know you were close to him. I'm sorry."

Billy looked confused. "Uncle Johnzie? He pass on? I ain't even know he was there. What was he doin' there?"

"He came for you, Billy. He wanted to make sure that you were being treated fairly."

Billy took a while trying to understand this. "You know, Miss Trudy, I ain't done nothin' to that man—that white farmer man. Why e'rybody sayin' I did?"

"I don't know. We're trying to figure that out."

This being the first opportunity to speak at length with Billy since the incident, Trudy asked him to tell her everything he could remember about that cold Tuesday afternoon in December. His memory was remarkably clear and detailed. He told her about Ninah-Lou giving him a whole dollar to give to the farmer for a ride to the tollhouse, and that Miss Trudy needed help with something and would meet him there. He remembered being surprised when Mr. Hill drove his wagon off without paying the toll. He described the fat man who wouldn't let him wait in the warm tollhouse, and instead told him to leave and even threatened him with a pistol. He said he waited as long as he could in the cold and then walked home, because it was already past his normal quitting time and he didn't think Mr. Dorsey would have any more work for him.

His story was thorough, unvarnished, and believable. Trudy wondered if the police had even bothered to interview him. She suspected not.

They sat a while in silence. Then Billy added, "That lawyer feller come see me last week. He say I gotta tell the judge I did it—that I beat that white man and took his money, else the judge gonna send me away for my whole life. He say if I fess up to the judge, maybe he gonna look kindly on me."

"But, Billy, that would be a lie. You didn't do it."

"I know, Miss Trudy, I know. But he say I got to. I don't like it much in jail, Miss Trudy. Folks ain't nice here. Even the colored folks ain't nice."

"Billy, don't confess—not yet anyway. We need to find out what really happened. Who is your lawyer, by the way? Do you remember his name?"

Billy shook his head. He didn't remember.

"Don't worry. I'll find out. I'll visit him and give him a piece of my mind."

Billy nodded his agreement.

"I spoke to the new judge. His name is Lilly. He said that you're going to stay here until grand jury session in March. You'll be safer here than you were back at home. Is that all right?"

Billy nodded again. "Food ain't much good. The string beans got worms in 'em. Sure could use some of Katie's bergoo."

This made Trudy laugh. Billy looked up, at last, with his endearing grin.

"Could use my banjo, too, but the guard says I might hurt somebody with it. How you gonna hurt somebody with a banjo?"

The guard approached. Their time had expired. The guard helped Billy to his feet and held one arm as he hobbled away on his bandaged foot.

Trudy waited a moment. A different guard came in to escort her out. They left the visiting room and began walking the long hallway to the main entrance.

"I'm Officer Leitch. Say, you're that lady that called last week from Ellicott City. I'm awful sorry about the mix-up. Nobody ever told me about a separate list for transfer prisoners."

Trudy looked up at him as they walked. He was a kindly looking, clean-shaven boy who couldn't have been more than twenty-five. "That's all right Officer. I made it here eventually."

Leitch said, by way of making conversation, "So I looked on the transfer list just now. We got another prisoner here from your town. He was transferred in just yesterday from the penitentiary because of overcrowding or something. By the name of Morgan."

This piqued Trudy's interest. She struggled to remember the first name. "Is it Marion? Marion Morgan?"

"Yes, ma'am, that's him. You know him?"

"No, not personally, but I attended his trial last summer. It was a curious case. Say, Officer Leitch, would it be possible for me to visit with Mr. Morgan while I'm here?" Trudy was thinking that, since the case had been big news in town last summer, perhaps she could write a follow-up piece for some future edition of the paper.

By that time, they had already reached the front desk, and Officer Leitch was in the process of signing her out. He stopped and said, "I don't see why not. Visiting hours go until five. You mind filling out the forms again?"

Trudy did so. She waited for twenty minutes and was then escorted back to the visiting room. Marion Morgan now sat at the same table where she had just met with Billy.

Morgan observed her with some puzzlement as she approached. His long, greasy hair was combed neatly. His face sported a two-day stubble. He looked calm, alert, and lucent—very different from the wild-eyed lunatic she had seen in the courtroom. She sat down opposite him.

"'Scuse me, ma'am." Morgan's voice was pure gravel. "Ma memory ain't so clear 'bout last year. I know you from someplace?"

"No, Mr. Morgan. We've never met. My name is Mrs. O'Flynn. I work at the Ellicott City Times. I've known the Ray sisters for many years. Mrs. Sanner is still quite nonplussed about what happened last year."

Morgan grunted and then looked down at the floor, evidently in shame. "Well, I tell ya, I ain't never been the sharpest saw in the mill. But a man gets a lot a time to think in prison, ya know? Things might be kinda fuzzy in ma mind 'bout last year, but I can tell ya this: I ain't never put no poison in that drinkin' bucket. Why would I go 'n do such a thing?"

Trudy thought back to the case. "The prosecution said it was a crime of passion—that you were angry for being evicted from your room."

Morgan paused to consider that. "Well I ain't gonna lie. I was fit to be tied, all right. But poison? It ain't never crossed ma mind. What'd I stand to gain by tryin' to poison poor old Mrs. Sanner? Nope. Nothin'. Like I say, I been turnin' this over in ma head for months. Only man that had anythin' to gain was that damned Hardin."

This surprised Trudy. "Hardin? The pharmacist? I know him—a little anyway. How would he benefit by poisoning the Rays?"

Morgan scratched the stubble on his cheek. "Not so much by poisoning the sisters, but by havin' me put away for it."

"I don't understand," said Trudy.

Morgan sat back in his chair and looked at the ceiling. "Well, lemme tell ya a story then. Mind ya now, I ain't blameless in all a this, but I figure I'm doin' ma time, so what's a man got to lose?

"It all goes back to that night last year. Late winter, early spring, I think. Like I said, ma mind's a bit fuzzy. I was sittin' at the table at the boardin' house, eatin' ma supper, when Hardin comes in dressed like a hobo. He didn't say nothin'. Just walked on through and out the door."

"A hobo?" Trudy wished she had some paper to take notes. She concentrated hard, trying to remember every word. "Go on."

"Right. Well, if ya know Hardin, then ya know he's mister dandy. Must a pained him awful to be wearin' those old duds.

"Now, I gotta confess, I spent most of that night down at Kramer's. Ya know the Rays don't allow no drinkin' on the premises. So, I had me a couple a beers, but I wasn't corned or nothin'. Came time I call it a night, and so I walk on out. Now, who do I see hobblin' by on the street? It's Mr. Everett Hardin. Only now he's limpin' on one leg and he ain't wearin' no coat or hat."

Something clicked in Trudy's mind. "Wait—you said early spring. Could this have been the same night that they found the dead man on the electric car tracks—you know, up in Oella?"

Morgan considered this. "Well now, I never made that connection, but I guess it could a been. That was some mischief there. Do ya think Hardin...?"

"I don't know, Mr. Morgan. It's possible. Go on," said Trudy with increasing interest.

Morgan took a moment to ponder this new information. At length he went on. "Anyway, I followed him home but I didn't talk to him or nothin'. He used to go out a lot at night. I started followin' him after that. Only he had his foot bandaged for weeks so he didn't go far for a while.

"Ya know, after a while, even a man as slow as me could figure it out. Mind you, he's got his self a pharmacy. So I figured he's sellin' drugs outside the law."

"Drugs," Trudy echoed. "What sort?"

"Beats me—heroin or cocaine powder, I 'spec most likely. That weren't so important to me. I figured I could get him to pay me to keep quiet all the same. Worked for a while, too—til I got greedy 'n asked for twenny dowars a week. After that, things are real hazy in ma mind."

"Let me understand, Mr. Morgan. You were blackmailing Mr. Hardin to keep quiet about his drug dealing?"

"That's right." Morgan chuckled. "That's ma crime. But that ain't never come out at the trial, now, did it?" He seemed to find this aspect of his case amusing. "And you know somethin' else?"

"What's that, Mr. Morgan?"

"When I first got here, they sent me to the jail hospital. The doc said I was carryin' on like someone with the DTs. He kept askin' me what kinda drugs I been takin'. I told 'im I didn't take nothin' but a beer every now and then, just for ma health, you know."

"They thought you were addicted to something?"

Morgan nodded. "Took me a while, but I finally figured it out. Hardin gave me a bunch a tins of fancy snuff. I used to dip all the time—finally quit though. I'm pretty sure Hardin put somethin' in ma snuff."

"You think Hardin was poisoning you, too?"

"Well, of a sort. From talkin' to other folks in jail, I figure it was cocaine. I remember the tingly feelin' I'd get from taking a dip."

Trudy put it together in her mind, "So, if I have this right, you saw Hardin leave Angelo Cottage last spring dressed as a ... hobo. You started following him after that and determined that he was selling some sort of drugs illegally. Instead of going to the police, you blackmailed him. He started slipping drugs to you and then framed you for the poisoning at Angelo Cottage. Is that about right?"

Morgan nodded. "When you lay it all out that way, I admit, it don't seem so likely. Makes Hardin sound like some kind of mastermind rather than what he is, a plain ol' bumpkin from Clarksville."

The guard came to the table indicating that the time for the interview had run out. Trudy started to stand, but then what Morgan had just said hit her. "Wait. Did you say Hardin is from Clarksville?"

"Yes, ma'am. Ol' Johanna Ray told me. Ya know, folks don't listen to her much. They reckon she's senile 'cause she don't say much. But she ain't. She's sharp as a tack."

Trudy thanked Mr. Morgan and agreed to take his heartfelt apology to Mrs. Sanner on his behalf.

She had a lot to think about on the ride home.

ALLEGED LYNCHER WINS SUIT

Fourteenth Amendment Does Not Apply, Supreme Court Says

Washington, Jan. 1.—The case of the United States vs. Robert Powell, involving the question whether the Fourteenth Amendment can be invoked in the United States courts to protect negroes against lynching, was decided by the Supreme Court of the United States today in favor of Powell on a writ of error bringing the case from the United States Circuit Court for the Northern District of Alabama.

Powell is under indictment on the charge of assisting a mob in the hanging of a negro named Horace Maples at Huntsville, Ala., the specific charge being that as a member of the lynching party Powell had deprived Maples of the right to a trial by due process of law. The Circuit Court held that the Fourteenth Amendment was not applicable to the case and declared that it could not be invoked unless the injustice complained of was inflicted by the State or its authorities. The Supreme Court's decision affirmed the decision of the lower tribunal.

[Baltimore Sun, January 12, 1909]

ELDER SISTER SURPRISINGLY LUCID

Wednesday Morning, January 13, 1909

After arriving at The Times on Wednesday morning, Trudy dug through the file cabinet and found the notes she had made the previous spring concerning the dead man on the tracks. At the bottom of the paper, under the lists of "What We Know" and "What We Don't Know," she had written free-form thoughts before filing the paper away. Her conclusions at the time were that Mr. D'Ignoto, the druggist from Catonsville, was almost certainly the victim. She had not determined a motive for the crime, and the only description she had of the likely assailant came from Billy: a white man with no coat or hat, limping across the covered bridge.

She had new items to add:

- Morgan saw Hardin limping through town late at night with no coat or hat. Same evening? Same man Billy saw?

- Morgan believes Hardin selling drugs illicitly

This wasn't a motive for murder exactly, but it did suggest that Hardin might have known D'Ignoto. They could have been competitors, or perhaps conspirators who had a falling out.

This evidence wasn't strong enough to take to the police, but Trudy had already made the conclusion that Hardin was indeed Billy's limping man on the bridge. The coincidence was just too striking.

So, if Morgan's description of Hardin, limping and coatless, corroborated Billy's account, it also went the other way: Billy's description of the limping man leant credence to Morgan's testimony—all of it.

She returned to the filing cabinet and retrieved her folder on the poisoning at Angelo Cottage in June. She found her notes from her interview with Mrs. Sanner the week after the incident. She remembered that Mrs. Sanner, always a prodigious talker, had been even more loquacious than usual, probably owing to the excitement of having such a scandalous event occur under her roof.

Trudy perused her half-legible jottings. She recalled writing as fast as she could, knowing that she was missing more than half of what Mrs. Sanner said. Most of it didn't seem important, but then near the end she read:

J – Mr. Hardin brought water from porch.

She remembered now—Johanna Ray had interrupted Mrs. Sanner's discourse to say that it was Mr. Hardin who had retrieved the pitcher of tainted water from the porch. She added this to her list.

As she wrote, Trudy was reminded of a conversation with Julius Wosch, in which he said that Hardin had supplied the emetic to the guests. He just happened to have a quantity of the curative in his room. So, if Hardin was the poisoner, he apparently did not intend to kill anyone.

But that didn't excuse any part of his actions. Someone *could* have been seriously hurt. Indeed, just yesterday The Baltimore Sun ran an article on the front page about a poisoning in Marydel, on the eastern shore of Maryland, where two people had died after ingesting muriatic acid.

She paused to consider the kind of callousness it would take to poison a house full of innocent people for the sole purpose of framing Mr. Morgan. If someone had been killed, Morgan could have been hanged. Such indifference to the well being of others was almost unthinkable. When she had met Hardin, he had seemed aloof and socially awkward, but could he really be such a monster?

She found that the more she thought about her interview with Morgan, the more she became convinced by his story: Hardin had to be responsible for the dead man on the tracks *and* the poisoning at Angelo Cottage. How strange it was that two such lurid events could be connected.

Trudy set the folders aside. She decided she would write up her findings as if it were to be a feature for the newspaper. If the Times wouldn't publish it, she would then take it to the police. Hopefully Chief Wosch would be back on the job soon.

But before she could begin writing, she would need more details. She decided to talk to Mrs. Sanner again, and then perhaps she would delicately interview Mr. Hardin himself without revealing what she knew or suspected.

In the early afternoon, she walked up the hill to Angelo Cottage, hoping Mr. Hardin would not be at home. Mrs. Sanner answered the door. "Trudy! What an unexpected pleasure. Come in out of the cold, dear. Dot was just fixing us tea. Dot! Put out another cup—Mrs. O'Flynn is here. Do come in dear."

"Thank you Roberta, I don't want to put you out."

"Nonsense. You are always welcome." They entered the front parlor. Johanna sat at her usual place at the end of the sofa. She was staring intently at a photograph of a small girl in a candy shop. Trudy had seen the photograph before but never knew where it came from or what Johanna found so fascinating about it. Perhaps it was from one of the case files at the courthouse.

"Good day, Johanna," Trudy said slowly. The older woman looked up with her thick glasses. She acknowledged the greeting with a nod but did not respond.

Trudy and Mrs. Sanner sat. Dot arrived with a silver tray and served a china cup of tea to each of the three ladies.

"'It's such a dreadful business in Italy," began Mrs. Sanner. "The paper this morning said it might be the worst earthquake disaster ever. I pity those poor people. Why I..."

"Indeed," agreed Trudy. "I hate to interrupt, dear, but my time is limited. I visited today because I have some news that is a bit closer to home. I went to the Baltimore City jail yesterday to see Billy Hatwood, and while I was there, I also had the opportunity to visit with Marion Morgan."

Mrs. Sanner shuddered involuntarily and almost dropped her teacup. She put it on the table and, silenced, looked expectantly at Trudy.

"He said to tell you both that he feels great remorse about his behavior last summer. He wanted..."

"Great remorse?" exclaimed Mrs. Sanner. "He tried to kill us all! If it weren't for Mr. Hardin we would all be..."

"Duplicity," declared Johanna loudly as she rolled her eyes. They waited for her to elaborate, but she did not.

Trudy went on, "He has an interesting story to tell that I found compelling. He still maintains that he had nothing to do with the poisoning."

Mrs. Sanner wasn't having it. "Trudy, we were all here. We all had to testify at that horrid trial. He was found guilty by a jury, and that's good enough for me. I'm just happy to be rid of him. Things have been peaceful here ever since he left—oh, aside from that business at Easton's hall down the hill, but that had nothing to do with..."

Trudy interrupted, "Yes, yes, but ... I was wondering if I might ask you a few questions about Mr. Hardin?"

"Mr. Hardin? Do you know where he is?" asked Mrs. Sanner.

Trudy was surprised by the question. "What do you mean? I assumed he was at his pharmacy. No?"

The two Ray sisters exchanged a look. "We haven't seen him for four days," said Mrs. Sanner. "Now, mind you, he does go out from time to time in the evenings, and on occasion he will spend a night in Baltimore, but he is fastidious about letting me know of his arrangements beforehand. He is very thoughtful that way. To tell you the truth, Trudy, I am becoming worried. I would have told the police about his absence already, but with them being short-handed with all the injuries, I thought I would wait until the end of the week before I alarmed anyone about..." Mrs. Sanner seemed to run out of steam.

"That is surprising," said Trudy. "But let me ask you—one of the things that Mr. Morgan told me is that Mr. Hardin is from Clarksville. Were you aware of that?"

Mrs. Sanner thought briefly. "Well, no, I don't think that is correct. I remember the form he filled out when he began boarding here. I can find it if you like. It's right over here in the bureau." Mrs. Sanner arose and went to the bureau, talking all the while. "I remember it quite clearly because I discussed it with him. He came here from another boarding house in west Baltimore. He said that he had relatives ... oh, here is the card." She examined it and handed the card to Trudy. "Yes, I was right. Look here. It says his previous address was..."

"Clarksville!" snapped Johanna.

Trudy and Mrs. Sanner looked at each other, both remembering the previous conversation in June when Johanna had interrupted in exactly the same manner.

Mrs. Sanner retrieved the card, looked at it again, and attempted to hand it to Johanna. "Look, dear. It says right here. Name—Everett Hardin. It says his previous address was..."

Johanna waved the card away, "Harriman. He went by his middle name, Emmett."

Trudy and Mrs. Sanner exchanged a puzzled look. Trudy said, "Johanna, dear, we don't understand. What are you saying about someone named ... Harriman?"

Johanna sighed and rolled her eyes. She spoke slowly, as if she were addressing someone with limited mental capacity. "Obviously, Hardin is an alias. Juvenile case in 1890, July. Drunk, disorderly conduct—that's your boarder. His best friend testified against him at the hearing—name of Charles Hill." She sipped her tea and resumed looking at her photograph.

ANOTHER VICTIM DEAD

Martin Rodey, of Ellicott City, Succumbs to Pneumonia.

Making the second fatality due indirectly to the collapse of the temporary courtroom at Ellicott City December 29, in which about 40 persons were injured, Martin Rodey, of Ellicott City, died yesterday morning at the University Hospital.

Rodey was brought to the hospital several hours after the accident suffering with a badly broken kneecap. The injury in itself was not fatal and readily responded to treatment until Monday, when pneumonia symptoms were discovered and caused his death.

Rodey was 70 years old and a shoemaker. He will be buried from his home.

State's Attorney Martin F. Burke, of Ellicott City, another of the victims of the accident, who is at the hospital, is said to be steadily improving. He is suffering with a broken leg.

[Baltimore Sun, January 14, 1909]

THE CHEMIST'S DISPOSITION

Tuesday, January 19, 1909

Chief Wosch's two fractured ribs and sprained lower back had turned out to be more serious than originally thought. The doctors were advising bed rest until at least the beginning of February. Sheriff Howard also remained out of commission due to his compound leg fracture.

Thus, Deputy Sheriff Hobbs was holding the fort alone at the police office on Main Street. He was overwhelmed by the many and diverse demands on his time. Hobbs had no time to listen to Trudy. He told her he didn't want to hear any cockamamie theories about cases that were out of his jurisdiction or already closed.

So Trudy resolved to follow through with her plan to write up her findings and either turn them over to the police, if she could find any that were interested, or publish them. There was one thing left to do—attempt to find and interview Hardin.

It was a cold day. In the early afternoon, she donned her overcoat and warmest hat. She ascended Main Street and walked past the Howard House, past the firehouse, past Yates' Grocery, past Gaither's livery and Dr. Sykes' house. She continued past Talbott's lumberyard and Court Avenue. She turned right onto Fels Lane and crossed the narrow wooden bridge over Hudson's branch. With determination, she turned left onto Mercer. Hardin's pharmacy was five doors down on the left.

As Trudy approached the building, she saw Hardin's prized buggy in the alleyway beside the shop. It had been half covered with a painter's cloth. The sight of the buggy wheel reminded her that she never did hear back from Chief Wosch about the axle cap she had found at the scene of the assault. It had been just before Billy's capture, and she supposed that he had gotten caught up in events and was never able to follow up on it.

The right rear wheel was visible outside of the cloth. It indeed had a decorative axle cap. It was hard to remember the small piece of wood she had handled almost a month ago, but it seemed to her that this one looked just like it. She walked around the buggy and lifted the canvas covering the other wheel. She was disappointed to see that it also had a cap.

Something in the way the sun caught the wood made her look more closely. There was a seam around the rim of the wood. She ran her finger over it. It was uneven. It appeared that the axle cap on this wheel had broken off and was then glued back on. Had Wosch already confronted Hardin? Why would he have given him the broken piece?

With renewed resolve, she dropped the cloth and marched to the front door of the shop. She didn't expect Hardin to be in, but she was hoping to find some clue as to his whereabouts. There was no sign on the shop of any kind, but from the discoloration on the door, it looked like one had been recently removed. To her surprise, the door was unlocked. She pulled it open and entered the pharmacy.

The interior was dim. A single electric bulb hung on a wire over the counter. A man sat near the back at a small table. He was smoking a cigar and reading a newspaper by a small lamp. A bell mounted on the door rang as she entered.

The man quickly put down the paper and stood. He was small in stature and wore a tight-fitting vest under his suspenders. His glossy black hair was slicked back over his spectacled face. His voice was high-pitched and breathy, his accent northern. "Yes, Hello? Miss, I think you may be in the wrong place, yeah?"

Trudy walked further into the smoky room. She screwed up her courage. In for a penny, in for a pound, her mother used to say. "Good day," she said with formality. "I was looking for Mr. Hardin. I was led to believe that this is his pharmacy."

The small man said nothing but seemed to look past Trudy. She heard the rustle of paper and the creak of a chair from behind her. She turned with surprise. Trudy had not seen the man sitting in the corner when she entered.

The man was large. She couldn't make out his features well because he was silhouetted in the front window of the shop. The man studied her for a moment and then said, "I've seen you someplace before."

Trudy was also experiencing a feeling of déjà vu. She had encountered this man in circumstances very similar to these.

"You got a name?" the large man asked as he struck a match to light his cigar. The flame briefly illuminated his fleshy jowls.

"I was asking about Mr. Hardin," maintained Trudy. "Is this his pharmacy, or am I mistaken?"

There was another pause as the two men looked at each other. It was plain that they were calculating what to say next. At length, the small man said, "Hardin ain't here. He sold the business to us. He left town."

Trudy was beginning to feel that it would be prudent to leave without delay. But she had been through too much, and she needed answers. She persisted. "Left town? That is surprising. He never checked out of his boarding house, and I believe that is his buggy out on the side of the building."

The larger man by the front door answered. "Lady, like my friend said, Mr. Hardin—he had to move. It was a family emergency. I believe he's gone back to ... New Jersey." The two men chuckled.

In a flash, she remembered where she had encountered this man before. Trudy quickly pushed her way past him, through the door and out onto the street. She kept walking rapidly toward the center of town, not slowing until she was certain that they weren't following her. She stopped and leaned against a building to catch her breath. She knew now that she would never see Hardin again. Nor would anyone else.

MR. WALLENHORST DEAD

Third Victim of Collapse Of Easton Hall At Ellicott City

OTHER STRUCTURES INSECURE

Town And Howard County Authorities Have Not Yet Agreed Upon A Plan Of Inspection.

On December 29 the second floor of Easton Hall at Ellicott City collapsed; 37 persons were seriously injured, and three have died since, the third yesterday, when Justice Bernard H. Wallenhorst succumbed at St. Joseph's Hospital, where he had lain in great pain for many days. He was presiding at the trial of William Hatwood, colored, when the floor went down.

Several days later Mayor Leishear told the City Council the crash was caused by defective or rotten joists, and that Ellicott City had no building inspector, who might have averted the disaster and saved three lives and many broken bones. The City Council talked it over and referred the question to its counsel, Edward M. Hammond, to see if the charter provided for such an official.

[Baltimore Sun, January 22, 1909]

MARCH
1909

A VISIT TO A SLEEPY TOWN

Thursday, March 4, 1909

Trudy had spent much of February in bed fighting a debilitating bout of the grippe. The disease had been going around Oella for months and had hit Trudy's family particularly hard. Everyone but the Old Man had succumbed, leaving him to minister to everyone's symptoms from his inexhaustible supply of remedies. For Trudy, he had prescribed Duffy's Pure Malt Whiskey, and although it allowed her to sleep more easily, she doubted that it had any curative effects.

Her fever finally broke on Sunday last, and she had been feeling quite well ever since. She decided it was time to take the much-delayed trip to Clarksville. She was going to visit Charles Hill with the faint hope that she could persuade him to revise his testimony concerning Billy Hatwood.

She held the reins of a borrowed one-horse buggy as she left town heading west on Frederick Turnpike. Just after eight o'clock, it was sunny and a not-unpleasant fifty degrees. Beside her on the bench she had wedged an oversized vase of hothouse flowers that Catherine Rodey had given her to place on her husband's grave. Having missed Martin's funeral due to her infirmity, Trudy agreed to the errand, as it would afford her a chance to pay her own respects.

A short distance west of the tenement houses for Burgess' mills, the cobblestones ended and the turnpike became a dirt and gravel road. The mud from the recent rain and the steadily rising terrain made the going slow. Trudy wasn't in a hurry. She was enjoying the fresh air and the opportunity to think, away from the fetid chaos of her crowded home.

In the past few days, she had been gradually picking up the various threads of her life. Her two sons had also fully recovered from the grippe. Sean was back in school, and Colin had resumed his work at Oella Mill. Trudy had gone to the newspaper office several times this week, but had yet to resume full-time work. She had also visited many of those afflicted by the building collapse. Bertha Wallenhorst was still taking her husband's death quite hard.

On Tuesday morning Trudy had gone to visit Katie Hatwood. The poor woman had become increasingly despondent and pessimistic. Billy still languished in the Baltimore jail awaiting his trial. Things still looked dire for him.

After visiting Katie, she had gone to Angelo Cottage to discover that, as expected, Hardin had never turned up. After Mrs. Sanner reported him missing, the police came to examine his abandoned room. They found few clues: He had not packed; his clothes were still in drawers; a suitcase sat unused in the closet; several books lay in a stack on his night table; a chess board with a half-finished game sat on the dresser by the window. They found one notebook, but it appeared to be written in some kind of code. The only thing notable was a sizable amount of cash, which they discovered in a shoebox in the back of the closet.

The police also visited Hardin's pharmacy, which they found empty—no supplies, no records—nothing. Even his prized Phaeton buggy had disappeared. The missing person case would be kept open, but they told Mrs. Sanner there was nothing further they could do.

A little over a mile out of town Trudy passed the tollhouse on her left. The proprietor, whom Trudy did not know, was digging in a flowerbed in the front yard.

She called out, "Excuse me, I have your quarter-dollar."

The man waved her through. "The governor declared no tolls today, ma'am. On account of inauguration day."

Trudy thanked the man. She shook the reins and continued up the long hill. With all of the bustle in her personal life, she had completely forgotten that William Howard Taft would become the president today. No doubt Edward and William Powell would prepare scathing reviews of his speech for Saturday's edition.

The police and sheriff's departments were still short-staffed due to injury and illness, but Julius Wosch had now been back on duty for several weeks. Trudy managed to speak with the busy man just yesterday. To her disappointment, he didn't give her much cause for hope concerning Billy. He told her that he had indeed confronted Hardin about the axle cap and had given it to him. He had originally planned to follow up on Hardin's whereabouts on the day in question, but then the events of Hatwood's capture and the disaster at Easton's hall had overtaken everything. Now with Hardin gone there was little that could be done. The only hope, he said, would be to have someone else confess to the crime, or have Charles Hill recant his testimony.

The latter was her mission today.

The ground finally leveled off and she turned onto the lane to St. John's Episcopal Church just past mile marker twelve. Two men in black coats stood at the corner of the stone building. One was pointing at something high up in the bell tower.

As she approached she recognized the shorter of the two. "Good morning Reverend Wegner. I'm glad that I found you here today."

Reverend Ignatius Wegner was the pastor at the German Lutheran Church in Ellicott City. He squinted in the sunlight as Trudy stopped her buggy on the lane. "Ah, yes, child. Mrs. ... O'Flynn, is it not?"

"Yes. Please call me Trudy."

"Very well, Trudy then," said the reverend. "And this," he said gesturing to the taller man, "is Archdeacon Helfenstein. He is the rector here at St. John's."

The clergyman nodded his head in an unctuous manner. His dark eyes and expression were unreadable.

"Good day ... archdeacon. I understand you have been here for some time. It is a pity I have not had the opportunity to make your acquaintance before."

Helfenstein again nodded his long head. "Indeed, madam."

Unsure of the protocol in such circumstances, Trudy returned the nod. She spoke again to Wegner. "Reverend, I have flowers for Martin Rodey. I've been ill and was not able to attend his funeral. Could you tell me where the grave is?"

Reverend Wegner directed her to an area in the far corner where the winter-brown grass had been recently disturbed. Trudy left the buggy and walked through well-tended rows of stone markers. Because Martin's granite headstone was still being fashioned, his grave was marked with a hand-painted wooden sign. Trudy set the vase next to the marker and fanned out the flowers in what she thought was an appealing bouquet. She said a silent prayer for the kind old man she had known for almost twenty years. She crossed herself and returned to her buggy.

She continued west on the Frederick Turnpike. After another mile she found the cutoff for the old Hammond road and turned left, heading southwest toward Clarksville. The trip to Dayton would be about fourteen miles each way. Except for the steep climb out of the Patapsco Valley, the road traversed gently rolling hills. Her plan was to be there well before noon, conduct her interview with Charles Hill, and then be home before dark.

Her thoughts drifted to her visit with Katie Hatwood the previous day. Katie had been out to visit Billy in the Baltimore jail every week since his arrest. She said that he was in good spirits considering his predicament. The last time she had visited—just last week—she met the lawyer who had been appointed to defend Billy. He was a young, ambitious man by the name of Waldo Payne. Katie and Billy were both dismayed that the man didn't seem at all interested in Billy's claim of innocence. He advised that, from a legal standpoint, it was an open-and-shut case, and Billy's only option was to plead guilty. He said he knew Judge Forsyth personally and could probably negotiate the sentence down to around ten years. This, he said, was quite lenient for the offense.

Trudy was also acquainted with Judge Forsyth and did not share the lawyer's optimism. She knew that the most painful thing to Billy about pleading guilty would be admitting to a lie. Billy was perhaps the most honest person she had ever known.

Embittered, Katie was now threatening that if he did plead guilty, she would leave town and return to her native North Carolina. She maintained, correctly Trudy thought, that if the shoe were on the other foot—if a white man stood accused of attacking a black man—the court would almost certainly give him the benefit of the doubt.

Yesterday, she had learned that a hearing for Billy would be held next Tuesday. This was essentially a second attempt of the ill-fated hearing in December, which had been interrupted by the building collapse before a judgment could be rendered. It would be held in the Ellicott City jail and would not be open to the public. After that, Billy would be held there until his trial later in the month. Agitation for his lynching seemed to have abated over time, so the police weren't expecting any trouble.

Trudy rode through Clarksville—a sleepy town consisting of a few blocks of frame houses and storefronts. She took the Linden road toward Dayton.

She had seen Charles Hill from afar when he arrived for the hearing in December but had never spoken with him. Near the beginning of February, she had sent a letter explaining that she was a writer for The Ellicott City Times, and that she was examining previously undisclosed aspects of the case. She wrote that his first-hand account of the incident would be invaluable to the piece, and promised that she would do her best to present him in a favorable light. To her surprise, he agreed.

She found the Hill family's estate set amid dormant cornfields several hundred yards off of the road. She directed her horse onto the muddy lane and approached the house.

When she drew near the house, a colored woman ran from the front door toward her. She was waving a hand towel. "Mr. Benjamin says that whatever y'all are sellin' we don't want none. Y'all ain't welcome here."

"But ... I wrote to Charles some weeks ago and he invited me to visit. I'm Mrs. O'Flynn from The Ellicott City Times. I promise you I am not selling anything."

"Mr. Benjamin know you comin'? He ain't said nothin' to me 'bout it."

After some negotiation, Trudy was admitted to the house. She was told to stand in the front hall while the maid went to fetch her employer. Several minutes later, she heard raised voices and the sound of glass shattering from somewhere in the house—the basement perhaps.

When he finally appeared at the far end of the hall, Benjamin Hill was much as Trudy remembered him from the first hearing at the courthouse in December. His stringy gray hair and beard were unkempt. His cotton overalls and shirt were covered in grime. The tall, thin man approached warily, squinting in the light of the hall after emerging from the basement. When he approached, Trudy recoiled at the reek of sweat and alcohol.

"So you're that writer from the city. Ain't heard a peep in weeks. We 'bout give up on you."

Trudy composed herself. "Yes, good morning Mr. Hill. I am Mrs. O'Flynn. I wrote to you some weeks ago. I regret that I was detained this long. And I thank you for agreeing to let me speak with your brother." She didn't want to mention the grippe. Some folks got spooked at the prospect of being around anyone ill or recently ill.

"Yeah, well, you can go on in there and have a sit." He motioned to a room off of the front hall. It contained four plain chairs around a wooden table. "I'll see if I can fetch 'im." He called to the interior of the house. "Hey Weezie, you know where Charley's at?"

Trudy heard the colored woman's shouted reply. "I ain't seen 'im. You look out by the shed? You know he like to just sit there and stare. Boy ain't right no more."

Trudy entered the front room and pulled a chair out from the table. She was about to sit when she noticed the only decoration in the room: A framed photograph hanging on the wall, behind a sheet of glass. She got up and studied the picture. It looked to be about ten years old. John Hill, the patriarch, stood to the side. The six grown children were in the center. None were smiling.

Trudy knew from looking up the court records that Charles Hill, or *Charley* as he was evidently called, was the youngest, having been born in September of 1876. In the photograph, he was a young man in his early twenties. Benjamin was about ten years older. He was recognizable in the picture, but apparently the years had not been kind to him.

"Found 'im," growled Benjamin. Charley, walking with a cane, followed his brother into the room. He sat at the head of the table while Benjamin took the chair across from Trudy. Charley's head was still bandaged, covering his left eye. Other than that, he looked well.

Charley cleared his throat and spat into a rag. Then he directed his attention to Trudy. He spoke slowly and softly, as one who is groggy after waking up from a long nap. "You're 'at lady from the paper in Ellicott City. Been a while since you wrote." He reached into a back pocket of his trousers and produced a crumpled paper, which he spread out in front of him on the table. "Took your time gettin' here."

Trudy recognized the paper as her letter from more than a month ago. "Thank you for agreeing to speak with me, Mr. Hill. You are looking much better than when I saw you before the hearing in December."

Charley rubbed his thigh with his fist. "I don't recollect I seen you afore today. Twisted my leg damned near off that day. Y'all make fun of us country folk, but at least our buildings don't fall down." When Trudy made no reply, he added, "So what's this about, then? Says you're writin' some kinda article?"

"Yes. Well, as I'm sure you're aware, the circuit court comes back into session next week, and your..."

"We know all that," interrupted Benjamin. "The lawyer, what's his name Burke—explained all that. He says we gotta have another preliminary hearing next Tuesday. Let's hope the courtroom is safe this time."

Trudy plowed ahead, "So, there will be renewed interest in the case, and my editor wants a follow-up piece. We're hoping for a new angle ... fresh information that hasn't appeared in print before. I'd like to go over the incident with you. You know, get a first hand account."

The brothers looked at each other. Charley shrugged. Benjamin said, "I don't know what kinda *angle* you're lookin' for, but go ahead and ask your questions."

Trudy got out her notepad and opened it. "Okay, let's start with when you first met Mr. Hatwood. Where was that, exactly?"

A perplexed expression came over Charley's face. After thinking for a minute he looked up questioningly at Benjamin.

Trudy had gone through all the newspaper accounts she could find about the attack. She realized that they were all very general, with few details. Furthermore, the details that were present—the amount of money stolen, the exact nature of the assault—seemed to shift from one telling to the next. She wasn't sure if this was due to sources—policemen and such—making assumptions, newspaper writers being creative and filling in the gaps, or the actual principals refining the story as time went by.

"I reckon it was when he asked me for a ride."

"Was it Mr. Hatwood who helped you load the wagon ... at the train depot?"

Again Charley looked to Benjamin, who just shrugged. "I don't ... I don't think so."

As she wrote in her notebook, she asked, "and did he say where he was going ... why he needed a ride?"

Again there was a long pause. When Trudy looked up, he said, "I don't know, I mean, who knows where his kind goes?"

"And when you arrived at the toll house, did Mr. Hatwood pay the toll, or did you?"

Charley thought hard about this one. "I did, I reckon. I don't recollect the negro having any money."

"No? One account said that Mr. Hatwood paid you a dollar for the ride."

Charley adjusted the bandage over his eye as he thought. Eventually he shrugged his shoulders.

Trudy went on, "No matter—perhaps whoever said that was wrong. So you say you paid the toll. Did you meet the toll man, or did you just leave the money in the box?"

Benjamin interjected, "Lady, I don't see what all this has to do with it. That negro made up some tall tale about some rocks lookin' like coal, then he goes and throws 'em at poor Charley here. Darn near killed 'im."

"Forgive me," said Trudy deferentially. "It's the little things that bring a story to life for the reader. But I don't mean to cause you any undue anguish. Let's change the subject." She looked at her notebook a moment. "Do you remember an August Harriman from your youth? I believe he went by the name Emmett."

Charley seemed to recoil at the mention of the name. He swallowed hard and said, "Emmett—sure I remember him. I ain't stupid. Funny you should ask about him."

"Why is that, Mr. Hill?"

"I don't know. It's just funny. He's been on ma mind lately. His face keeps poppin' into ma head."

"When did you last see Emmett?"

Charley looked to Benjamin again. He seemed reluctant to answer. At length he said, "Well, I guess it was at that hearin' in Ellicott City when they sent 'im away. I always felt bad about what happened. That must be, what? Twenny years ago?"

"Sixteen," said Trudy. "Are you sure you haven't seen him since then?"

Benjamin sighed heavily. "Lady, I can't say I get what you're goin' on about, but what's this got..."

"Are you aware," Trudy asked Charley, "that Emmett was living in Ellicott City until very recently? He had changed his name to Hardin. I'm wondering if perhaps you saw him when you came through town."

Charley adjusted his bandage again and then scratched his beard. "I ... I don't think so. I can't say I'd even recognize 'im now. We was just boys when I knew 'im."

Trudy had been hoping that the mention of his childhood friend would jog some memory in the poor man's mind. She wished she had a photograph of Mr. Hardin to show Charley. She considered describing the man to Charley, but his features were so common—so ordinary, that she doubted it would do any good.

She pursed her lips, deciding to press the point. She placed her hand over Charley's as a sympathetic gesture. "I know it's difficult, Mr. Hill, and I'm sorry to cause you trouble, but it's important. A man's life is at stake. Think hard. Are you positive it wasn't Emmett that attacked you that day?"

Charley and Benjamin both looked up in surprise. Trudy's cards were on the table.

"A man's life," echoed Benjamin. "You mean that negro? You ride all the way out here ahead of the hearing tryin' to put strange notions into Charley's head. Lady, I didn't trust you when you wrote that letter, but Charley didn't think it would do no harm. I think you better get on back to town now."

HATWOOD HELD FOR COURT

Negro Who Nearly Killed Mr. C. E. Hill Has A Hearing

Ellicott City, Md., March 9.–The preliminary hearing of William Hatwood, the negro assailant of Charles E. Hill, which was so interrupted here on December 29, 1908, by the giving away of the floor of Easton's Hall, where the case was being heard, was taken up today before Justice William F. Lilly. The hearing was held at the county jail, and only the officers and witnesses were present.

Mr. Hill testified that on December 15 last, on leaving Ellicott City for his home near Dayton, he was accosted by Hatwood, who asked for a ride. Mr. Hill took him up. When the wagon reached a point between Little River and Leishear's gate on the Columbia pike Hatwood got out and picked up two large stones, remarking that they resembled coal. Approaching him, the negro hurled the stones at him, striking him squarely in the face.

At the time of the assault Mr. Hill had in his possession $35, which was taken from him while he was unconscious from the blow.

Dr. Thomas B. Owings, who dressed the injured man's wounds, testified to their nature and extent.

Hatwood was held for the action of the grand jury, which convenes Monday, March 15, on the charge of robbery and assault with attempt to kill. His bail is fixed at $1,000 for each charge.

[Baltimore Sun, March 10, 1909]

QUITE A DEVIOUS MAN

Monday, March 29, 1909

When Trudy arrived at her desk just after the lunch hour on Monday afternoon, she found a single folded piece of paper. It was closed in the old fashioned manner with an ornate wax seal. A name was written on the outside: T. O'Flynn.

She broke the seal and opened it:

Dear T.,

Please do me the honor of meeting me this afternoon at four o'clock at Angelo Cottage. Johanna Ray suggested that I speak with you. I have important information regarding the man you know as E. Hardin.

Truly yours,

R. Knibbs

Trudy glanced at the clock on the wall. She had almost three hours. She put aside the note and decided to get started on a piece William Powell wanted for this Saturday's edition. The paper was planning to endorse a "law and order ticket" in the upcoming municipal elections. William had left her a stack of hand-written jottings to compile into some semblance of order. She got to work.

She made some headway, but it was slow going. She simply could not concentrate on mundane political platitudes. It had been a season of disappointment. Everything Trudy had attempted concerning Billy's case had resulted in failure: The broken axle cap had been lost, Hardin had disappeared, and Charles Hill had stuck to his original story accusing Billy of the attack. And that awful lawyer, Mr. Payne, had been urging Billy to plead guilty for months, saying that the longer they waited, the worse it would look.

Trudy finally convinced Payne last week to file a request to have the trial moved to a different jurisdiction. The disagreeable man gave it minimal effort, writing a one-sentence, barely legible request and filing it with Mr. Gissell, the clerk of the court. He had even delayed doing this until just before close of business on Wednesday afternoon, the day before Billy's presentment. As expected, it was summarily denied.

At the presentment the next day, Payne took it upon himself to argue to Judge Forsythe that Billy was *non compos mentis*, and he entered a plea of guilty on Billy's behalf. Grand jury proceedings were not open to the public, so neither Trudy nor Katie were there to object. The jury returned a true bill indicting Billy and accepting his guilty plea before he even understood what was happening.

Consequently, there would be no trial. Billy was already guilty and was now awaiting sentencing. Katie Hatwood, disgusted, had announced her intention to move back to North Carolina and had already begun packing.

At a quarter to four, Trudy donned her hat and coat and began walking toward Angelo Cottage. When she turned the corner, it was strange to see an empty lot at the bottom of Church Road where Easton's Hall had stood for as long as she had lived in this town. She continued up the hill and knocked on the door of Angelo Cottage. Mrs. Sanner's daughter answered almost immediately.

"Hello Dot. I'm here to see a Mr. Knibbs. I was told to meet him at four."

Dot appeared confused for a moment and then said, "Mister? Oh, yes ... Knibbs. On the roof—follow me."

Dot led Trudy through the house to the upper floor. In a back storage room there was a steep staircase—more of a ladder really—that led up to an open trapdoor through which she saw blue sky. Chagrined, she set her hat on a shelf, hitched up her ankle-length skirt, and carefully ascended. When she was halfway through the trapdoor, she saw a short man in a dark suit and top hat at the edge of the building. He had his back to her.

"Excuse me—Mr. Knibbs? Could you please give me a hand?"

The man turned and approached. Trudy saw him only in silhouette as the sun was behind his left shoulder. He offered her a white-gloved hand and assisted her onto the roof.

When she was standing solidly on the roof, he brushed his hand over her left shoulder. "Dear, you've got dirt all over your sleeve."

Trudy recoiled in surprise at the tone of the voice. She looked more closely: R. Knibbs was a woman. She had short-cropped hair and was dressed in a man's formal suit. "Goodness, you're ... you're..."

"Yes, yes," said Knibbs, a smile spreading across her face. "Apologies for the subterfuge. It's a habit of mine. I find that I am taken more seriously if I am thought to be male." She had a tanned, well-weathered but youthful face devoid of wrinkles. She removed her hat revealing dark hair with just a few strands of gray.

"Allow me to introduce myself. I am Rebecca Lee Knibbs. And I take it that you are Gertrude O'Flynn. May I call you Trudy?"

Trudy nodded, unable to find her voice.

"Excellent. And you may call me Lee, as do all my friends." She took Trudy by the arm and led her to the eastern edge of the building. Trudy stopped short, remaining a yard from the edge.

"Ah, a touch of acrophobia? No matter. Stay where you are. It is a marvelous view. Mr. Harriman—or Hardin as you knew him—used to come up here often to smoke his pipe. He described it to me in a letter last year, but I must say his description does not do it justice."

Trudy recovered her voice. "So, Missus ... Miss?"

Knibbs waved her hand dismissively. "Please—Lee. I don't use titles."

"Lee, then. So, who are you, exactly?"

"Who am I?" Lee Knibbs laughed. "Where to begin? I suppose that, like all of us, I play different roles in different situations. Let's see ... I trained as a surgeon in Boston, so if you insist on a title, you may call me Doctor Knibbs. I am the author of twenty-three books—a few of them are not bad. I have tried marriage twice and found that I don't have the patience or desire for it. But, I suppose what you are really asking is why am I here, and why have I contacted you?"

Trudy nodded.

Lee went on. "Johanna Ray, on whose roof we are now standing, is a wonderful researcher whom I have had the pleasure of engaging on a freelance basis from time to time. She has a rare talent for finding the needle in the haystack of tedious court documents. I was traveling from Washington to my home in New York and decided to stop by—a purely social call. It was she who suggested I contact you. I believe it has to do with your unfortunate involvement with Mr. Harriman."

"Unfortunate indeed," said Trudy ruefully. "The man wreaked havoc in this town for the past year, and no one neither knows nor cares."

Lee's eyes widened. "I perceive that you already know more than I anticipated about our miscreant—perhaps even more than I do about his recent activities. Let me give you some background."

"Please," prompted Trudy.

"Where to start ... I suppose after completing my medical studies." Lee rubbed her chin for a moment as she collected her thoughts. "Early in my career, I became interested in the workings of the human mind and have since made a career of it. At the outset of my work, I discovered the writings of Dr. Sigmund Freud. Do you know of him?"

"I have read articles about him."

"Ah, you should read his new book on the interpretation of dreams—most interesting. He is observant and insightful—qualities unusual in a male—although, like most men, he is incurably preoccupied with sex. Anyway, his early work suggests ways of using hypnosis to unlock truths hidden deep within a mind. Using Freud's method, I began using hypnosis extensively on my psychological subjects when I was under contract to the State of Maryland in the nineties. That is how I made the acquaintance of your Mr. Hardin."

"Mr. Hardin was a patient—or subject—of yours? Where?"

Still in possession of Trudy's arm, Lee led her toward the southern end of the building, overlooking the back of Rodey's Hall and Main Street. It was a strange feeling being led about by a woman in man's clothing. The top hat made her seem taller than she actually was.

"I was hired by the State of Maryland in the early nineties. I'm afraid I am older than I look. I credit the Cherokee blood from my maternal grandmother for my youthful appearance. But never mind that, you want to know about Mr. Hardin. My task was to do a long-term study of the criminal mind—particularly how it developed—where it went astray. To that end, I met with many inmates at the Maryland House of Refuge over a number of years to determine which boys could be redeemed, and which were destined for a life of lawlessness. Mr. Hardin—or Harriman, which was his original name—let's just call him Emmett—was a particularly interesting case. He would often want to play chess during our interviews, even under hypnosis."

"Chess?"

"Yes. Emmett fancied himself quite the mastermind. He liked to believe himself always two or three moves ahead of everyone else—guards, teachers, administrators—whom he typically referred as his adversaries or opponents. I believe he included me in that category near the end. His modus operandi was to perpetrate some elaborate bit of mischief in such a way that it would be blamed on someone else. He was quite good at it. Many fellow inmates and more than one guard were punished after being framed by Emmett for some infraction—sometimes quite harmful infractions, too. Emmett seemed quite indifferent to the consequences his actions had on innocent people. Oh, here, I have something for you." She reached into an inside coat pocket and produced a small book, which she handed to Trudy.

Trudy squinted in the fading sunlight to read the title on the cloth binding. "*Calamitous Life of A. Emmett Harriman.* Oh—you are the author."

"One and the same," replied Lee. "I find that my psychological studies provide endless material for fiction." She took Trudy's arm again and led her to the west, overlooking the backs of the stone buildings on Main Street. "Oh, and please forgive the colloquial style of the writing. I am more than a bit embarrassed by it, but my publisher insisted that it would increase sales.

"The book explains it all, starting in his early childhood. He became institutionalized when he was fourteen, and I daresay he had a rough time of it. He was shuttled back and forth between the House of Refuge and Bayview Sanitarium numerous times. He was in fights constantly and spent most of his time in the infirmary. He was sick often—twice with influenza and once with consumption. They tried various 'cures' on him, addicting him at different times to both morphine and cocaine. They gave him the 'Keeley Gold Cure' for alcoholism—yes the same treatment that you advertise in your paper. The only efficacy I've been able to find for it is that it makes its victims too nauseated to eat or drink. In fact, a recent study claims that the injections at one time contained mercury. Thus poor Emmett could well have been rendered 'mad as a hatter.'

"Anyway, I came to realize that Emmett was growing into quite a devious man. He had originally been incarcerated not for an offense, but simply because he was an orphan. With all of his trips between institutions and the infirmaries, his paperwork was fouled up with another inmate. I was the one who discovered the clerical error that kept him behind bars until he was twenty-four. The state had no cause to hold him any longer."

"My goodness—twenty-four!"

"Indeed. I kept up sporadic correspondence with him after he became free. He changed his name legally to Hardin—which is easier than you might think—and moved here to Ellicott City. He wrote to me about this view. And he wrote to me about you, my dear. It seems that he was quite taken with you last spring."

Trudy frowned. "I met him once socially—at a public gathering. It was nothing."

"Nothing to you," replied Lee. "Anyway, when he mentioned that he had resumed his pharmacy trade and was making quite a bit of money, I had my suspicions. Then I became alarmed when he wrote to me September last. He seemed quite proud of some recent misdeeds, which he described only in a vague manner. He was careful never to incriminate himself in his letters."

"Morgan," guessed Trudy.

Lee looked at Trudy with new appreciation. "I am impressed. I only determined that this afternoon after deciphering his journal. How did you learn of it?"

Trudy then spoke at length, going back over a year to the discovery of the dead man on the tracks and her own investigation that led her to the pharmacy in Catonsville. She told Lee about her suspicions that something wasn't right in the Morgan case, but she never knew what it was until her serendipitous interview with Morgan in January at the Baltimore jail. She explained that Morgan had been blackmailing Hardin because of his knowledge of Hardin's illicit drug business.

"My goodness," exclaimed Lee. "You have it all worked out. I had not yet determined what Emmett's motive was, but you make a convincing case."

They stood a while in silence, arm in arm. At length, Lee continued. "As for Emmett's involvement with the attack on Hill, I have no hard evidence—only the striking coincidence, as I believe Johanna has already told you, that they were childhood companions in Clarksville. I can also tell you, from my hypnosis sessions with Emmett, that he continued to harbor a deep resentment toward Hill throughout his incarceration.

"I'm very sorry, Trudy, but I don't think any information I have could exonerate your friend, Mr. Hatwood, especially now that, in the eyes of the court, he has confessed to the crime."

Trudy nodded her head. She had come to the same conclusion.

Lee reached over and wiped a tear from Trudy's cheek. They had returned to the eastern edge of the building and now looked out over the river in the orange glow of twilight. Across the river, several men were unloading a wagon in the lumberyard. A whistle blew as a shift ended at the flouring mills. They heard a squeal of brakes as the five-thirty electric car clattered onto the trestle bridge on its way eastward toward Baltimore.

The air had become chilly. Lee bent down and picked up a discarded matchbook from the roof. She showed it to Trudy. It bore a drawing of the ornate grillwork on the front of the Howard House Hotel, with the slogan "Cuisine Unexcelled."

She offered Trudy her hand. "Come. You shall dine with me tonight. We have much to discuss."

ACKNOWLEDGEMENTS

I am indebted to generous friends and family members who endured early drafts of this book. They made invaluable suggestions and pointed out many errors that I really ought to have fixed myself: Dan Beekman, Susan Carlson, Barry Eigen, Brad Howard, Kate Howard, Susan Little, Maura Maloney, Mary Gertrude Maloney, Terry Maloney, Lisa Ragland, Stuart Ragland, and Susan Maloney.

The Howard County Historical Society can be found online at hchsmd.org. They have a wonderful collection of books, letters, photographs, court records, and other materials. Their volunteers are numerous, cheerful, and extremely helpful.

Thanks to Charles Wagandt for sitting with me and answering my questions about textile mills in general and Oella Mill in particular. Mr. Wagandt is the grandson of William J. Dickey, who purchased Oella Mill in 1887. He now runs The Oella Company (www.oellacompany.com).

Books that I found particularly helpful include:

Joetta M. Cramm. *Howard County, A Pictorial History.* Virginia Beach, VA, 2004.

Jerre Garrett. *A Pictorial History of Oella Maryland.* Oella, MD, 2007.

Alison Kahn and Peggy Fox. *Patapsco – Life Along Maryland's Historic River Valley.* Center for American Places at Columbia College Chicago, 2008.

B. H. Shipley Jr. *Remembrances of Passing Days, A Pictorial History of Ellicott City and It's Fire Department.* Ellicott City, MD, 1997.

Finally, thanks to Susan Maloney for indulging me while I spent all my free time doing this, and for the many fun conversations we had about characters and plot.

ABOUT THE AUTHOR

Michael Maloney currently resides in Catonsville, Maryland. Except for brief stints in Boston and San Diego, he is a lifelong Marylander. He attended the Peabody Conservatory and Johns Hopkins University in Baltimore.

He is also the author of *The Secrets of Miryam*, available at Amazon and Barnes & Noble.

www.michaelmaloneyauthor.com

83422158R00161

Made in the USA
Middletown, DE
11 August 2018